LIFE'S LITTLE IRONIES

LIFE'S LITTLE IRONIES

A Set of Tales

WITH
SOME COLLOQUIAL SKETCHES
ENTITLED
A FEW CRUSTED CHARACTERS

BY

THOMAS HARDY

GYAN

Published by

GYAN

Gyan Publishing House
5, Ansari Road
Daryaganj, New Delhi-110002
Phone: 011-47034999, 9811692060
E-mail: books@gyanbooks.com

Distribution Network
gyanbooks.com
India, USA, Canada, UK, Australia

ISBN: 978-81-212-7625-2 (PB)
First Published, 1894

2nd Impression 2024

Printed at: Gyan Press, Delhi.

LIFE'S LITTLE IRONIES
Author: THOMAS HARDY

LIFE'S LITTLE IRONIES

A Set of Tales

WITH

SOME COLLOQUIAL SKETCHES

ENTITLED

A FEW CRUSTED CHARACTERS

BY

THOMAS HARDY

AUTHOR OF "TESS OF THE D'URBERVILLES"
"A GROUP OF NOBLE DAMES" ETC.

NEW YORK

HARPER & BROTHERS PUBLISHERS

CONTENTS

PAGE

THE SON'S VETO 3
FOR CONSCIENCE' SAKE 22
A TRAGEDY OF TWO AMBITIONS 44
ON THE WESTERN CIRCUIT 76
TO PLEASE HIS WIFE 107
THE MELANCHOLY HUSSAR OF THE GERMAN LEGION . . . 129
THE FIDDLER OF THE REELS 152
A TRADITION OF 1804 175
A FEW CRUSTED CHARACTERS 187
TONY KYTES, THE ARCH-DECEIVER 193
THE HISTORY OF THE HARDCOMES 205
THE SUPERSTITIOUS MAN'S STORY 218
ANDREY SATCHEL AND THE PARSON AND CLERK . 223
OLD ANDREY'S EXPERIENCE AS A MUSICIAN . . . 234
ABSENT-MINDEDNESS IN A PARISH CHOIR 238
THE WINTERS AND THE PALMLEYS 243
INCIDENT IN THE LIFE OF MR. GEORGE CROOK-HILL 254
NETTY SARGENT'S COPYHOLD 260

THE SON'S VETO

I

To the eyes of a man viewing it from behind, the nut-brown hair was a wonder and a mystery. Under the black beaver hat, surmounted by its tuft of black feathers, the long locks, braided and twisted and coiled like the rushes of a basket, composed a rare, if somewhat barbaric, example of ingenious art. One could understand such weavings and coilings being wrought to last intact for a year, or even a calendar month; but that they should be all demolished regularly at bedtime, after a single day of permanence, seemed a reckless waste of successful fabrication.

And she had done it all herself, poor thing. She had no maid, and it was almost the only accomplishment she could boast of. Hence the unstinted pains.

She was a young invalid lady—not so very much of an invalid—sitting in a wheeled chair, which had been pulled up in the front part of a green enclosure, close to a band-stand, where a concert was going on, during a warm June afternoon. It had place in one of the minor parks or private gardens that are to be found in the suburbs of London, and was the effort of a local association to raise money for some charity. There are worlds within worlds in the great city, and though nobody outside the immediate district had ever heard of the charity, or the band, or the garden, the enclosure was filled with an interested audience sufficiently informed on all these.

As the strains proceeded many of the listeners observed the chaired lady, whose back hair, by reason of her prominent position, so challenged inspection. Her face was not easily discernible, but the aforesaid cunning tress-weavings, the white ear and poll, and the curve of a cheek which was neither flaccid nor sallow, were signals that led to the expectation of good beauty in front. Such expectations are not infrequently disappointed as soon as the disclosure comes; and in the present case, when the lady, by a turn of the head, at length revealed herself, she was not so handsome as the people behind her had supposed, and even hoped—they did not know why.

For one thing (alas! the commonness of this complaint), she was less young than they had fancied her to be. Yet attractive her face unquestionably was, and not at all sickly. The revelation of its details came each time she turned to talk to a boy of twelve or thirteen who stood beside her, and the shape of whose hat and jacket implied that he belonged to a well-known public school. The immediate by-standers could hear that he called her "Mother."

When the end of the programme was reached, and the audience withdrew, many chose to find their way out by passing at her elbow. Almost all turned their heads to take a full and near look at the interesting woman, who remained stationary in the chair till the way should be clear enough for her to be wheeled out without obstruction. As if she expected their glances, and did not mind gratifying their curiosity, she met the eyes of several of her observers by lifting her own, showing these to be soft, brown, and affectionate orbs, a little plaintive in their regard.

She was conducted out of the garden, and passed

along the pavement till she disappeared from view, the school-boy walking beside her. To inquiries made by some persons who watched her away, the answer came that she was the second wife of the incumbent of a neighboring parish, and that she was lame. She was generally believed to be a woman with a story—an innocent one, but a story of some sort or other.

In conversing with her on their way home the boy who walked at her elbow said that he hoped his father had not missed them.

"He have been so comfortable these last few hours that I am sure he cannot have missed us," she replied.

"*Has*, dear mother—not *have!*" exclaimed the public-school boy, with an impatient fastidiousness that was almost harsh. "Surely you know that by this time!"

His mother hastily adopted the correction, and did not resent his making it, or retaliate, as she might well have done, by bidding him to wipe that crumby mouth of his, whose condition had been caused by surreptitious attempts to eat a piece of cake without taking it out of the pocket wherein it lay concealed. After this the pretty woman and the boy went onward in silence.

That question of grammar bore upon her history, and she fell into reverie, of a somewhat sad kind to all appearance. It might have been assumed that she was wondering if she had done wisely in shaping her life as she had shaped it, to bring out such a result as this.

In a remote nook in North Wessex, forty miles from London, near the thriving county-town of Aldbrickham, there stood a pretty village with its church and parsonage, which she knew well enough, but her son had never seen. It was her native village, Gaymead, and the first event bearing upon her present situation had occurred at that place when she was only a girl of nineteen.

How well she remembered it, that first act in her little tragi-comedy, the death of her reverend husband's first wife. It happened on a spring evening, and she who now and for many years had filled that first wife's place was then parlor-maid in the parson's house.

When everything had been done that could be done, and the death was announced, she had gone out in the dusk to visit her parents, who were living in the same village, to tell them the sad news. As she opened the white swing-gate and looked towards the trees which rose westward, shutting out the pale light of the evening sky, she discerned, without much surprise, the figure of a man standing in the hedge, though she roguishly exclaimed, as a matter of form, "Oh, Sam, how you frightened me!"

He was a young gardener of her acquaintance. She told him the particulars of the late event, and they stood silent, these two young people, in that elevated, calmly philosophic mind which is engendered when a tragedy has happened close at hand, and has not happened to the philosophers themselves. But it had its bearings upon their relations.

"And will you stay on now at the Vicarage, just the same?" asked he.

She had hardly thought of that. "Oh yes—I suppose," she said. "Everything will be just as usual, I imagine."

He walked beside her towards her mother's. Presently his arm stole round her waist. She gently removed it; but he placed it there again, and she yielded the point. "You see, dear Sophy, you don't know that you'll stay on; you may want a home; and I shall be ready to offer one some day, though I may not be ready just yet."

"Why, Sam, how can you be so fast? I've never even said I liked 'ee; and it is all your own doing, coming after me."

"Still, it is nonsense to say I am not to have a try at you, like the rest." He stooped to kiss her a farewell, for they had reached her mother's door.

"No, Sam; you sha'n't!" she cried, putting her hand over his mouth. "You ought to be more serious on such a night as this." And she bade him adieu without allowing him to kiss her or to come indoors.

The vicar just left a widower was at this time a man about forty years of age, of good family, and childless. He had led a secluded existence in this college living, partly because there were no resident landowners; and his loss now intensified his habit of withdrawal from outward observation. He was still less seen than heretofore, kept himself still less in time with the rhythm and racket of the movements called progress in the world without. For many months after his wife's decease the economy of his household remained as before; the cook, the house-maid, the parlor-maid, and the man out-of-doors performed their duties or left them undone, just as nature prompted them—the vicar knew not which. It was then represented to him that his servants seemed to have nothing to do in his small family of one. He was struck with the truth of this representation, and decided to cut down his establishment. But he was forestalled by Sophy, the parlor-maid, who said one evening that she wished to leave him.

"And why?" said the parson.

"Sam Hobson has asked me to marry him, sir."

"Well—do you want to marry?"

"Not much. But it would be a home for me. And we have heard that one of us will have to leave."

A day or two after she said: "I don't want to

leave just yet, sir, if you don't wish it. Sam and I have quarrelled."

He looked up at her. He had hardly ever observed her before, though he had been frequently conscious of her soft presence in the room. What a kitten-like, flexuous, tender creature she was! She was the only one of the servants with whom he came into immediate and continuous relation. What should he do if Sophy were gone?

Sophy did not go, but one of the others did, and things proceeded quietly again.

When Mr. Twycott, the vicar, was ill, Sophy brought up his meals to him, and she had no sooner left the room one day than he heard a noise on the stairs. She had slipped down with the tray, and so twisted her foot that she could not stand. The village surgeon was called in; the vicar got better, but Sophy was incapacitated for a long time; and she was informed that she must never again walk much or engage in any occupation which required her to stand long on her feet. As soon as she was comparatively well she spoke to him alone. Since she was forbidden to walk and bustle about, and, indeed, could not do so, it became her duty to leave. She could very well work at something sitting down, and she had an aunt a seamstress.

The parson had been very greatly moved by what she had suffered on his account, and he exclaimed, "No, Sophy; lame or not lame, I cannot let you go. You must never leave me again."

He came close to her, and, though she could never exactly tell how it happened, she became conscious of his lips upon her cheek. He then asked her to marry him. Sophy did not exactly love him, but she had a respect for him which almost amounted to veneration. Even if she had wished to get away from him she hardly dared refuse a personage so reverend and august in her eyes, and she assented forthwith to be his wife.

Thus it happened that one fine morning, when the doors of the church were naturally open for ventilation, and the singing birds fluttered in and alighted on the tie-beams of the roof, there was a marriage-service at the communion rails which hardly a soul knew of. The parson and a neighboring curate had entered at one door, and Sophy at another, followed by two necessary persons, whereupon in a short time there emerged a newly-made husband and wife.

Mr. Twycott knew perfectly well that he had committed social suicide by this step, despite Sophy's spotless character, and he had taken his measures accordingly. An exchange of livings had been arranged with an acquaintance who was incumbent of a church in the south of London, and as soon as possible the couple removed thither, abandoning their pretty country home with trees and shrubs and glebe for a narrow, dusty house in a long, straight street, and their fine peal of bells for the wretchedest one-tongued clangor that ever tortured mortal ears. It was all on her account. They were, however, away from every one who had known her former position, and also under less observation from without than they would have had to put up with in any country parish.

Sophy the woman was as charming a partner as a man could possess, though Sophy the lady had her deficiencies. She showed a natural aptitude for little domestic refinements, so far as related to things and manners; but in what is called culture she was less intuitive. She had now been married more than fourteen years, and her husband had taken much trouble with her education; but she still held confused ideas on the use of "was" and "were," which did not beget a respect for her among the few acquaintances she made.

Her great grief in this relation was that her only child, on whose education no expense had been or would be spared, was now old enough to perceive these deficiencies in his mother, and not only to see them but to feel irritated at their existence.

Thus she lived on in the city, and wasted hours in braiding her beautiful hair, till her once apple cheeks waned to pink of the very faintest. Her foot had never regained its natural strength after the accident, and she was mostly obliged to avoid walking altogether. Her husband had grown to like London for its freedom and its domestic privacy; but he was twenty years his Sophy's senior, and had latterly been seized with a serious illness. On this day, however, he had seemed to be well enough to justify her accompanying her son Randolph to the concert.

II

The next time we get a glimpse of her is when she appears in the mournful attire of a widow.

Mr. Twycott had never rallied, and now lay in a well-packed cemetery to the south of the great city, where, if all the dead it contained had stood erect and alive, not one would have known him or recognized his name. The boy had dutifully followed him to the grave, and was now again at school.

Throughout these changes Sophy had been treated like the child she was in nature though not in years. She was left with no control over anything that had been her husband's beyond her modest personal income. In his anxiety lest her inexperience should be overreached he had safeguarded with trustees all he possibly could. The completion of the boy's course at the public school, to be followed in due time by Oxford and ordination, had been all previsioned and arranged, and she really had nothing to occupy her in the world but to eat and drink, and make a business of indolence, and go on weaving and coiling the nut-brown hair, merely keeping a home open for the son whenever he came to her during vacations.

Foreseeing his probable decease long years before her, her husband in his lifetime had purchased for her use a semi-detached villa in the same long, straight road whereon the church and parsonage faced, which was to be hers as long as she chose to live in it. Here she now resided, looking out upon the fragment of lawn in front, and through the railings at the ever-flowing traffic ; or, bending forward over the window-sill on the first floor, stretching her eyes far up and down the vista of sooty trees, hazy air, and drab house façades, along which echoed the noises common to a suburban main thoroughfare.

Somehow, her boy, with his aristocratic school-knowledge, his grammars, and his aversions, was losing those wide infantine sympathies, extending as far as to the sun and moon themselves, with which he, like other children, had been born, and which his mother, a child of nature herself, had loved in him ; he was reducing their compass to a population of a few thousand wealthy and titled people, the mere veneer of a thousand million or so of others who did not interest him at all. He drifted further and further away from her. Sophy's *milieu* being a suburb of minor tradesmen and under-clerks, and her almost only companions the two servants of her own house, it was not surprising that after her husband's death she soon lost the little artificial tastes she had acquired from him, and became—in her son's eyes—a mother whose mistakes and origin it was his painful lot as a gentleman to blush for. As yet he was far from being man enough — if he ever would be — to rate these sins of hers at their true infinitesimal value beside the yearning fondness that welled up and remained penned in her heart till it should be more fully accepted by him, or by some other person or thing. If he had lived at home with her he would have had all of it; but he seemed to require so very little in present circumstances, and it remained stored.

Her life became insupportably dreary; she could not take walks, and had no interest in going for drives, or, indeed, in travelling anywhere. Nearly two years passed without an event, and still she looked on that suburban road, thinking of the village in which she had been born, and whither she would have gone back—oh, how gladly!—even to work in the fields.

Taking no exercise, she often could not sleep, and would rise in the night or early morning and look out upon the then vacant thoroughfare, where the lamps stood like sentinels waiting for some procession to go by. An approximation to such a procession was indeed made every early morning about one o'clock, when the country vehicles passed up with loads of vegetables for Covent Garden market. She often saw them creeping along at this silent and dusky hour—wagon after wagon, bearing green bastions of cabbages nodding to their fall, yet never falling; walls of baskets enclosing masses of beans and pease; pyramids of snow-white turnips, swaying howdahs of mixed produce — creeping along behind aged night-horses, who seemed ever patiently wondering between their hollow coughs why they had always to work at that still hour when all other sentient creatures were privileged to rest. Wrapped in a cloak, it was soothing to watch and sympathize with them when depression and nervousness hindered sleep, and to see how the fresh green-stuff brightened to life as it came opposite the lamp, and how the sweating animals steamed and shone with their miles of travel.

They had an interest, almost a charm, for Sophy, these semi-rural people and vehicles moving in an urban atmosphere, leading a life quite distinct from that of the daytime toilers on the same road. One morning a man who accompanied a wagon-load of potatoes gazed rather hard at the house fronts as he passed, and with a curious emotion she thought his form was familiar to her. She looked out for him again. His being an old-fashioned conveyance with a yellow front, it was easily recognizable, and on the third night after she saw it a second time. The man alongside was, as she had fancied, Sam Hobson, formerly gardener at Gaymead, who would at one time have married her.

She had occasionally thought of him, and wondered if life in a cottage with him would not have been a happier lot than the life she had accepted. She had not thought of him passionately, but her now dismal situation lent an interest to his resurrection—a tender interest which it is impossible to exaggerate. She went back to bed, and began thinking. When did these market-gardeners, who travelled up to town so regularly at one or two in the morning, come back? She dimly recollected seeing their empty wagons, hardly noticeable among the ordinary day-traffic, passing down at some hour before noon.

It was only April, but that morning, after breakfast, she had the window opened, and sat looking out, the feeble sun shining full upon her. She affected to sew, but her eyes never left the street. Between ten and eleven the desired wagon, now unladen, reappeared on its return journey. But Sam was not looking round him then, and drove on in a reverie.

"Sam!" cried she.

Turning with a start, his face lighted up. He called to him a little boy to hold the horse, alighted, and came and stood under her window.

"I can't come down easily, Sam, or I would!" she said. "Did you know I lived here?"

"Well, Mrs. Twycott, I knew you lived along here somewhere. I have often looked out for 'ee."

He briefly explained his own presence on the scene. He had long since given up his gardening in the village near Aldbrickham, and was now manager at a market-gardener's on the south side of London, it being part of his duty to go up to Covent Garden with wagon-loads of produce two or three times a week. In answer to her curious inquiry, he admitted that he had come to this particular district because he had seen in the Aldbrickham paper a year or two before the announcement of the death in South London of the aforetime vicar of Gaymead, which had revived an interest in her dwelling-place that he could not extinguish, leading him to hover about the locality till his present post had been secured.

They spoke of their native village in dear old North Wessex, the spots in which they had played together as children. She tried to feel that she was a dignified personage now, that she must not be too confidential with Sam. But she could not keep it up, and the tears hanging in her eyes were indicated in her voice.

"You are not happy, Mrs. Twycott, I'm afraid," he said.

"Oh, of course not! I lost my husband only the year before last."

"Ah! I meant in another way. You'd like to be home again?"

"This is my home—for life. The house belongs to me. But I understand"— She let it out then.

"Yes, Sam. I long for home—*our* home! I *should* like to be there, and never leave it, and die there." But she remembered herself. "That's only a momentary feeling. I have a son, you know, a dear boy. He's at school now."

"Somewhere handy, I suppose? I see there's lots on 'em along this road."

"Oh no! Not in one of these wretched holes! At a public school—one of the most distinguished in England."

"Chok it all! of course! I forget, ma'am, that you've been a lady for so many years."

"No, I am not a lady," she said, sadly. "I never shall be. But he's a gentleman, and that—makes it—oh, how difficult for me!"

III

The acquaintance thus oddly reopened proceeded apace. She often looked out to get a few words with him, by night or by day. Her sorrow was that she could not accompany her one old friend on foot a little way, and talk more freely than she could do while he paused before the house. One night, at the beginning of June, when she was again on the watch after an absence of some days from the window, he entered the gate and said, softly, "Now, wouldn't some air do you good? I've only half a load this morning. Why not ride up to Covent Garden with me? There's a nice seat on the cabbages, where I've spread a sack. You can be home again in a cab before anybody is up."

She refused at first, and then, trembling with excitement, hastily finished her dressing, and wrapped herself up in cloak and veil, afterwards sidling down-stairs by the aid of the handrail, in a way she could adopt on an emergency. When she had opened the door she found Sam on the step, and he lifted her bodily on his strong arm across the little forecourt into his vehicle. Not a soul was visible or audible in the infinite length of the straight, flat highway, with its ever-waiting lamps converging to points in each direction. The air was fresh as country air at this hour, and the stars shone, except to the north-eastward, where there was a whitish light — the dawn. Sam carefully placed her in the seat and drove on.

They talked as they had talked in old days, Sam pulling himself up now and then, when he thought himself too familiar. More than once she said with misgiving that she wondered if she ought to have indulged in the freak. "But I am so lonely in my house," she added, "and this makes me so happy!"

"You must come again, dear Mrs. Twycott. There is no time o' day for taking the air like this."

It grew lighter and lighter. The sparrows became busy in the streets, and the city waxed denser around them. When they approached the river it was day, and on the bridge they beheld the full blaze of morning sunlight in the direction of St. Paul's, the river glistening towards it, and not a craft stirring.

Near Covent Garden he put her into a cab, and they parted, looking into each other's faces like the very old friends they were. She reached home without adventure, limped to the door, and let herself in with her latch-key unseen.

The air and Sam's presence had revived her; her cheeks were quite pink—almost beautiful. She had something to live for in addition to her son. A woman of pure instincts, she knew there had been nothing really wrong in the journey, but supposed it conventionally to be very wrong indeed.

Soon, however, she gave way to the temptation of going with him again, and on this occasion their conversation was distinctly tender, and Sam said he never should forget her, notwithstanding that she had served him rather badly at one time. After much hesitation he told her of a plan it was in his power to carry out, and one he should like to take in hand, since he did not care for London work; it was to set up as a master greengrocer down at Aldbrickham, the county-town of their native place. He knew of an opening—a shop kept by aged people who wished to retire.

"And why don't you do it, then, Sam?" she asked, with a slight heart-sinking.

"Because I'm not sure if—you'd join me. I know you wouldn't—couldn't! Such a lady as ye've been so long, you couldn't be a wife to a man like me."

"I hardly suppose I could!" she assented, also frightened at the idea.

"If you could," he said, eagerly, "you'd on'y have to sit in the back parlor and look through the glass partition when I was away sometimes—just to keep an eye on things. The lameness wouldn't hinder that. I'd keep you as genteel as ever I could, dear Sophy—if I might think of it," he pleaded.

"Sam, I'll be frank," she said, putting her hand on his. "If it were only myself I would do it, and gladly, though everything I possess would be lost to me by marrying again."

"I don't mind that. It's more independent."

"That's good of you, dear, dear Sam. But there's something else. I have a son. I almost fancy when I am miserable sometimes that he is not really mine, but one I hold in trust for my late husband. He seems to belong so little to me personally, so entirely to his dead father. He is so much educated and I so little that I do not feel dignified enough to be his mother. Well, he would have to be told."

"Yes. Unquestionably." Sam saw her thought and her fear. "Still, you can do as you like, Sophy —Mrs. Twycott," he added. "It is not you who are the child, but he."

"Ah, you don't know! Sam, if I could, I would marry you, some day. But you must wait awhile, and let me think."

It was enough for him, and he was blithe at their parting. Not so she. To tell Randolph seemed impossible. She could wait till he had gone up to Oxford, when what she did would affect his life but little. But would he ever tolerate the idea? And if not, could she defy him?

She had not told him a word when the yearly cricket-match came on at Lord's between the public schools, though Sam had already gone back to Aldbrickham. Mrs. Twycott felt stronger than usual. She went to the match with Randolph, and was able to leave her chair and walk about occasionally. The bright idea occurred to her that she could casually broach the subject while moving round among the spectators, when the boy's spirits were high with interest in the game, and he would weigh domestic matters as feathers in the scale beside the day's victory. They promenaded under the lurid July sun, this pair, so wide apart, yet so near, and Sophy saw the large proportion of boys like her own, in their broad white collars and dwarf hats, and all around the rows of great coaches under which was jumbled the débris of luxurious luncheons—bones, pie-crusts, champagne-bottles, glasses, plates, napkins, and the family silver; while on the coaches sat the proud fathers and mothers; but never a poor mother like her. If Randolph had not appertained to these, had not centred all his interests in them, had not cared exclusively for the class they belonged to, how happy would things have been! A great huzza at some small performance with the bat burst from the multitude of relatives, and Randolph jumped wildly into the air to see what had happened. Sophy fetched up the sentence that had been already shaped; but she could not get it out. The occasion was, perhaps, an inopportune one. The contrast between her story and the display of fashion to which Randolph had grown to regard himself as akin would be fatal. She awaited a better time.

It was on an evening when they were alone in their plain suburban residence, where life was not blue but brown, that she ultimately broke silence, qualifying her announcement of a probable second marriage by assuring him that it would not take place for a long time to come, when he would be living quite independently of her.

The boy thought the idea a very reasonable one, and asked if she had chosen anybody. She hesitated; and he seemed to have a misgiving. He hoped his step-father would be a gentleman, he said.

"Not what you call a gentleman," she answered, timidly. "He'll be much as I was before I knew your father;" and by degrees she acquainted him with the whole. The youth's face remained fixed for a moment; then he flushed, leaned on the table, and burst into passionate tears.

His mother went up to him, kissed all of his face that she could get at, and patted his back as if he were still the baby he once had been, crying herself the while. When he had somewhat recovered from his paroxysm he went hastily to his own room and fastened the door.

Parleyings were attempted through the key-hole,

outside which she waited and listened. It was long before he would reply, and when he did it was to say sternly at her from within: "I am ashamed of you! It will ruin me! A miserable boor! a churl! a clown! It will degrade me in the eyes of all the gentlemen of England!"

"Say no more—perhaps I am wrong! I will struggle against it!" she cried, miserably.

Before Randolph left her that summer a letter arrived from Sam to inform her that he had been unexpectedly fortunate in obtaining the shop. He was in possession; it was the largest in the town, combining fruit with vegetables, and he thought it would form a home worthy even of her some day. Might he not run up to town to see her?

She met him by stealth, and said he must still wait for her final answer. The autumn dragged on, and when Randolph was home at Christmas for the holidays she broached the matter again. But the young gentleman was inexorable.

It was dropped for months; renewed again; abandoned under his repugnance; again attempted, and thus the gentle creature reasoned and pleaded till four or five long years had passed. Then the faithful Sam revived his suit with some peremptoriness. Sophy's son, now an undergraduate, was down from Oxford one Easter, when she again opened the subject. As soon as he was ordained, she argued, he would have a home of his own, wherein she, with her bad grammar and her ignorance, would be an encumbrance to him. Better obliterate her as much as possible.

He showed a more manly anger now, but would not agree. She on her side was more persistent, and he had doubts whether she could be trusted in his absence. But by indignation and contempt for her taste he completely maintained his ascendency; and finally taking her before a little cross and shrine that he had erected in his bedroom for his private devotions, there bade her kneel, and swear that she would not wed Samuel Hobson without his consent. "I owe this to my father!" he said.

The poor woman swore, thinking he would soften as soon as he was ordained and in full swing of clerical work. But he did not. His education had by this time sufficiently ousted his humanity to keep him quite firm; though his mother might have led an idyllic life with her faithful fruiterer and green-grocer, and nobody have been anything the worse in the world.

Her lameness became more confirmed as time went on, and she seldom or never left the house in the long southern thoroughfare, where she seemed to be pining her heart away. "Why mayn't I say to Sam that I'll marry him? Why mayn't I?" she would murmur plaintively to herself when nobody was near.

Some four years after this date a middle-aged man was standing at the door of the largest fruiterer's shop in Aldbrickham. He was the proprietor, but to-day, instead of his usual business attire, he wore a neat suit of black; and his window was partly shuttered. From the railway-station a funeral procession was seen approaching: it passed his door and went out of the town towards the village of Gaymead. The man, whose eyes were wet, held his hat in his hand as the vehicles moved by; while from the mourning coach a young smooth-shaven priest in a high waistcoat looked black as a cloud at the shopkeeper standing there.

December, 1891.

FOR CONSCIENCE' SAKE

I

WHETHER the utilitarian or the intuitive theory of the moral sense be upheld, it is beyond question that there are a few subtle-souled persons with whom the absolute gratuitousness of an act of reparation is an inducement to perform it; while exhortation as to its necessity would breed excuses for leaving it undone. The case of Mr. Millborne and Mrs. Frankland particularly illustrated this, and perhaps something more.

There were few figures better known to the local crossing-sweeper than Mr. Millborne's, in his daily comings and goings along a familiar and quiet London street, where he lived inside the door marked eleven, though not as householder. In age he was fifty at least, and his habits were as regular as those of a person can be who has no occupation but the study of how to keep himself employed. He turned almost always to the right on getting to the end of his street, then he went onward down Bond Street to his club, whence he returned by precisely the same course about six o'clock, on foot; or, if he went to dine, later on in a cab. He was known to be a man of some means, though apparently not wealthy. Being a bachelor he seemed to prefer his present mode of living as a lodger in Mrs. Towney's best rooms, with the use of furniture which he had bought ten times over in rent during his tenancy, to having a house of his own.

None among his acquaintance tried to know him well, for his manner and moods did not excite curiosity or deep friendship. He was not a man who seemed to have anything on his mind, anything to conceal, anything to impart. From his casual remarks it was generally understood that he was country-born, a native of some place in Wessex; that he had come to London as a young man in a banking-house, and had risen to a post of responsibility; when, by the death of his father, who had been fortunate in his investments, the son succeeded to an income which led him to retire from a business life somewhat early.

One evening, when he had been unwell for several days, Dr. Bindon came in after dinner from the adjoining medical quarter, and smoked with him over the fire. The patient's ailment was not such as to require much thought, and they talked together on indifferent subjects.

"I am a lonely man, Bindon—a lonely man," Millborne took occasion to say, shaking his head gloomily. "You don't know such loneliness as mine. . . . And the older I get the more I am dissatisfied with myself. And to-day I have been, through an accident, more than usually haunted by what, above all other events of my life, causes that dissatisfaction—the recollection of an unfulfilled promise made some twenty years ago. In ordinary affairs I have always been considered a man of my word; and perhaps it is on that account that a particular vow I once made and did not keep comes back to me with a magnitude out of all proportion (I dare say) to its real gravity, especially at this time of day. You know the discomfort caused at night by the half-sleeping sense that a door or window has been left unfastened, or in the day by the remembrance of unanswered letters. So does that promise haunt me from time to time, and has done to-day particularly."

There was a pause, and they smoked on. Millborne's eyes, though fixed on the fire, were really regarding attentively a town in the West of England.

"Yes," he continued, "I have never quite forgotten it, though during the busy years of my life it was shelved and buried under the pressure of my pursuits. And, as I say, to-day in particular an incident in the law report of a somewhat similar kind has brought it back again vividly. However, what it was I can tell you in a few words, though no doubt you, as a man of the world, will smile at the thinness of my skin when you hear it. . . . I came up to town at one-and-twenty, from Toneborough, in Outer Wessex, where I was born, and where, before I left, I had won the heart of a young woman of my own age. I promised her marriage, took advantage of my promise, and—am a bachelor."

"The old story."

The other nodded.

"I left the place, and thought at the time I had done a very clever thing in getting so easily out of an entanglement. But I have lived long enough for that promise to return to bother me—to be honest, not altogether as a pricking of the conscience, but as a dissatisfaction with myself as a specimen of the heap of flesh called humanity. If I were to ask you to lend me fifty pounds, which I would repay you next midsummer, and I did not repay you, I should consider myself a shabby sort of fellow, especially if you wanted the money badly. Yet I promised that girl just as distinctly, and then coolly broke my word, as if doing so were rather smart conduct than a mean action; for which the poor victim herself, encumbered with a child, and not I, had really to pay the penalty, in spite of certain pecuniary aid that was given. . . . There, that's the retrospective trouble that I am always unearthing; and you may hardly believe that though so many years have elapsed, and it is all gone by and done with, and she must be getting on for an old woman now, as I am for an old man, it really often destroys my sense of self-respect still."

"Oh, I can understand it. All depends upon the temperament. Thousands of men would have forgotten all about it; so would you, perhaps, if you had married and had a family. Did she ever marry?"

"I don't think so. Oh no — she never did. She left Toneborough, and later on appeared under another name at Exonbury, in the next county, where she was not known. It is very seldom that I go down into that part of the country, but in passing through Exonbury on one occasion I learned that she was quite a settled resident there, as a teacher of music or something of the kind. That much I casually heard when I was there two or three years ago. But I have never set eyes on her since our original acquaintance, and should not know her if I met her."

"Did the child live?" asked the doctor.

"For several years, certainly," replied his friend. "I cannot say if she is living now. It was a little girl. She might be married by this time as far as years go."

"And the mother—was she a decent, worthy young woman?"

"Oh yes; a sensible, quiet girl, neither attractive nor unattractive to the ordinary observer; simply commonplace. Her position at the time of our acquaintance was not so good as mine. My father was a solicitor, as I think I have told you. She was a young girl in a music-shop; and it was represented to me that it would be beneath my position to marry her. Hence the result."

"Well, all I can say is that after twenty years it is probably too late to think of mending such a matter. It has doubtless by this time mended itself. You had better dismiss it from your mind as an evil past your control. Of course, if mother and daughter are alive, or either, you might settle something upon them, if you were inclined, and had it to spare."

"Well, I haven't much to spare, and I have relations in narrow circumstances — perhaps narrower than theirs. But that is not the point. Were I ever so rich I feel I could not rectify the past by money. I did not promise to enrich her. On the contrary, I told her it would probably be dire poverty for both of us. But I did promise to make her my wife."

"Then find her and do it," said the doctor, jocularly, as he rose to leave.

"Ah, Bindon. That, of course, is the obvious jest. But I haven't the slightest desire for marriage; I am quite content to live as I have lived. I am a bachelor by nature and instinct and habit and everything. Besides, though I respect her still (for she was not an atom to blame), I haven't any shadow of love for her. In my mind she exists as one of those women you think well of, but find uninteresting. It would be purely with the idea of putting wrong right that I should hunt her up, and propose to do it off-hand."

"You don't think of it seriously?" said his surprised friend.

"I sometimes think that I would, if it were practicable; simply, as I say, to recover my sense of being a man of honor."

"I wish you luck in the enterprise," said Dr. Bindon. "You'll soon be out of that chair, and then you can put your impulse to the test. But—after twenty years of silence—I should say, don't!"

II

The doctor's advice remained counterpoised in Millborne's mind by the aforesaid mood of seriousness and sense of principle, approximating often to religious sentiment, which had been evolving itself in his breast for months, and even years.

The feeling, however, had no immediate effect upon Mr. Millborne's actions. He soon got over his trifling illness, and was vexed with himself for having, in a moment of impulse, confided such a case of conscience to anybody.

But the force which had prompted it, though latent, remained with him, and ultimately grew stronger. The upshot was that about four months after the date of his illness and disclosure, Millborne found himself on a mild spring morning at Paddington Station, in a train that was starting for the west. His many intermittent thoughts on his broken promise from time to time, in those hours when loneliness brought him face to face with his own personality, had at last resulted in this course.

The decisive stimulus had been given when, a day or two earlier, on looking into a post-office directory, he learned that the woman he had not met for twenty years was still living on at Exonbury under the name she had assumed when, a year or two after her disappearance from her native town and his, she had returned from abroad as a young widow with a child, and taken up her residence at the former city. Her condition was apparently but little changed, and her daughter seemed to be with her, their names standing in the directory as "Mrs. Leonora Frankland and Miss Frankland, Teachers of Music and Dancing."

Mr. Millborne reached Exonbury in the afternoon, and his first business, before even taking his luggage into the town, was to find the house occupied by the teachers. Standing in a central and open place it was not difficult to discover, a well-burnished brass door-plate bearing their names prominently. He hesitated to enter without further knowledge, and ultimately took lodgings over a toy-shop opposite, securing a sitting-room which faced a similar drawing or sitting room at the Franklands', where the dancing lessons were given. Installed here he was enabled to make indirectly, and without suspicion, inquiries and observations on the character of the ladies over the way, which he did with much deliberateness.

He learned that the widow, Mrs. Frankland, with her one daughter, Frances, was of cheerful and excellent repute, energetic and painstaking with her pupils, of whom she had a good many, and in whose tuition her daughter assisted her. She was quite a recognized townswoman, and though the dancing branch of her profession was perhaps a trifle worldly, she was really a serious-minded lady who, being obliged to live by what she knew how to teach, balanced matters by lending a hand at charitable bazaars, assisting at sacred concerts, and giving musical recitations in aid of funds for bewildering happy savages, and other such enthusiasms of this enlightened country. Her daughter was one of the foremost of the bevy of young women who decorated the churches at Easter and Christmas, was organist in one of those edifices, and had subscribed to the testimonial of a silver broth-basin that was presented to the Rev. Mr. Walker as a token of gratitude for his faithful and arduous intonations of six months as sub-precentor in the cathedral. Altogether, mother and daughter appeared to be a typical and innocent pair among the genteel citizens of Exonbury.

As a natural and simple way of advertising their profession they allowed the windows of the music-room to be a little open, so that you had the pleasure of hearing all along the street at any hour between sunrise and sunset fragmentary gems of classical music as interpreted by the young people of twelve or fourteen who took lessons there. But it was said that Mrs. Frankland made most of her income by letting out pianos on hire, and by selling them as agent for the makers.

The report pleased Millborne ; it was highly creditable, and far better than he had hoped. He was curious to get a view of the two women who led such blameless lives.

He had not long to wait to gain a glimpse of Leonora. It was when she was standing on her own door-step, opening her parasol, on the morning after his arrival. She was thin, though not gaunt ; and a good, well-wearing, thoughtful face had taken the place of the one which had temporarily attracted him in the days of his nonage. She wore black, and it became her in her character of widow. The daughter next appeared; she was a smoothed and rounded copy of her mother, with the same decision in her mien that Leonora had, and a bounding gait in which he traced a faint resemblance to his own at her age.

For the first time he absolutely made up his mind to call on them. But his antecedent step was to send Leonora a note the next morning, stating his proposal to visit her, and suggesting the evening as the time, because she seemed to be so greatly occupied in her professional capacity during the day. He purposely worded his note in such a form as not to require an answer from her which would be possibly awkward to write.

No answer came. Naturally he should not have been surprised at this; and yet he felt a little checked, even though she had only refrained from volunteering a reply that was not demanded.

At eight, the hour fixed by himself, he crossed over and was passively admitted by the servant. Mrs. Frankland, as she called herself, received him in the large music and dancing room on the first floor front, and not in any private little parlor as he had expected. This cast a distressingly business-like color over their first meeting after so many years of severance. The woman he had wronged stood before him, well-dressed, even to his metropolitan eyes, and her manner as she came up to him was dignified even to hardness. She certainly was not glad to see him. But what could he expect after a neglect of twenty years!

"How do you do, Mr. Millborne?" she said, cheerfully, as to any chance caller. "I am obliged to receive you here because my daughter has a friend downstairs."

"Your daughter—and mine."

"Ah—yes, yes," she replied, hastily, as if the addition had escaped her memory. "But perhaps the less said about that the better, in fairness to me. You will consider me a widow, please."

"Certainly, Leonora—" He could not get on, her manner was so cold and indifferent. The expected scene of sad reproach, subdued to delicacy by the run of years, was absent altogether. He was obliged to come to the point without preamble.

"You are quite free, Leonora—I mean as to marriage? There is nobody who has your promise, or—"

"Oh yes; quite free, Mr. Millborne," she said, somewhat surprised.

"Then I will tell you why I have come. Twenty years ago I promised to make you my wife, and I am here to fulfil that promise. Heaven forgive my tardiness!"

Her surprise was increased, but she was not agitated. She seemed to become gloomy, disapproving. "I could not entertain such an idea at this time of life," she said, after a moment or two. "It would complicate matters too greatly. I have a very fair income, and require no help of any sort. I have no wish to marry. . . . What could have induced you to come on such an errand now? It seems quite extraordinary, if I may say so."

"It must—I dare say it does," Millborne replied, vaguely; "and I must tell you that impulse—I mean in the sense of passion—has little to do with it. I wish to marry you, Leonora; I much desire to marry you. But it is an affair of conscience, a case of fulfilment. I promised you, and it was dishonorable of me to go away. I want to remove that sense of dishonor before I die. No doubt we might get to love each other as warmly as we did in old times."

She dubiously shook her head. "I appreciate your motives, Mr. Millborne; but you must consider my position, and you will see that, short of the personal wish to marry, which I don't feel, there is no reason why I should change my state, even though by so doing I should ease your conscience. My position in this town is a respected one; I have built it up by my own hard labors, and, in short, I don't wish to alter it. My daughter, too, is just on the verge of an engagement to be married to a young man who will make her an excellent husband. It will be in every way a desirable match for her. He is down-stairs now."

"Does she know—anything about me?"

"Oh no, no; God forbid! Her father is dead and buried to her. So that, you see, things are going on smoothly, and I don't want to disturb their progress."

He nodded. "Very well," he said, and rose to go. At the door, however, he came back again.

"Still, Leonora," he urged, "I have come on purpose, and I don't see what disturbance would be caused. You would simply marry an old friend. Won't you reconsider? It is no more than right that we should be united, remembering the girl."

She shook her head, and patted with her foot nervously.

"Well, I won't detain you," he added. "I shall not be leaving Exonbury yet. You will allow me to see you again?"

"Yes; I don't mind," she said, reluctantly.

The obstacles he had encountered, though they did not reanimate his dead passion for Leonora, did certainly make it appear indispensable to his peace of mind to overcome her coldness. He called frequently. The first meeting with the daughter was a trying ordeal, though he did not feel drawn towards her as he had expected to be; she did not excite his sympathies. Her mother confided to Frances the errand of "her old friend," which was viewed by the daughter with strong disfavor. His desire being thus uncongenial to both, for a long time Millborne made not the least impression upon Mrs. Frankland. His attentions pestered her rather than pleased her. He was surprised at her firmness, and it was only when he hinted at moral reasons for their union that she was ever shaken. "Strictly speaking," he would say, "we ought, as honest persons, to marry; and that's the truth of it, Leonora."

"I have looked at it in that light," she said, quickly. "It struck me at the very first. But I don't see the force of the argument. I totally deny that after this interval of time I am bound to marry you for honor's sake. I would have married you, as you know well enough, at the proper time. But what is the use of remedies now?"

They were standing at the window. A scantily-whiskered young man in clerical attire called at the door below. Leonora flushed with interest.

"Who is he?" asked Mr. Millborne.

"My Frances's lover. I am so sorry—she is not at home! Ah! they have told him where she is, and he has gone to find her. I hope that suit will prosper, at any rate!"

"Why shouldn't it?"

"Well, he cannot marry yet; and Frances sees but little of him now he has left Exonbury. He was formerly doing duty here, but now he is curate of St. John's, Ivell, fifty miles up the line. There is a tacit agreement between them, but—there have been friends of his who object, because of our vocation. However, he sees the absurdity of such an objection as that, and is not influenced by it."

"Your marriage with me would help the match, instead of hindering it, as you have said."

"Do you think it would?"

"It certainly would, by taking you out of this business altogether."

By chance he had found the way to move her somewhat, and he followed it up. This view was imparted to Mrs. Frankland's daughter, and it led her to soften her opposition. Millborne, who had given up his lodging in Exonbury, journeyed to and fro regularly, till at last he overcame her negations, and she expressed a reluctant assent.

They were married at the nearest church; and the good-will—whatever that was—of the music-and-dancing connection was sold to a successor only too ready to jump into the place, the Millbornes having decided to live in London.

III

Millborne was a householder in his old district, though not in his old street, and Mrs. Millborne and their daughter had turned themselves into Londoners. Frances was well reconciled to the removal by her lover's satisfaction at the change. It suited him better to travel from Ivell a hundred miles to see her in London, where he frequently had other engagements, than fifty in the opposite direction where nothing but herself required his presence. So here they were, furnished up to the attics, in one of the small but popular streets of the West district, in a house whose front, till lately of the complexion of a chimney-sweep, had been scraped to show to the surprised wayfarer the bright yellow and red brick that had lain lurking beneath the soot of fifty years.

The social lift that the two women had derived from the alliance was considerable; but when the exhilaration which accompanies a first residence in London, the sensation of standing on a pivot of the world, had passed, their lives promised to be somewhat duller than when, at despised Exonbury, they had enjoyed a nodding acquaintance with three-fourths of the town. Mr. Millborne did not criticise his wife; he could not. Whatever defects of hardness and acidity his original treatment and the lapse of years might have developed in her, his sense of a realized idea, of a re-established self-satisfaction, was always thrown into the scale on her side, and outweighed all objections.

It was about a month after their settlement in town that the household decided to spend a week at a watering-place in the Isle of Wight, and while there the Rev. Percival Cope (the young curate aforesaid) came to see them, Frances in particular. No formal engagement of the young pair had been announced as yet, but it was clear that their mutual understanding could not end in anything but marriage without grievous disappointment to one of the parties at least. Not that Frances was sentimental. She was rather of the imperious sort, indeed ; and, to say all, the young girl had not fulfilled her father's expectations of her. But he hoped and worked for her welfare as sincerely as any father could do.

Mr. Cope was introduced to the new head of the family, and stayed with them in the island two or three days. On the last day of his visit they decided to venture on a two hours' sail in one of the small yachts which lay there for hire. The trip had not progressed far before all except the curate found that sailing in a breeze did not quite agree with them ; but as he seemed to enjoy the experience, the other three bore their condition as well as they could without grimace or complaint, till the young man, observing their discomfort, gave immediate directions to tack about. On the way back to port they sat silent, facing each other.

Nausea in such circumstances, like midnight watching, fatigue, trouble, fright, has this marked effect upon the countenance—that it often brings out strongly the divergences of the individual from the norm of his race, accentuating superficial peculiarities to radical distinctions. Unexpected physiognomies will uncover themselves at these times in well-known faces; the aspect becomes invested with the spectral presence of entombed and forgotten ancestors ; and family lineaments of special or exclusive cast, which in ordinary moments are masked by a stereotyped expression and mien, start up with crude insistence to the view.

Frances, sitting beside her mother's husband, with Mr. Cope opposite, was naturally enough much regarded by the curate during the tedious sail home; at first with sympathetic smiles. Then, as the middle-aged father and his child grew each gray-faced, as the pretty blush of Frances disintegrated into spotty stains, and the soft rotundities of her features diverged from their familiar and reposeful beauty into elemental lines, Cope was gradually struck with the resemblance between a pair in their discomfort who in their ease presented nothing to the eye in common. Mr. Millborne and Frances in their indisposition were strangely, startlingly alike.

The inexplicable fact absorbed Cope's attention quite. He forgot to smile at Frances, to hold her hand; and when they touched the shore he remained sitting for some moments like a man in a trance.

As they went homeward, and recovered their complexions and contours, the similarities one by one disappeared, and Frances and Mr. Millborne were again masked by the commonplace differences of sex and age. It was as if, during the voyage, a mysterious veil had been lifted, temporarily revealing a strange pantomime of the past.

During the evening he said to her, casually: "Is your step-father a cousin of your mother, dear Frances?"

"Oh no," said she; "there is no relationship. He was only an old friend of hers. Why did you suppose such a thing?"

He did not explain, and the next morning started to resume his duties at Ivell.

Cope was an honest young fellow, and shrewd

withal. At home in his quiet rooms in St. Peter's Street, Ivell, he pondered long and unpleasantly on the revelations of the cruise. The tale it told was distinct enough, and for the first time his position was an uncomfortable one. He had met the Franklands at Exonbury as parishioners, had been attracted by Frances, and had floated thus far into an engagement which was indefinite only because of his inability to marry just yet. The Franklands' past had apparently contained mysteries, and it did not coincide with his judgment to marry into a family whose mystery was of the sort suggested. So he sat and sighed between his reluctance to lose Frances and his natural dislike of forming a connection with people whose antecedents would not bear the strictest investigation.

A passionate lover of the old-fashioned sort might possibly never have halted to weigh these doubts; but though he was in the Church, Cope's affections were fastidious—distinctly tempered with the alloys of the century's decadence. He delayed writing to Frances for some while, simply because he could not tune himself up to enthusiasm when worried by suspicions of such a kind.

Meanwhile the Millbornes had returned to London, and Frances was growing anxious. In talking to her mother of Cope she had innocently alluded to his curious inquiry if her mother and her step-father were connected by any tie of cousinship. Mrs. Millborne made her repeat the words. Frances did so, and watched with inquisitive eyes their effect upon her elder.

"What is there so startling in his inquiry, then?" she asked. "Can it have anything to do with his not writing to me?"

Her mother flinched, but did not inform her, and Frances also was now drawn within the atmosphere of suspicion. That night, when standing by chance outside the chamber of her parents, she heard for the first time their voices engaged in a sharp altercation.

The apple of discord had, indeed, been dropped into the house of the Millbornes. The scene within the chamber door was Mrs. Millborne standing before her dressing-table, looking across to her husband in the dressing-room adjoining, where he was sitting down, his eyes fixed on the floor.

"Why did you come and disturb my life a second time?" she harshly asked. "Why did you pester me with your conscience till I was driven to accept you to get rid of your importunity? Frances and I were doing well: the one desire of my life was that she should marry that good young man. And now the match is broken off by your cruel interference! Why did you show yourself in my world again, and raise this scandal upon my hard-won respectability—won by such weary years of labor as none will ever know!" She bent her face upon the table and wept passionately.

There was no reply from Mr. Millborne. Frances lay awake nearly all that night, and when at breakfast-time the next morning still no letter appeared from Mr. Cope, she entreated her mother to go to Ivell and see if the young man were ill.

Mrs. Millborne went, returning the same day. Frances, anxious and haggard, met her at the station.

Was all well? Her mother could not say it was; though he was not ill.

One thing she had found out—that it was a mistake to hunt up a man when his inclinations were to hold aloof. Returning with her mother in the cab, Frances insisted upon knowing what the mystery was which plainly had alienated her lover. The precise words which had been spoken at the interview with him that day at Ivell Mrs. Millborne could not be induced to repeat; but thus far she admitted—that the estrangement was fundamentally owing to Mr. Millborne having sought her out and married her.

"And why did he seek you out—and why were you obliged to marry him?" asked the distressed girl. Then the evidences pieced themselves together in her acute mind, and, her color gradually rising, she asked her mother if what they pointed to was indeed the fact. Her mother admitted that it was.

A flush of mortification succeeded to the flush of shame upon the young woman's face. How could a scrupulously correct clergyman and lover like Mr. Cope ask her to be his wife after this discovery of her irregular birth? She covered her eyes with her hands in a silent despair.

In the presence of Mr. Millborne they at first suppressed their anguish. But by-and-by their feelings got the better of them, and when he was asleep in his chair after dinner, Mrs. Millborne's irritation broke out. The imbittered Frances joined her in reproaching the man who had come as the spectre to their intended feast of Hymen, and turned its promise to ghastly failure.

"Why were you so weak, mother, as to admit such an enemy to your house—one so obviously your evil genius—much less accept him as a husband, after so long? If you had only told me all, I could have advised you better! But I suppose I have no right to reproach him, bitter as I feel, and even though he has blighted my life forever!"

"Frances, I did hold out; I saw it was a mistake to have any more to say to a man who had been such an unmitigated curse to me. But he would not listen; he kept on about his conscience and mine till I was bewildered, and said, 'Yes.' . . . Bringing us away from a quiet town where we were known and respected—

what an ill-considered thing it was! Oh, the content of those days! We had society there, people in our own position, who did not expect more of us than we expected of them. Here, where there is so much, there is nothing! He said London society was so bright and brilliant that it would be like a new world. It may be to those who are in it; but what is that to us two lonely women? we only see it flashing past! . . . Oh, the fool, the fool that I was!"

Now Millborne was not so soundly asleep as to prevent his hearing these animadversions that were almost execrations, and many more of the same sort. As there was no peace for him at home, he went again to his club, where, since his reunion with Leonora, he had seldom if ever been seen. But the shadow of the troubles in his household interfered with his comfort here also; he could not, as formerly, settle down into his favorite chair with the evening paper, reposeful in the celibate's sense that where he was his world's centre had its fixture. His world was now an ellipse, with a dual centrality, of which his own was not the major.

The young curate of Ivell still held aloof, tantalizing Frances by his elusiveness. Plainly he was waiting upon events. Millborne bore the reproaches of his wife and daughter almost in silence, but by degrees he grew meditative, as if revolving a new idea. The bitter cry about blighting their existence at length became so impassioned that one day Millborne calmly proposed to return again to the country; not necessarily to Exonbury, but, if they were willing, to a little old manor-house which he had found was to be let, standing a mile from Mr. Cope's town of Ivell.

They were surprised, and, despite their view of him as the bringer of ill, were disposed to accede. "Though I suppose," said Mrs. Millborne to him, "it will end in Mr. Cope's asking you flatly about the past, and your being compelled to tell him, which may dash all my hopes for Frances. She gets more and more like you every day, particularly when she is in a bad temper. People will see you together and notice it, and I don't know what may come of it!"

"I don't think they will see us together," he said; but he entered into no argument when she insisted otherwise. The removal was eventually resolved on; the town-house was disposed of, and again came the invasion by furniture-men and vans, till all the movables and servants were whisked away. He sent his wife and daughter to a hotel while this was going on, taking two or three journeys himself to Ivell to superintend the refixing, and the improvement of the grounds. When all was done he returned to them in town.

The house was ready for their reception, he told them, and there only remained the journey. He accompanied them and their personal luggage to the station only, having, he said, to remain in town a short time on business with his lawyer. They went, dubious and discontented, for the much-loved Cope had made no sign.

"If we were going down to live here alone," said Mrs. Millborne to her daughter in the train; "and there was no intrusive telltale presence! But let it be!"

The house was a lovely little place in a grove of elms, and they liked it much. The first person to call upon them as new residents was Mr. Cope. He was delighted to find that they had come so near, and (though he did not say this) meant to live in such excellent style. He had not, however, resumed the manner of a lover.

"Your father spoils all!" murmured Mrs. Millborne.

But three days later she received a letter from her husband which caused her no small degree of astonishment. It was written from Boulogne.

It began with a long explanation of settlements of his property, in which he had been engaged since their departure. The chief feature in the business was that Mrs. Millbourne found herself the absolute owner of a comfortable sum in personal estate, and Frances of a life-interest in a larger sum, the principal to be afterwards divided among her children, if she had any. The remainder of his letter ran as hereunder:

"I have learned that there are some derelictions of duty which cannot be blotted out by tardy accomplishment. Our evil actions do not remain isolated in the past, waiting only to be reversed; like locomotive plants they spread and reroot, till to destroy the original stem has no material effect in killing them. I made a mistake in searching you out; I admit it; whatever the remedy may be in such cases it is not marriage, and the best thing for you and me is that you do not see me more. You had better not seek me, for you will not be likely to find me; you are well provided for, and we may do ourselves more harm than good by meeting again. F. M."

Millborne, in short, disappeared from that day forward. But a searching inquiry would have revealed that, soon after the Millbornes went to Ivell, an Englishman who did not give the name of Millborne took up his residence in Brussels; a man who might have been recognized by Mrs. Millborne if she had met him. One afternoon in the ensuing summer, when this gentleman was looking over the English papers, he saw the announcement of Miss Frances Frankland's marriage. She had become the Rev. Mrs. Cope.

"Thank God!" said the gentleman.

But his momentary satisfaction was far from being

happiness. As he formerly had been weighted with a bad conscience, so now was he burdened with the heavy thought which oppressed Antigone, that by honorable observance of a rite he had obtained for himself the reward of dishonorable laxity. Occasionally he had to be helped to his lodgings by his servant from the *cercle* he frequented, through having imbibed a little too much liquor to be able to take care of himself. But he was harmless, and even when he had been drinking said little.

March, 1891.

A TRAGEDY OF TWO AMBITIONS

I

THE shouts of the village-boys came in at the window, accompanied by broken laughter from loungers at the inn door; but the brothers Halborough worked on.

They were sitting in a bedroom of the master-millwright's house, engaged in the untutored reading of Greek and Latin. It was no tale of Homeric blows and knocks, Argonautic voyaging, or Theban family woe that inflamed their imaginations and spurred them onward. They were plodding away at the Greek Testament, immersed in a chapter of the idiomatic and difficult Epistle to the Hebrews.

The dog-day sun in its decline reached the low ceiling with slanting sides, and the shadows of the great goat's-willow swayed and interchanged upon the walls like a spectral army manœuvring. The open casement which admitted the remoter sounds now brought the voice of some one close at hand. It was their sister, a pretty girl of fourteen, who stood in the court below.

"I can see the tops of your heads! What's the use of staying up there? I like you not to go out with the street-boys; but do come and play with me!"

They treated her as an inadequate interlocutor, and

put her off with some slight word. She went away disappointed. Presently there was a dull noise of heavy footsteps at the side of the house, and one of the brothers sat up. "I fancy I hear him coming," he murmured, his eyes on the window.

A man in the light drab clothes of an old-fashioned country tradesman approached from round the corner, reeling as he came. The elder son flushed with anger, rose from his books, and descended the stairs. The younger sat on, till, after the lapse of a few minutes, his brother re-entered the room.

"Did Rosa see him?"

"No."

"Nor anybody?"

"No."

"What have you done with him?"

"He's in the straw-shed. I got him in with some trouble, and he has fallen asleep. I thought this would be the explanation of his absence! No stones dressed for Miller Kench, the great wheel of the saw-mill waiting for new float-boards, even the poor folk not able to get their wagons wheeled."

"What *is* the use of poring over this!" said the younger, shutting up Donnegan's *Lexicon* with a slap. "Oh, if we had only been able to keep mother's seven hundred pounds, what we could have done!"

"How well she had estimated the sum necessary! Three hundred and fifty each, she thought. And I have no doubt that we could have done it on that with care."

This loss of the seven hundred pounds was the sharp thorn of their crown. It was a sum which their mother had amassed with great exertion and self-denial, by adding to a chance legacy such other small amounts as she could lay hands on from time to time; and she had intended with the hoard to indulge the dear wish of her heart—that of sending her sons, Joshua and Cornelius, to one of the universities, having been informed that from three hundred to three hundred and fifty each might carry them through their terms with such great economy as she knew she could trust them to practise. But she had died a year or two before this time, worn out by too keen a strain towards these ends; and the money, coming unreservedly into the hands of their father, had been nearly dissipated. With its exhaustion went all opportunity and hope of a university degree for the sons.

"It drives me mad when I think of it," said Joshua, the elder. "And here we work and work in our own bungling way, and the utmost we can hope for is a term of years as national school-masters, and possible admission to a theological college, and ordination as despised licentiates."

The anger of the elder was reflected as simple sadness in the face of the other. "We can preach the gospel as well without a hood on our surplices as with one," he said, with feeble consolation.

"Preach the gospel—true," said Joshua, with a slight pursing of mouth. "But we can't rise."

"Let us make the best of it, and grind on."

The other was silent, and they drearily bent over their books again.

The cause of all this gloom, the millwright Halborough, now snoring in the shed, had been a thriving master-machinist, notwithstanding his free and careless disposition, till a taste for a more than adequate quantity of strong liquor took hold of him; since when his habits had interfered with his business sadly. Already millers went elsewhere for their gear, and only one set of hands was now kept going, though there were formerly two. Already he found a difficulty in meeting his men at the week's end, and though they had been reduced in number, there was barely enough work to do for those who remained.

The sun dropped lower and vanished, the shouts of the village children ceased to resound, darkness cloaked the students' bedroom, and all the scene outwardly breathed peace. None knew of the fevered youthful ambitions that throbbed in two breasts within the quiet creeper-covered walls of the millwright's house.

In a few months the brothers left the village of their birth to enter themselves as students in a training college for school-masters; first having placed their young sister Rosa under as efficient a tuition at a fashionable watering-place as the means at their disposal could command.

II

A man in semi-clerical dress was walking along the road which led from the railway station into a provincial town. As he walked he read persistently, only looking up once now and then to see that he was keeping on the foot-track and to avoid other passengers. At those moments, whoever had known the former students at the millwright's would have perceived that one of them, Joshua Halborough, was the peripatetic reader here.

What had been simple force in the youth's face was energized judgment in the man's. His character was gradually writing itself out in his countenance. That he was watching his own career with deeper and deeper interest, that he continually "heard his days before him," and cared to hear little else, might have been hazarded from what was seen there. His ambitions were, in truth, passionate, yet controlled; so that the germs of many more plans than ever blossomed to maturity had place in him; and forward visions were kept purposely in twilight to avoid distraction.

Events so far had been encouraging. Shortly after assuming the mastership of his first school he had obtained an introduction to the bishop of a diocese far from his native county, who had looked upon him as a promising young man and taken him in hand. He was now in the second year of his residence at the theological college of the cathedral town, and would soon be presented for ordination.

He entered the town, turned into a back street, and then into a yard, keeping his book before him till he set foot under the arch of the latter place. Round the arch was written "National School," and the stone-work of the jambs was worn away as nothing but boys and the waves of the ocean will wear it. He was soon amid the sing-song accents of the scholars.

His brother Cornelius, who was the school-master here, laid down the pointer with which he was directing attention to the capes of Europe, and came forward.

"That's his brother Jos!" whispered one of the sixth-standard boys. "He's going to be a pa'son. He's now at college."

"Corney is going to be one, too, when he's saved enough money," said another.

After greeting his brother, whom he had not seen for several months, the junior began to explain his system of teaching geography.

But Halborough the elder took no interest in the subject. "How about your own studies?" he asked. "Did you get the books I sent?"

Cornelius had received them, and he related what he was doing.

"Mind you work in the morning. What time do you get up?"

The younger replied: "Half-past five."

"Half-past four is not a minute too soon this time of the year. There is no time like the morning for construing. I don't know why, but when I feel even too dreary to read a novel I can translate—there is something mechanical about it, I suppose. Now, Cornelius, you are rather behindhand, and have some heavy reading before you if you mean to get out of this next Christmas."

"I am afraid I have."

"We must soon sound the bishop. I am sure you will get a title without difficulty when he has heard all. The subdean, the principal of my college, says that the best plan will be for you to come there when his lordship is present at an examination, and he'll get you a personal interview with him. Mind you make a good impression upon him. I found in my case that that was everything, and doctrine almost nothing. You'll do for a deacon, Corney, if not for a priest."

The younger remained thoughtful. "Have you heard from Rosa lately?" he asked; "I had a letter this morning."

"Yes. The little minx writes rather too often. She is homesick — though Brussels must be an attractive place enough. But she must make the most of her time over there. I thought a year would be enough for her, after that high-class school at Sandbourne; but I have decided to give her two, and make a good job of it, expensive as the establishment is."

Their two rather harsh faces had softened directly they began to speak of their sister, whom they loved more ambitiously than they loved themselves.

"But where is the money to come from, Joshua?"

"I have already got it." He looked round, and

finding that some boys were near withdrew a few steps. "I have borrowed it at five per cent. from the farmer who used to occupy the farm next our field. You remember him."

"But about paying him?"

"I shall pay him by degrees out of my stipend. No, Cornelius, it was no use to do the thing by halves. She promises to be a most attractive, not to say beautiful, girl. I have seen that for years; and if her face is not her fortune, her face and her brains together will be, if I observe and contrive aright. That she should be, every inch of her, an accomplished and refined woman, was indispensable for the fulfilment of her destiny, and for moving onward and upward with us; and she'll do it, you will see. I'd half starve myself rather than take her away from that school now."

They looked round the school they were in. To Cornelius it was natural and familiar enough; but to Joshua, with his limited human sympathies, who had just dropped in from a superior sort of place, the sight jarred unpleasantly, as being that of something he had left behind. "I shall be glad when you are out of this," he said, "and in your pulpit, and well through your first sermon."

"You may as well say, inducted into my fat living, while you are about it."

"Ah, well; don't think lightly of the Church. There's a fine work for any man of energy in the Church, as you'll find," he said, fervidly. "Torrents of infidelity to be stemmed, new views of old subjects to be expounded, truths in spirit to be substituted for truths in the letter. . . ." He lapsed into reverie with the vision of his career, persuading himself that it was ardor for Christianity which spurred him on, and not pride of place. He had shouldered a body of doctrine, and was prepared to defend it tooth and nail, solely for the honor and glory that warriors win.

"If the Church is elastic, and stretches to the shape of the time, she'll last, I suppose," said Cornelius. "If not— Only think, I bought a copy of Paley's *Evidences*, best edition, broad margins, excellent preservation, at a book-stall the other day for—ninepence; and I thought that at this rate Christianity must be in rather a bad way."

"No, no!" said the other, almost angrily. "It only shows that such defences are no longer necessary. Men's eyes can see the truth without extraneous assistance. Besides, we are in for Christianity, and must stick to her, whether or no. I am just now going right through Pusey's *Library of the Fathers*."

"You'll be a bishop, Joshua, before you have done!"

"Ah!" said the other, bitterly, shaking his head. "Perhaps I might have been—I might have been! But where is my D.D. or LL.D.? and how be a bishop without that kind of appendage? Archbishop Tillotson was the son of a Sowerby clothier, but he was sent to Clare College. To hail Oxford or Cambridge as *alma mater* is not for me—for us! My God! when I think of what we should have been—what fair promise has been blighted by that cursed, worthless—"

"Hush, hush! . . . But I feel it, too, as much as you. I have seen it more forcibly lately. You would have obtained your degree long before this time—possibly fellowship — and I should have been on my way to mine."

"Don't talk of it," said the other. "We must do the best we can."

They looked out of the window sadly through the dusty panes, so high up that only the sky was visible. By degrees the haunting trouble loomed again, and

Cornelius broke the silence with a whisper: "He has called on me!"

The living pulses died on Joshua's face, which grew arid as a clinker. "When was that?" he asked, quickly.

"Last week."

"How did he get here—so many miles?"

"Came by railway. He came to ask for money."

"Ah!"

"He says he will call on you."

Joshua replied resignedly. The theme of their conversation spoiled his buoyancy for that afternoon. He returned in the evening, Cornelius accompanying him to the station; but he did not read in the train which took him back to the Fountall Theological College, as he had done on the way out. That ineradicable trouble still remained as a squalid spot in the expanse of his life. He sat with the other students in the cathedral choir next day; and the recollection of the trouble obscured the purple splendor thrown by the panes upon the floor.

It was afternoon. All was as still in the close as a cathedral green can be between the Sunday services, and the incessant cawing of the rooks was the only sound. Joshua Halborough had finished his ascetic lunch, and had gone into the library, where he stood for a few moments looking out of the large window facing the green. He saw walking slowly across it a man in a fustian coat and a battered white hat with a much-ruffled nap, having upon his arm a tall gypsy woman wearing long brass ear-rings. The man was staring quizzically at the west front of the cathedral, and Halborough recognized in him the form and features of his father. Who the woman was he knew not. Almost as soon as Joshua became conscious of these things, the subdean, who was also the principal of the college, and of whom the young man stood in more awe than of the bishop himself, emerged from the gate and entered a path across the close. The pair met the dignitary, and to Joshua's horror his father turned and addressed the subdean.

What passed between them he could not tell. But as he stood in a cold sweat he saw his father place his hand familiarly on the subdean's shoulder; the shrinking response of the latter, and his quick withdrawal, told his feeling. The woman seemed to say nothing, but when the subdean had passed by they came on towards the college gate.

Halborough flew along the corridor and out at a side door, so as to intercept them before they could reach the front entrance, for which they were making. He caught them behind a clump of laurel.

"By Jerry, here's the very chap! Well, you're a fine fellow, Jos, never to send your father as much as a twist o' baccy on such an occasion, and to leave him to travel all these miles to find ye out!"

"First, who is this?" said Joshua Halborough, with pale dignity, waving his hand towards the buxom woman with the great ear-rings.

"Dammy, the mis'ess! Your step-mother. Didn't you know I'd married? She helped me home from market one night, and we came to terms, and struck the bargain. Didn't we, Selinar?"

"Oi, by the great Lord an' we did!" simpered the lady.

"Well, what sort of a place is this you are living in?" asked the millwright. "A kind of house of correction, apparently."

Joshua listened abstractedly, his features set to resignation. Sick at heart he was going to ask them if they were in want of any necessary, any meal, when his father cut him short by saying, "Why, we've called to ask ye to come round and take pot-luck with us at the Cock and Bottle, where we've put up for the day, on our way to see mis'ess's friends at Binegar Fair, where they'll be lying under canvas for a night or two. As for the victuals at the Cock I can't testify to 'em at all; but for the drink, they've the rarest drop of Old Tom that I've tasted for many a year."

"Thanks; but I am a teetotaler, and I have lunched," said Joshua, who could fully believe his father's testimony to the gin from the odor of his breath. "You see we have to observe regular habits here, and I couldn't be seen at the Cock and Bottle just now."

"Oh, dammy, then don't come, your reverence. Perhaps you won't mind standing treat for those who can be seen there."

"Not a penny," said the younger, firmly. "You've had enough already."

"Thank you for nothing. By-the-bye, who was that spindle-legged, shoe-buckled parson feller we met by now? He seemed to think we should poison him."

Joshua remarked coldly that it was the principal of his college, guardedly inquiring, "Did you tell him whom you were come to see?"

His father did not reply. He and his strapping gypsy wife—if she were his wife—stayed no longer, and disappeared in the direction of the High Street. Joshua Halborough went back to the library. Determined as was his nature, he wept hot tears upon the books, and was immeasurably more wretched that afternoon than the unwelcome millwright. In the evening he sat down and wrote a letter to his brother, in which, after stating what had happened, and expatiating upon this new disgrace in the gypsy wife, he propounded a plan for raising money sufficient to induce the couple to emigrate to Canada. "It is our only chance," he said. "The case as it stands is maddening. For a successful painter, sculptor, musician, author, who takes society by storm, it is no drawback; it is sometimes even a romantic recommendation to hail from outcasts and profligates. But for a clergyman of the Church of England! Cornelius, it is fatal! To succeed in the Church, people must believe in you, first of all, as a gentleman, secondly as a man of means, thirdly as a scholar, fourthly as a preacher, fifthly perhaps as a Christian—but always first as a gentleman, with all their heart and soul and strength. I would have faced the fact of being a small machinist's son, and have taken my chance, if he'd been in any sense respectable and decent. The essence of Christianity is humility, and by the help of God I would have brazened it out. But this terrible vagabondage and disreputable connection! If he does not accept my terms and leave the country, it will extinguish us and kill me. For how can we live and relinquish our high aim and bring down our dear sister Rosa to the level of a gypsy's step-daughter?"

III

There was excitement in the parish of Narrobourne one day. The congregation had just come out from morning service, and the whole conversation was of the new curate, Mr. Halborough, who had officiated for the first time, in the absence of the rector.

Never before had the feeling of the villagers approached a level which could be called excitement on such a matter as this. The droning which had been the rule in that quiet old place for a century seemed ended at last. They repeated the text to each other as a refrain: "O Lord, be thou my helper!" Not within living memory till to-day had the subject of the sermon formed the topic of conversation from the church door to church-yard gate, to the exclusion of personal remarks on those who had been present, and on the week's news in general.

The thrilling periods of the preacher hung about their minds all that day. The parish being steeped in indifferentism, it happened that when the youths and maidens, middle-aged and old people, who had attended church that morning, recurred as by a fascination to what Halborough had said, they did so more or less indirectly, and even with the subterfuge of a light laugh that was not real, so great was their shyness under the novelty of their sensations.

What was more curious than that these unconventional villagers should have been excited by a preacher of a new school after forty years of familiarity with the old hand who had had charge of their souls, was the effect of Halborough's address upon the occupants of the manor-house pew, including the owner of the estate. These thought they knew how to discount the mere sensational sermon, how to minimize flash oratory to its bare proportions; but they had yielded like the rest of the assembly to the charm of the new-comer.

Mr. Fellmer, the land-owner, was a young widower whose mother, still in the prime of life, had returned to her old position in the family mansion since the death of her son's wife in the year after her marriage, at the birth of a fragile little girl. From the date of his loss to the present time, Fellmer had led an inactive existence in the seclusion of the parish; a lack of motive seemed to leave him listless. He had gladly reinstated his mother in the gloomy house, and his main occupation now lay in stewarding his estate, which was not large. Mrs. Fellmer, who had sat beside him under Halborough this morning, was a cheerful, straightforward woman, who did her marketing and her alms-giving in person; was fond of old-fashioned flowers, and walked about the village on very wet days visiting the parishioners. These, the only two great ones of Narrobourne, were impressed by Joshua's eloquence as much as the cottagers.

Halborough had been briefly introduced to them on his arrival some days before, and, their interest being kindled, they waited a few moments till he came out of the vestry, to walk down the church-yard path with him. Mrs. Fellmer spoke warmly of the sermon, of the good-fortune of the parish in his advent, and hoped he had found comfortable quarters.

Halborough, faintly flushing, said that he had obtained very fair lodgings in the roomy house of a farmer, whom he named.

She feared he would find it very lonely, especially in the evenings, and hoped they would see a good deal of him. When would he dine with them? Could he not come that day—it must be so dull for him the first Sunday evening in country lodgings?

Halborough replied that it would give him much pleasure, but that he feared he must decline. "I am not altogether alone," he said, "My sister, who has just returned from Brussels, and who felt, as you do, that I should be rather dismal by myself, has accompanied me hither to stay a few days till she has put my rooms in order and set me going. She was too fatigued to come to church, and is waiting for me now at the farm."

"Oh, but bring your sister—that will be still better! I shall be delighted to know her. How I wish I had been aware! Do tell her, please, that we had no idea of her presence."

Halborough assured Mrs. Fellmer that he would certainly bear the message; but as to her coming he was not so sure. The real truth was, however, that the matter would be decided by him, Rosa having an almost filial respect for his wishes. But he was uncertain as to the state of her wardrobe, and had determined that she should not enter the manor-house at a disadvantage that evening, when there would probably be plenty of opportunities in the future of her doing so becomingly.

He walked to the farm in long strides. This, then, was the outcome of his first morning's work as curate here. Things had gone fairly well with him. He had been ordained; he was in a comfortable parish, where he would exercise almost sole supervision, the rector being infirm. He had made a deep impression at starting, and the absence of a hood seemed to have done him no harm. Moreover, by considerable persuasion and payment, his father and the dark woman had been shipped off to Canada, where they were not likely to interfere greatly with his interests.

Rosa came out to meet him. "Ah! you should have gone to church like a good girl," he said.

"Yes—I wished I had afterwards. But I do so hate church as a rule that even your preaching was underestimated in my mind. It was too bad of me!"

The girl who spoke thus playfully was fair, tall, and sylph-like, in a muslin dress, and with just the coquettish *dêsinvolture* which an English girl brings home from abroad, and loses again after a few months of native life. Joshua was the reverse of playful; the world was too important a concern for him to indulge in light moods. He told her in decided, practical phraseology of the invitation.

"Now, Rosa, we must go—that's settled—if you've a dress that can be made fit to wear all on the hop like this. You didn't, of course, think of bringing an evening dress to such an out-of-the-way place?"

But Rosa had come from the wrong city to be caught napping in those matters. "Yes, I did," said she. "One never knows what may turn up."

"Well done! Then off we go at seven."

The evening drew on, and at dusk they started on foot, Rosa pulling up the edge of her skirt under her cloak out of the way of the dews, so that it formed a great wind-bag all round her, and carrying her satin shoes under her arm. Joshua would not let her wait till she got in-doors before changing them, as she proposed, but insisted on her performing that operation under a tree, so that they might enter as if they had not walked. He was nervously formal about such trifles, while Rosa took the whole proceeding—walk, dressing, dinner, and all—as a pastime. To Joshua it was a serious step in life.

A more unexpected kind of person for a curate's sister was never presented at a dinner. The surprise of Mrs. Fellmer was unconcealed. She had looked forward to a Dorcas, or Martha, or Rhoda at the outside, and a shade of misgiving crossed her face. It was possible that, had the young lady accompanied her brother to church, there would have been no dining at Narrobourne House that day.

Not so with the young widower, her son. He resembled a sleeper who had awaked in a summer noon expecting to find it only dawn. He could scarcely help stretching his arms and yawning in their faces, so strong was his sense of being suddenly aroused to an unforeseen thing. When they had sat down to table he at first talked to Rosa somewhat with the air of a ruler in the land; but the woman lurking in the acquaintance soon brought him to his level, and the girl from Brussels saw him looking at her mouth, her hands, her contour, as if he could not quite comprehend how they got created; then he dropped into the more satisfactory stage which discerns no particulars.

He talked but little; she said much. The homeliness of the Fellmers, to her view, though they were regarded with such awe down here, quite disembarrassed her. The squire had become so unpractised, had dropped so far into the shade during the last year or so of his life, that he had almost forgotten what the world contained till this evening reminded him. His mother, after her first moments of doubt, appeared to think that he must be left to his own guidance, and gave her attention to Joshua.

With all his foresight and doggedness of aim, the result of that dinner exceeded Halborough's expectations. In weaving his ambitions he had viewed his sister Rosa as a slight, bright thing to be helped into notice by his abilities; but it now began to dawn upon him that the physical gifts of nature to her might do more for them both than nature's intellectual gifts to himself. While he was patiently boring the tunnel Rosa seemed about to fly over the mountain.

He wrote the next day to his brother, now occupying his own old rooms in the theological college, telling him exultingly of the unanticipated début of Rosa at the manor-house. The next post brought him a reply of congratulation, dashed with the counteracting intelligence that his father did not like Canada—that his wife had deserted him, which made him feel so dreary that he thought of returning home.

In his recent satisfaction at his own successes Joshua Halborough had wellnigh forgotten his chronic trouble—latterly screened by distance. But it now returned upon him; he saw more in this brief announcement than his brother seemed to see. It was the cloud no bigger than a man's hand.

IV

The following December, a day or two before Christmas, Mrs. Fellmer and her son were walking up and down the broad gravel path which bordered the east front of the house. Till within the last half-hour the morning had been a drizzling one, and they had just emerged for a short turn before luncheon.

"You see, dear mother," the son was saying, "it is the peculiarity of my position which makes her appear to me in such a desirable light. When you consider how I have been crippled at starting, how my life has been maimed; that I feel anything like publicity distasteful, that I have no political ambition, and that my chief aim and hope lie in the education of the little thing Annie has left me, you must see how desirable a wife like Miss Halborough would be, to prevent my becoming a mere vegetable."

"If you adore her, I suppose you must have her," replied his mother, with dry indirectness. "But you'll find that she will not be content to live on here as you do, giving her whole mind to a young child."

"That's just where we differ. Her very disqualification, that of being a nobody, as you call it, is her recommendation in my eyes. Her lack of influential connections limits her ambition. From what I know of her, a life in this place is all that she would wish for. She would never care to go outside the park gates if it were necessary to stay within."

"Being in love with her, Albert, and meaning to marry her, you invent your practical reasons to make the case respectable. Well, do as you will; I have no authority over you, so why should you consult me? You mean to propose on this very occasion, no doubt. Don't you, now?"

"By no means. I am merely revolving the idea in my mind. If on further acquaintance she turns out to be as good as she has hitherto seemed—well, I shall see. Admit now, that you like her."

"I readily admit it. She is very captivating at first sight. But as a step-mother to your child! You seem mighty anxious, Albert, to get rid of me!"

"Not at all. And I am not so reckless as you think. I don't make up my mind in a hurry. But the thought having occurred to me, I mention it to you at once, mother. If you dislike it, say so."

"I don't say anything. I will try to make the best of it if you are determined. When does she come?"

"To-morrow."

All this time there were great preparations in train at the curate's, who was now a householder. Rosa, whose two or three weeks' stay on two occasions earlier in the year had so affected the squire, was coming again, and at the same time her younger brother Cornelius, to make up a family party. Rosa, who journeyed from the Midlands, could not arrive till late in the evening, but Cornelius was to get there in the afternoon, Joshua going out to meet him in his walk across the fields from the railway.

Everything being ready in Joshua's modest abode he started on his way, his heart buoyant and thankful, if ever it was in his life. He was of such good report himself that his brother's path into holy orders promised to be unexpectedly easy; and he longed to compare experiences with him, even though there was on hand a more exciting matter still. From his youth he had held that, in old-fashioned country places, the Church conferred social prestige up to a certain point at a cheaper price than any other profession or pursuit; and events seemed to be proving him right.

He had walked about half an hour when he saw

Cornelius coming along the path, and in a few minutes the two brothers met. The experiences of Cornelius had been less immediately interesting than those of Joshua, but his personal position was satisfactory, and there was nothing to account for the singularly subdued manner that he exhibited, which at first Joshua set down to the fatigue of over-study; and he proceeded to the subject of Rosa's arrival in the evening, and the probable consequences of this her third visit. "Before next Easter she'll be his wife, my boy," said Joshua, with grave exultation.

Cornelius shook his head. "She comes too late," he returned.

"What do you mean?"

"Look here." He produced the Fountall paper, and placed his finger on a paragraph, which Joshua read. It appeared under the report of Petty Sessions, and was a commonplace case of disorderly conduct, in which a man was sent to prison for seven days for breaking windows in that town.

"Well?" said Joshua.

"It happened during an evening that I was in the street; and the offender is our father."

"Not—how—I sent him more money on his promising to stay in Canada?"

"He is home, safe enough." Cornelius in the same gloomy tone gave the remainder of his information. He had witnessed the scene, unobserved of his father, and had heard him say that he was on his way to see his daughter, who was going to marry a rich gentleman. The only good-fortune attending the untoward incident was that the millwright's name had been printed as Joshua Alborough.

"Beaten! We are to be beaten on the eve of our expected victory!" said the elder brother. "How did he guess that Rosa was likely to marry? Good Heaven! Cornelius, you seem doomed to bring bad news always, do you not?"

"I do," said Cornelius. "Poor Rosa!"

It was almost in tears, so great was their heart-sickness and shame, that the brothers walked the remainder of the way to Joshua's dwelling. In the evening they set out to meet Rosa, bringing her to the village in a fly; and when she had come into the house, and was sitting down with them, they almost forgot their secret anxiety in contemplating her, who knew nothing about it.

Next day the Fellmers came, and the two or three days after that were a lively time. That the squire was yielding to his impulses—making up his mind—there could be no doubt. On Sunday Cornelius read the lessons and Joshua preached. Mrs. Fellmer was quite maternal towards Rosa, and it appeared that she had decided to welcome the inevitable with a good grace. The pretty girl was to spend yet another afternoon with the elder lady, superintending some parish treat at the house in observance of Christmas, and afterwards to stay on to dinner, her brothers to fetch her in the evening. They were also invited to dine, but they could not accept owing to an engagement.

The engagement was of a sombre sort. They were going to meet their father, who would that day be released from Fountall Jail, and try to persuade him to keep away from Narrobourne. Every exertion was to be made to get him back to Canada, to his old home in the Midlands—anywhere, so that he would not impinge disastrously upon their courses, and blast their sister's prospect of the auspicious marriage which was just then hanging in the balance.

As soon as Rosa had been fetched away by her friends at the manor-house her brothers started on their expedition, without waiting for dinner or tea. Cornelius, to whom the millwright always addressed his letters when he wrote any, drew from his pocket and reread as he walked the curt note which had led to this journey being undertaken; it was despatched by their father the night before, immediately upon his liberation, and stated that he was setting out for Narrobourne at the moment of writing; that having no money he would be obliged to walk all the way; that he calculated on passing through the intervening town of Ivell about six on the following day, where he should sup at the Castle Inn, and where he hoped they would meet him with a carriage-and-pair, or some other such conveyance, that he might not disgrace them by arriving like a tramp.

"That sounds as if he gave a thought to our position," said Cornelius.

Joshua knew the satire that lurked in the paternal words, and said nothing. Silence prevailed during the greater part of their journey. The lamps were lighted in Ivell when they entered the streets, and Cornelius, who was quite unknown in this neighborhood, and who, moreover, was not in clerical attire, decided that he should be the one to call at the Castle Inn. Here, in answer to his inquiry under the darkness of the archway, they told him that such a man as he had described left the house about a quarter of an hour earlier, after making a meal in the kitchen settle. He was rather the worse for liquor.

"Then," said Joshua, when Cornelius joined him outside with this intelligence, "we must have met and passed him. And now that I think of it, we did meet some one who was unsteady in his gait under the trees on the other side of Hendcome Hill, where it was too dark to see him."

They rapidly retraced their steps; but for a long

stretch of the way home could discern nobody. When, however, they had gone about three-quarters of the distance, they became conscious of an irregular footfall in front of them, and could see a whitish figure in the gloom. They followed dubiously. The figure met another wayfarer—the single one that had been encountered upon this lonely road—and they distinctly heard him ask the way to Narrobourne. The stranger replied—what was quite true—that the nearest way was by turning in at the stile by the next bridge, and following the foot-path which branched thence across the meadows.

When the brothers reached the stile they also entered the path, but did not overtake the subject of their worry till they had crossed two or three meads, and the lights from Narrobourne manor-house were visible before them through the trees. Their father was no longer walking; he was seated against the wet bank of an adjoining hedge. Observing their forms he shouted, "I'm going to Narrobourne; who may you be?"

They went up to him, and revealed themselves, reminding him of the plan which he had himself proposed in his note, that they should meet him at Ivell.

"By Jerry, I'd forgot it!" he said. "Well, what do you want me to do?" His tone was distinctly quarrelsome.

A long conversation followed, which became imbittered at the first hint from them that he should not come to the village. The millwright drew a quart bottle from his pocket, and challenged them to drink if they meant friendly and called themselves men. Neither of the two had touched alcohol for years, but for once they thought it best to accept, so as not to needlessly provoke him.

"What's in it?" said Joshua.

"A drop of weak gin-and-water. It won't hurt ye. Drink from the bottle." Joshua did so, and his father pushed up the bottom of the vessel so as to make him swallow a good deal in spite of himself. It went down into his stomach like molten lead.

"Ha, ha, that's right!" said old Halborough. "But 'twas raw spirit—ha, ha!"

"Why should you take me in so!" said Joshua, losing his self-command, try as he would to keep calm.

"Because you took me in, my lad, in banishing me to that cursed country under pretence that it was for my good. You were a pair of hypocrites to say so. It was done to get rid of me—no more nor less. But, by Jerry, I'm a match for ye now! I'll spoil your souls for preaching. My daughter is going to be married to the squire here. I've heard the news—I saw it in a paper!"

"It is premature—"

"I know it is true; and I'm her father, and I shall give her away, or there'll be a hell of a row, I can assure ye! Is that where the gennleman lives?"

Joshua Halborough writhed in impotent despair. Fellmer had not yet positively declared himself, his mother was hardly won round; a scene with their father in the parish would demolish as fair a palace of hopes as was ever builded. The millwright rose. "If that's where the squire lives I'm going to call. Just arrived from Canady with her fortune—ha, ha! I wish no harm to the gennleman, and the gennleman will wish no harm to me. But I like to take my place in the family, and stand upon my rights, and lower people's pride!"

"You've succeeded already! Where's that woman you took with you—"

"Woman! She was my wife as lawful as the Constitution—a sight more lawful than your mother was till some time after you were born!"

Joshua had for many years before heard whispers that his father had cajoled his mother in their early acquaintance, and had made somewhat tardy amends; but never from his father's lips till now. It was the last stroke, and he could not bear it. He sank back against the hedge. "It is over!" he said. "He ruins us all!"

The millwright moved on, waving his stick triumphantly, and the two brothers stood still. They could see his drab figure stalking along the path, and over his head the lights from the conservatory of Narrobourne House, inside which Albert Fellmer might possibly be sitting with Rosa at that moment, holding her hand, and asking her to share his home with him.

The staggering whitey-brown form, advancing to put a blot on all this, had been diminishing in the shade; and now suddenly disappeared beside a wear. There was the noise of a flounce in the water.

"He has fallen in!" said Cornelius, starting forward to run for the place at which his father had vanished.

Joshua, awaking from the stupefied reverie into which he had sunk, rushed to the other's side before he had taken ten steps. "Stop, stop, what are you thinking of?" he whispered, hoarsely, grasping Cornelius's arm.

"Pulling him out!"

"Yes, yes—so am I. But—wait a moment—"

"But, Joshua!"

"Her life and happiness, you know—Cornelius—and your reputation and mine—and our chance of rising together, all three—"

He clutched his brother's arm to the bone; and as they stood breathless the splashing and floundering in the wear continued; over it they saw the hopeful lights from the manor-house conservatory winking through the trees as their bare branches waved to and fro.

The floundering and splashing grew weaker, and they could hear gurgling words: "Help—I'm drownded! Rosie—Rosie!"

"We'll go—we *must* save him. Oh, Joshua!"

"Yes, yes, we must!"

Still they did not move, but waited, holding each other, each thinking the same thought. Weights of lead seemed to be affixed to their feet, which would no longer obey their wills. The mead became silent. Over it they fancied they could see figures moving in the conservatory. The air up there seemed to emit gentle kisses.

Cornelius started forward at last, and Joshua almost simultaneously. Two or three minutes brought them to the brink of the stream. At first they could see nothing in the water, though it was not so deep nor the night so dark but that their father's light kerseymere coat would have been visible if he had lain at the bottom. Joshua looked this way and that.

"He has drifted into the culvert," he said.

Below the foot-bridge of the wear the stream suddenly narrowed to half its width, to pass under a barrel arch or culvert constructed for wagons to cross into the middle of the mead in hay-making time. It being at present the season of high water the arch was full to the crown, against which the ripples clucked every now and then. At this point he had just caught sight of a pale object slipping under. In a moment it was gone.

They went to the lower end, but nothing emerged. For a long time they tried at both ends to effect some communication with the interior, but to no purpose.

"We ought to have come sooner!" said the conscience-stricken Cornelius, when they were quite exhausted, and dripping wet.

"I suppose we ought," replied Joshua, heavily. He perceived his father's walking-stick on the bank; hastily picking it up he stuck it into the mud among the sedge. Then they went on.

"Shall we—say anything about this accident?" whispered Cornelius as they approached the door of Joshua's house.

"What's the use? It can do no good. We must wait until he is found."

They went in-doors and changed their clothes; after which they started for the manor-house, reaching it about ten o'clock. Besides their sister there were only three guests: an adjoining land-owner and his wife, and the infirm old rector.

Rosa, although she had parted from them so recently, grasped their hands in an ecstatic, brimming, joyful manner, as if she had not seen them for years. "You look pale," she said.

The brothers answered that they had had a long walk, and were somewhat tired. Everybody in the room seemed charged full with some sort of interesting knowledge; the squire's neighbor and his wife looked wisely around, and Fellmer himself played the part of host with a preoccupied bearing which approached fervor. They left at eleven, not accepting the carriage offered, the distance being so short and the roads dry. The squire came rather farther into the dark with them than he need have done, and wished Rosa good-night in a mysterious manner, slightly apart from the rest.

When they were walking along Joshua said, with a desperate attempt at joviality, "Rosa, what's going on?"

"Oh, I—" she began, between a gasp and a bound. "He—"

"Never mind—if it disturbs you."

She was so excited that she could not speak connectedly at first, the practised air which she had brought home with her having disappeared. Calming herself she added, "I am not disturbed, and nothing has happened. Only he said he wanted to ask me something, some day; and I said never mind that now. He hasn't asked yet, and is coming to speak to you about it. He would have done so to-night, only I asked him not to be in a hurry. But he will come to-morrow, I am sure!"

V

It was summer-time, six month's later, and mowers and hay-makers were at work in the meads. The manor-house, being opposite them, frequently formed a peg for conversation during these operations; and the doings of the squire, and the squire's young wife, the curate's sister—who was at present the admired of most of them, and the interest of all—met with their due amount of criticism.

Rosa was happy, if ever woman could be said to be so. She had not learned the fate of her father, and sometimes wondered—perhaps with a sense of relief—why he did not write to her from his supposed home in Canada. Her brother Joshua had been presented to a living in a small town, shortly after her marriage, and Cornelius had thereupon succeeded to the vacant curacy of Narrobourne.

These two had awaited in deep suspense the discovery of their father's body, and yet the discovery had not been made. Every day they expected a man or a boy to run up from the meads with the intelligence; but he had never come. Days had accumulated to weeks and months; the wedding had come and gone; Joshua had tolled and read himself in at his new parish, and never a shout of amazement over the millwright's remains.

But now, in June, when they were mowing the meads, the hatches had to be drawn and the water let out of its channels for the convenience of the mowers. It was thus that the discovery was made. A man, stooping low with his scythe, caught a view of the culvert lengthwise, and saw something entangled in the recently bared weeds of its bed. A day or two after there was an inquest; but the body was unrecognizable. Fish and flood had been busy with the millwright; he had no watch or marked article which could be identified, and a verdict of the accidental drowning of a person unknown settled the matter.

As the body was found in Narrobourne parish, there it had to be buried. Cornelius wrote to Joshua, begging him to come and read the service, or to send some one; he himself could not do it. Rather than let in a stranger Joshua came, and silently scanned the coroner's order handed him by the undertaker:

"I, Henry Giles, Coroner for the Mid-Division of Outer Wessex, do hereby order the Burial of the Body now shown to the Inquest Jury as the Body of an Adult Male Person Unknown . . ." etc.

Joshua Halborough got through the service in some way, and rejoined his brother Cornelius at his house. Neither accepted an invitation to lunch at their sister's; they wished to discuss parish matters together. In the afternoon she came down, though they had already called on her, and had not expected to see her again. Her bright eyes, brown hair, flowery bonnet, lemon-colored gloves, and flush beauty were like an irradiation into the apartment, which they in their gloom could hardly bear.

"I forgot to tell you," she said, "of a curious thing which happened to me a month or two before my marriage—something which I have thought may have had a connection with the accident to the poor man you have buried to-day. It was on that evening I was at the manor-house waiting for you to fetch me; I was in the winter-garden with Albert, and we were sitting silent together, when we fancied we heard a cry. We opened the door, and while Albert ran to fetch his hat, leaving me standing there, the cry was repeated, and my excited senses made me think I heard my own name. When Albert came back all was silent, and we decided that it was only a drunken shout, and not a cry for help. We both forgot the incident, and it never has occurred to me till since the funeral to-day that it might have been this stranger's cry. The name of course was only fancy, or he might have had a wife or child with a name something like mine, poor man!"

When she was gone the brothers were silent till Cornelius said, "Now mark this, Joshua. Sooner or later she'll know."

"How?"

"From one of us. Do you think human hearts are iron-cased safes, that you suppose we can keep this secret forever?"

"Yes, I think they are, sometimes," said Joshua.

"No. It will out. We shall tell."

"What, and ruin her—kill her? Disgrace her children, and pull down the whole auspicious house of Fellmer about our ears? No! May I—drown where he was drowned before I do it! Never, never. Surely you can say the same, Cornelius?"

Cornelius seemed fortified, and no more was said. For a long time after that day he did not see Joshua, and before the next year was out a son and heir was born to the Fellmers. The villagers rang the three bells every evening for a week and more, and were made merry by Mr. Fellmer's ale; and when the christening came on Joshua paid Narrobourne another visit.

Among all the people who assembled on that day the brother clergymen were the least interested. Their minds were haunted by a spirit in kerseymere. In the evening they walked together in the fields.

"She's all right," said Joshua. "But here are you doing journey-work, Cornelius, and likely to continue at it till the end of the day, as far as I can see. I, too, with my petty living—what am I, after all?... To tell the truth, the Church is a poor forlorn hope for people without influence, particularly when their enthusiasm begins to flag. A social regenerator has a better chance outside, where he is unhampered by dogma and tradition. As for me, I would rather have gone on mending mills, with my crust of bread and liberty."

Almost automatically they had bent their steps along the margin of the river; they now paused. They were standing on the brink of the well-known wear. There were the hatches, there was the culvert; they could see the pebbly bed of the stream through the pellucid water. The notes of the church-bells were audible, still jangled by the enthusiastic villagers.

"It was there I hid his walking-stick," said Joshua, looking towards the sedge. The next moment, during a passing breeze, something flashed white on the spot they regarded.

From the sedge rose a straight little silver-poplar,

and it was the leaves of this sapling which caused the flicker of whiteness.

"His walking-stick has grown!" said Cornelius. "It was a rough one—cut from the hedge, I remember."

At every puff of wind the tree turned white, till they could not bear to look at it; and they walked away.

"I see him every night," Cornelius murmured. . . . "Ah, we read our *Hebrews* to little account, Jos! Ὑπέμεινε σταυρόν, αἰσχύνης καταφρονήσας. To have *endured* the cross, *despising* the shame—there lay greatness! But now I often feel that I should like to put an end to trouble here in this self-same spot."

"I have thought of it myself," said Joshua.

"Perhaps we shall, some day," murmured his brother.

"Perhaps," said Joshua, moodily.

With that contingency to consider in the silence of their nights and days they bent their steps homeward.

December, 1888.

ON THE WESTERN CIRCUIT

I

The man who played the disturbing part in the two quiet lives hereafter depicted—no great man, in any sense, by-the-way—first had knowledge of them on an October evening in the city of Melchester. He had been standing in the close, vainly endeavoring to gain amid the darkness a glimpse of the most homogeneous pile of mediæval architecture in England, which towered and tapered from the damp and level sward in front of him. While he stood the presence of the cathedral walls was revealed rather by the ear than by the eyes; he could not see them, but they reflected sharply a roar of sound which entered the close by a street leading from the city square, and, falling upon the building, was flung back upon him.

He postponed till the morrow his attempt to examine the deserted edifice, and turned his attention to the noise. It was compounded of steam barrel-organs, the clanging of gongs, the ringing of hand-bells, the clack of rattles, and the undistinguishable shouts of men. A lurid light hung in the air in the direction of the tumult. Thitherward he went, passing under the arched gateway, along a straight street, and into the square.

He might have searched Europe over for a greater

contrast between juxtaposed scenes. The spectacle was that of the eighth chasm of the Inferno as to color and flame, and, as to mirth, a development of the Homeric heaven. A smoky glare, of the complexion of brass filings, ascended from the fiery tongues of innumerable naphtha lamps affixed to booths, stalls, and other temporary erections which crowded the spacious market-square. In front of this irradiation scores of human figures, more or less in profile, were darting athwart and across, up, down, and around, like gnats against a sunset.

Their motions were so rhythmical that they seemed to be moved by machinery. And it presently appeared that they were moved by machinery indeed, the figures being those of the patrons of swings, see-saws, flying-leaps, above all of the three steam roundabouts which occupied the centre of the position. It was from the latter that the din of steam-organs came.

Throbbing humanity in full light was, on second thoughts, better than ecclesiology in the dark. The young man, lighting a short pipe, and putting his hat on one side and one hand in his pocket, to throw himself into harmony with his new environment, drew near to the largest and most patronized of the steam circuses, as the roundabouts were called by their owners. This was one of brilliant finish, and it was now in full revolution. The musical instrument around which and to whose tones the riders revolved, directed its trumpet-mouths of brass upon the young man, and the long plate-glass mirrors set at angles, which revolved with the machine, flashed the gyrating personages and hobby-horses kaleidoscopically into his eyes.

It could now be seen that he was unlike the majority of the crowd. A gentlemanly young fellow, one of the species found in large towns only, and London particularly, built on delicate lines, well, though not fashionably dressed, he appeared to belong to the professional class; he had nothing square or practical about his look, much that was curvilinear and sensuous. Indeed, some would have called him a man not altogether typical of the middle-class male of a century wherein sordid ambition is the master-passion that seems to be taking the time-honored place of love.

The revolving figures passed before his eyes with an unexpected and quiet grace in a throng whose natural movements did not suggest gracefulness or quietude as a rule. By some contrivance there was imparted to each of the hobby-horses a motion which was really the triumph and perfection of roundabout inventiveness — a galloping rise and fall, so timed that, of each pair of steeds, one was on the spring while the other was on the pitch. The riders were quite fascinated by these equine undulations in this most delightful holiday game of our times. There were riders as young as six, and as old as sixty years, with every age between. At first it was difficult to catch a personality, but by-and-by the observer's eyes centred on the prettiest girl out of the several pretty ones revolving.

It was not that one with the light frock and light hat whom he had been at first attracted by; no, it was the one with the black cape, gray skirt, light gloves, and — no, not even she, but the one behind her; she with the crimson skirt, dark jacket, brown hat, and brown gloves. Unmistakably that was the prettiest girl.

Having finally selected her, this idle spectator studied her as well as he was able during each of her brief transits across his visual field. She was absolutely unconscious of everything save the act of riding: her features were rapt in an ecstatic dreaminess; for the moment she did not know her age or her history or her lineaments, much less her troubles. He himself was full of vague latter-day glooms and popular melancholies, and it was a refreshing sensation to behold this young thing, then and there, absolutely as happy as if she were in a Paradise.

Dreading the moment when the inexorable stoker, grimly lurking behind the glittering rococo-work, should decide that this set of riders had had their pennyworth, and bring the whole concern of steam-engine, horses, mirrors, trumpets, drums, cymbals, and such like to pause and silence, he waited for her every reappearance, glancing indifferently over the intervening forms, including the two plainer girls, the old woman and child, the two youngsters, the newly-married couple, the old man with a clay pipe, the sparkish youth with a ring, the young ladies in the chariot, the pair of journeyman carpenters, and others, till his select country beauty followed on again in her place. He had never seen a fairer product of nature, and at each round she made a deeper mark in his sentiments. The stoppage then came, and the sighs of the riders were audible.

He moved round to the place at which he reckoned she would alight; but she retained her seat. The empty saddles began to refill, and she plainly was deciding to have another turn. The young man drew up to the side of her steed, and pleasantly asked her if she had enjoyed her ride.

"Oh yes!" she said, with dancing eyes. "It has been quite unlike anything I have ever felt in my life before!"

It was not difficult to fall into conversation with her. Unreserved — too unreserved — by nature, she was not experienced enough to be reserved by art, and after a little coaxing she answered his remarks readily. She had come to live in Melchester from a village on the Great Plain, and this was the first time that she had ever seen a steam-circus; she could not understand how such wonderful machines were made. She had come to the city on the invitation of Mrs. Harnham, who had taken her into her household to train her as a servant if she showed any aptitude. Mrs. Harnham was a young lady who before she married had been Miss Edith White, living in the country near the speaker's cottage; she was now very kind to her through knowing her in childhood so well. She was even taking the trouble to educate her. Mrs. Harnham was the only friend she had in the world, and being without children had wished to have her near her in preference to anybody else, though she had only lately come; allowed her to do almost as she liked, and to have a holiday whenever she asked for it. The husband of this kind young lady was a rich wine-merchant of the town, but Mrs. Harnham did not care much about him. In the daytime you could see the house from where they were talking. She, the speaker, liked Melchester better than the lonely country, and she was going to have a new hat for next Sunday that was to cost fifteen and ninepence.

Then she inquired of her acquaintance where he lived, and he told her in London, that ancient and smoky city, where everybody lived who lived at all, and died because they could not live there. He came into Wessex two or three times a year for professional reasons; he had arrived from Wintoncester yesterday, and was going on into the next county in a day or two. For one thing he did like the country better than the town, and it was because it contained such girls as she.

Then the pleasure-machine started again, and, to the light-hearted girl, the figure of the handsome young man, the market-square with its lights and crowd, the houses beyond, and the world at large, began moving round as before, countermoving in the revolving mirrors on her right hand, she being as it were the fixed point in an undulating, dazzling, lurid universe, in which loomed forward most prominently of all the form of her late interlocutor. Each time that she approached the half of her orbit that lay nearest him they gazed at each other with smiles, and with that unmistakable expression which means so little at the moment, yet so often leads up to passion, heartache, union, disunion, devotion, overpopulation, drudgery, content, resignation, despair.

When the horses slowed anew he stepped to her side and proposed another heat. "Hang the expense for once," he said. "I'll pay!"

She laughed till the tears came.

"Why do you laugh, dear?" said he.

"Because—you are so genteel that you must have plenty of money, and only say that for fun!" she returned.

"Ha-ha!" laughed the young man in unison, and gallantly producing his money she was enabled to whirl on again.

As he stood smiling there in the motley crowd, with his pipe in his hand, and clad in the rough pea-jacket and wide-awake that he had put on for his stroll, who would have supposed him to be Charles Bradford Raye, Esquire, stuff-gownsman, educated at Wintoncester, called to the bar at Lincoln's Inn, now going the Western Circuit, merely detained in Melchester by a small arbitration after his brethren had moved on to the next county-town?

II

The square was overlooked from its remoter corner by the house of which the young girl had spoken, a dignified residence of considerable size, having several windows on each floor. Inside one of these, on the first floor, the apartment being a large drawing-room, sat a lady, in appearance from twenty-eight to thirty years of age. The blinds were still undrawn, and the lady was absently surveying the weird scene without, her cheek resting on her hand. The room was unlit from within, but enough of the glare from the market-place entered it to reveal the lady's face. She was what is called an interesting creature rather than a handsome woman; dark-eyed, thoughtful, and with sensitive lips.

A man sauntered into the room from behind and came forward.

"Oh, Edith, I didn't see you," he said. "Why are you sitting here in the dark?"

"I am looking at the fair," replied the lady, in a languid voice.

"Oh? Horrid nuisance every year! I wish it could be put a stop to."

"I like it."

"H'm. There's no accounting for taste."

For a moment he gazed from the window with her, for politeness' sake, and then went out again.

In a few minutes she rang.

"Hasn't Anna come in?" asked Mrs. Harnham.

"No, m'm."

"She ought to be in by this time. I meant her to go for ten minutes only."

"Shall I go and look for her, m'm?" said the house-maid, alertly.

"No. It is not necessary: she is a good girl and will come soon."

However, when the servant had gone Mrs. Harnham arose, went up to her room, cloaked and bonneted herself, and proceeded down-stairs, where she found her husband.

"I want to see the fair," she said, "and I am going to look for Anna. I have made myself responsible for her, and must see she comes to no harm. She ought to be in-doors. Will you come with me?"

"Oh, she's all right. I saw her on one of those whirligig things, talking to her young man as I came in. But I'll go if you wish, though I'd rather go a hundred miles the other way."

"Then please do so. I shall come to no harm alone."

She left the house and entered the crowd which thronged the market-place, where she soon discovered Anna, seated on the revolving horse. As soon as it stopped Mrs. Harnham advanced and said, severely, "Anna, how can you be such a wild girl? You were only to be out for ten minutes."

Anna looked blank, and the young man, who had dropped into the background, came to her assistance.

"Please don't blame her," he said, politely. "It is my fault that she has stayed. She looked so graceful on the horse that I induced her to go round again. I assure you that she has been quite safe."

"In that case I'll leave her in your hands," said Mrs. Harnham, turning to retrace her steps.

But this for the moment it was not so easy to do. Something had attracted the crowd to a spot in their rear, and the wine-merchant's wife, caught by its sway, found herself pressed against Anna's acquaintance without power to move away. Their faces were within a few inches of each other, his breath fanned her cheek as well as Anna's. They could do no other than smile at the accident; but neither spoke, and each waited passively. Mrs. Harnham then felt a man's hand clasping her fingers, and from the look of consciousness on the young fellow's face she knew the hand to be his; she also knew that from the position of the girl he had no other thought than that the imprisoned hand was Anna's. What prompted her to refrain from undeceiving him she could hardly tell. Not content with holding the hand, he playfully slipped two of his fingers inside her glove, against her palm. Thus matters continued till the pressure lessened; but several minutes passed before the crowd thinned sufficiently to allow Mrs. Harnham to withdraw.

"How did they get to know each other, I wonder?" she mused as she retreated. "Anna is really very forward—and he very wicked and nice."

She was so gently stirred with the stranger's manner and voice, with the tenderness of his idle touch, that instead of re-entering the house she turned back again and observed the pair from a screened nook. Really, she argued (being little less impulsive than Anna herself), it was very excusable in Anna to encourage him, however she might have contrived to make his acquaintance; he was so gentlemanly, so fascinating, had such beautiful eyes. The thought that he was several years her junior produced a reasonless sigh.

At length the couple turned from the roundabout towards the door of Mrs. Harnham's house, and the young man could be heard saying that he would accompany her home. Anna, then, had found a lover, apparently a very devoted one. Mrs. Harnham was quite interested in him. When they drew near the door of the wine-merchant's house, a comparatively deserted spot by this time, they stood invisible for a little while in the shadow of a wall, where they separated, Anna going on to the entrance, and her acquaintance returning across the square.

"Anna," said Mrs. Harnham, coming up. "I've been looking at you! That young man kissed you at parting, I am almost sure."

"Well," stammered Anna, "he said if I didn't mind, it would do me no harm, and—and—him a great deal of good!"

"Ah, I thought so! And he was a stranger till to-night?"

"Yes, ma'am."

"Yet I warrant you told him your name and everything about yourself?"

"He asked me."

"But he didn't tell you his?"

"Yes, ma'am, he did!" cried Anna, victoriously. "It is Charles Bradford, of London."

"Well, if he's respectable, of course I've nothing to say against your knowing him," remarked her mistress, prepossessed, in spite of general principles, in the young man's favor. "But I must reconsider all that if he attempts to renew your acquaintance. A country-bred girl like you, who has never lived in Melchester till this month, who had hardly ever seen a black-coated man till you came here, to be so sharp as to capture a young Londoner like him!"

"I didn't capture him. I didn't do anything," said Anna, in confusion.

When she was in-doors and alone Mrs. Harnham thought what a well-bred and chivalrous young man Anna's companion had seemed. There had been a magic in his wooing touch of her hand, and she wondered how he had come to be attracted by the girl.

The next morning the emotional Edith Harnham

went to the usual week-day service in Melchester cathedral. In crossing the close through the fog she again perceived him who had interested her the previous evening, gazing up thoughtfully at the high-piled architecture of the nave; and as soon as she had taken her seat he entered and sat down in a stall opposite hers.

He did not particularly heed her; but Mrs Harnham was continually occupying her eyes with him, and wondered more than ever what had attracted him in her unfledged maid-servant. The mistress was almost as unaccustomed as the maiden herself to the end-of-the-age young man, or she might have wondered less. Raye, having looked about him awhile, left abruptly, without regard to the service that was proceeding; and Mrs. Harnham — lonely, impressionable creature that she was—took no further interest in praising the Lord. She wished she had married a London man who knew the subtleties of love-making as they were evidently known to him who had mistakenly caressed her hand.

III

The calendar at Melchester had been light, occupying the court only a few hours; and the assizes at Casterbridge, the next county-town on the Western Circuit, having no business for Raye, he had not gone thither. At the next town after that they did not open till the following Monday, trials to begin on Tuesday morning. In the natural order of things Raye would have arrived at the latter place on Monday afternoon; but it was not till the middle of Wednesday that his gown and gray wig, curled in tiers, in the best fashion of Assyrian bass-reliefs, were seen blowing and bobbing behind him as he hastily walked up the High Street from his lodgings. But though he entered the assize building, there was nothing for him to do; and sitting at the blue baize table in the well of the court, he mended pens with a mind far away from the case in progress. Thoughts of unpremeditated conduct, of which a week earlier he would not have believed himself capable, threw him into a mood of dissatisfied depression.

He had contrived to see again the pretty rural maiden Anna the day after the fair, had walked out of the city with her to the earthworks of Old Melchester, and, feeling a violent fancy for her, had remained in Melchester all Sunday, Monday, and Tuesday; by persuasion obtaining walks and meetings with the young girl six or seven times during the interval; had in brief won her, body and soul.

He supposed it must have been owing to the seclusion in which he had lived of late in town that he had given way so unrestrainedly to a passion for an artless creature whose inexperience had, from the first, led her to place herself unreservedly in his hands. Much he deplored trifling with her feelings for the sake of a passing desire; and he could only hope that she might not live to suffer on his account.

She had begged him to come to her again; entreated him; wept. He had promised that he would do so, and he meant to carry out that promise. He could not desert her now. Awkward as such unintentional connections were, the interspace of a hundred miles—which to a girl of her limited capabilities was like a thousand—would effectually hinder this summer fancy from greatly encumbering his life; while thought of her simple love might do him the negative good of keeping him from idle pleasures in town when he wished to work hard. His circuit journeys would take him to Melchester three or four times a year, and then he could always see her.

The pseudonym, or rather partial name, that he had given her as his before knowing how far the acquaintance was going to carry him, had been spoken on the spur of the moment, without any ulterior intention whatever. He had not afterwards disturbed Anna's error, but on leaving her he had felt bound to give her an address at a stationer's not far from his chambers, at which she might write to him under the initials "C. B."

In due time Raye returned to his London abode, having called at Melchester on his way and spent a few additional hours with his fascinating child of nature. In town he lived monotonously every day. Often he and his rooms were enclosed by a tawny fog from all the world besides, and when he lighted the gas to read or write by, his situation seemed so unnatural that he would look into the fire and think of that trusting girl at Melchester again and again. Often, oppressed by absurd fondness for her, he would enter the dim religious nave of the Law Courts by the north door, elbow other juniors habited like himself, and like him unretained; edge himself into this or that crowded court where a sensational case was going on, just as if he were in it, though the police officers at the door knew as well as he knew himself that he had no more concern with the business in hand than the patient idlers at the gallery door outside, who had waited to enter since eight in the morning because, like him, they belonged to the classes that live without working. But he would do these things to no purpose, and think how greatly the characters in such scenes contrasted with the pink and breezy Anna.

An unexpected feature in that peasant maiden's conduct was that she had not as yet written to him, though he had told her she might do so if she wished. Surely a young creature had never before been so reticent in such circumstances. At length he sent her a brief line, positively requesting her to write. There was no answer by the return post, but the day after a letter in a neat feminine hand, and bearing the Melchester postmark, was handed to him by the stationer.

The fact alone of its arrival was sufficient to satisfy his imaginative sentiment. He was not anxious to open the epistle, and in truth did not begin to read it for nearly half an hour, anticipating readily its terms of affectionate retrospect and tender adjuration. When at last he turned his feet to the fireplace and unfolded the sheet, he was surprised and pleased to find that neither extravagance nor vulgarity were there. It was the most charming little missive he had ever received from woman. To be sure the language was simple, and the ideas were slight; but it was so self-possessed, so purely that of a young girl who felt her womanhood to be enough for her dignity that he read it through twice. Four sides were filled, and a few lines written across, after the fashion of former days; the paper, too, was common, and not of the latest shade and surface. But what of those things? He had received letters from women who were fairly called ladies, but never so sensible, so human a letter as this. He could not single out any one sentence and say it was at all remarkable or clever; the *ensemble* of the letter it was which won him; and beyond the one request that he would write or come to her again soon there was nothing to show her sense of a claim upon him.

To write again and develop a correspondence was the last thing Raye would have preconceived as his conduct in such a situation; yet he did send a short, encouraging line or two, signed with his pseudonym, in which he asked for another letter, and cheeringly promised that he would try to see her again on some near day, and would never forget how much they had been to each other during their short acquaintance.

IV

To return now to the moment at which Anna, at Melchester, had received Raye's letter.

It had been put into her own hand by the postman on his morning rounds. She flushed down to her neck on receipt of it, and turned it over and over. "It is mine?" she said.

"Why, yes, can't you see it is?" said the postman, smiling as he guessed the nature of the document and the cause of the confusion.

"Oh yes, of course!" replied Anna, looking at the letter, forcedly tittering, and blushing still more.

Her look of embarrassment did not leave her with the postman's departure. She opened the envelope, kissed its contents, put away the letter in her pocket, and remained musing till her eyes filled with tears.

A few minutes later she carried up a cup of tea to Mrs. Harnham in her bed-chamber. Anna's mistress looked at her, and said: "How dismal you seem this morning, Anna. What's the matter?"

"I'm not dismal, I'm glad; only I—" She stopped to stifle a sob.

"Well?"

"I've got a letter—and what good is it to me if I can't read a word in it?"

"Why, I'll read it, child, if necessary."

"But this is from somebody—I don't want anybody to read it but myself!" Anna murmured.

"I shall not tell anybody. Is it from that young man?"

"I think so." Anna slowly produced the letter, saying: "Then will you read it to me, ma'am?"

This was the secret of Anna's embarrassment and flutterings. She could neither read nor write. She had grown up under the care of an aunt by marriage, at one of the lonely hamlets on the Great Mid-Wessex Plain where, even in days of national education, there had been no school within a distance of two miles. Her aunt was an ignorant woman; there had been nobody to investigate Anna's circumstances, nobody to care about her learning the rudiments, though, as often in such cases, she had been well fed and clothed and not unkindly treated. Since she had come to live at Melchester with Mrs. Harnham, the latter, who took a kindly interest in the girl, had taught her to speak correctly, in which accomplishment Anna showed considerable readiness, as is not unusual with the illiterate; and soon became quite fluent in the use of her mistress's phraseology. Mrs. Harnham also insisted upon her getting a spelling and copy book, and beginning to practise in these. Anna was slower in this branch of her education, and meanwhile here was the letter.

Edith Harnham's large dark eyes expressed some interest in the contents, though, in her character of mere interpreter, she threw into her tone as much as she could of mechanical passiveness. She read the short epistle on to its concluding sentence, which idly requested Anna to send him a tender answer.

"Now — you'll do it for me, won't you, dear mistress?" said Anna, eagerly. "And you'll do it as well as ever you can, please? Because I couldn't bear him to think I am not able to do it myself. I should sink into the earth with shame if he knew that!"

From some words in the letter Mrs. Harnham was led to ask questions, and the answers she received confirmed her suspicions. Deep concern filled Edith's heart at perceiving how the girl had committed her happiness to the issue of this new-sprung attachment. She blamed herself for not interfering in a flirtation which had resulted so seriously for the poor little creature in her charge; though at the time of seeing the pair together she had a feeling that it was hardly within her province to nip young affection in the bud. However, what was done could not be undone, and it behooved her now, as Anna's only protector, to help her as much as she could. To Anna's eager request that she, Mrs. Harnham, should compose and write the answer to this young London man's letter, she felt bound to accede, to keep alive his attachment to the girl if possible; though in other circumstances she might have suggested the cook as an amanuensis.

A tender reply was thereupon concocted, and set down in Edith Harnham's hand. This letter it had been which Raye had received and delighted in. Written in the presence of Anna it certainly was, and on Anna's humble note-paper, and in a measure indited by the young girl; but the life, the spirit, the individuality, were Edith Harnham's.

"Won't you at least put your name yourself?" she said. "You can manage to write that by this time?"

"No, no," said Anna, shrinking back. "I should do it so bad. He'd be ashamed of me, and never see me again!"

The note, so prettily requesting another from him, had, as we have seen, power enough in its pages to bring one. He declared it to be such a pleasure to hear from her that she must write every week. The same process of manufacture was accordingly repeated by Anna and her mistress, and continued for several weeks in succession, each letter being penned and suggested by Edith, the girl standing by; the answer read and commented on by Edith, Anna standing by and listening again.

Late on a winter evening, after the despatch of the sixth letter, Mrs. Harnham was sitting alone by the remains of her fire. Her husband had retired to bed, and she had fallen into that fixity of musing which takes no count of hour or temperature. The state of mind had been brought about in Edith by a strange thing which she had done that day. For the first time since Raye's visit Anna had gone to stay over a night or two with her cottage friends on the Plain, and in her absence had arrived, out of its time, a letter from Raye. To this Edith had replied on her own responsibility, from the depths of her own heart, without waiting for her maid's collaboration. The luxury of writing to him what would be known to no consciousness but his was great, and she had indulged herself therein.

Why was it a luxury?

Edith Harnham led a lonely life. Influenced by the belief of the British parent that a bad marriage with its aversions is better than free womanhood with its interests, dignity, and leisure, she had consented to marry the elderly wine-merchant as a *pis aller*, at the age of seven-and-twenty—some three years before this date—to find afterwards that she had made a mistake. That contract had left her still a woman whose deeper nature had never been stirred.

She was now clearly realizing that she had become possessed to the bottom of her soul with the image of a man to whom she was hardly so much as a shape. From the first he had attracted her by his looks and voice, by his tender touch; and, with these as generators, the writing of letter after letter and the reading of their soft answers had insensibly developed on her side an emotion which fanned his; till there had resulted a magnetic reciprocity between the correspondents, notwithstanding that one of them wrote in a character not her own.

They were her own impassioned and pent-up ideas—lowered to monosyllabic phraseology in order to keep up the disguise—that Edith put into letters signed with another name, much to the shallow Anna's delight, who, unassisted, could not for the world have conceived such pretty fancies for winning him, even had she been able to write them. Edith found that it was these, her own foisted-in sentiments, to which the young barrister mainly responded. The few sentences occasionally added from Anna's own lips made apparently no impression upon him.

The letter-writing in her absence Anna never discovered; but on her return the next morning she declared she wished to see her lover about something at once, and begged Mrs. Harnham to ask him to come.

There was a strange anxiety in her manner which did not escape Mrs. Harnham, and ultimately resolved itself into a flood of tears. Sinking down at Edith's knees, she made confession that the result of her relations with her lover it would soon become necessary to disclose.

Edith Harnham was generous enough to be very far from inclined to cast Anna adrift at this conjuncture. No true woman is ever so inclined from her own personal point of view, however prompt she may be in taking such steps to safeguard those dear to her. Although she had written to Raye so short a time previously, she instantly penned another Anna-note hinting clearly though delicately the state of affairs.

Raye replied by a hasty line to say how much he was affected by her news: he felt that he must run down to see her almost immediately.

But a week later the girl came to her mistress's room with another note, which on being read informed her that, after all, he could not find time for the journey. Anna was broken with grief; but by Mrs. Harnham's counsel strictly refrained from hurling at him the reproaches and bitterness customary from young women so situated. One thing was imperative: to keep the young man's romantic interest in her alive. Rather therefore did Edith, in the name of her protégée, request him on no account to be distressed about the looming event, and not to inconvenience himself to hasten down. She desired above everything to be no weight upon him in his career, no clog upon his high activities. She had wished him to know what had befallen; he was to dismiss it again from his mind. Only he must write tenderly as ever, and when he should come again on the spring circuit it would be time enough to discuss what had better be done.

It may well be supposed that Anna's own feelings had not been quite in accord with these generous expressions; but the mistress's judgment had ruled, and Anna had acquiesced. "All I want is that *niceness* you can so well put into your letters, my dear, dear mistress, and that I can't for the life o' me make up out of my own head; though I mean the same thing and feel it exactly when you've written it down!"

When the letter had been sent off, and Edith Harnham was left alone, she bowed herself on the back of her chair and wept.

"I wish it was mine—I wish it was!" she murmured. "Yet how can I say such a wicked thing!"

V

The letter moved Raye considerably when it reached him. The intelligence itself had affected him less than her unexpected manner of treating him in relation to it. The absence of any word of reproach, the devotion to his interests, the self-sacrifice apparent in every line, all made up a nobility of character that he had never dreamed of finding in womankind.

"God forgive me!" he said, tremulously. "I have been a wicked wretch. I did not know she was such a treasure as this!"

He reassured her instantly; declaring that he would not of course desert her, that he would provide a home for her somewhere. Meanwhile she was to stay where she was as long as her mistress would allow her.

But a misfortune supervened in this direction. Whether an inkling of Anna's circumstances reached the knowledge of Mrs. Harnham's husband or not cannot be said, but the girl was compelled, in spite of Edith's entreaties, to leave the house. By her own choice she decided to go back for a while to the cottage on the Plain. This arrangement led to a consultation as to how the correspondence should be carried on; and in the girl's inability to continue personally what had been begun in her name, and in the difficulty of their acting in concert as heretofore, she requested Mrs. Harnham—the only well-to-do friend she had in the world—to receive the letters and reply to them off-hand, sending them on afterwards to herself on the Plain, where she might at least get some neighbor to read them to her, though disqualified from replying for her because of the hand. Anna and her box then departed for the Plain.

Thus it befell that Edith Harnham found herself in the strange position of having to correspond, under no supervision by the real woman, with a man not her husband, in terms which were virtually those of a wife, concerning a condition that was not Edith's at all; the man being one for whom, mainly through the sympathies involved in playing this part, she secretly cherished a predilection, subtle and imaginative truly, but strong and absorbing. She opened each letter, read it as if intended for herself, and replied from the promptings of her own heart and no other.

Throughout this correspondence, carried on in the girl's absence, the high-strung Edith Harnham lived in the ecstasy of fancy; the vicarious intimacy engendered such a flow of passionateness as was never exceeded. For conscience' sake Edith at first sent on each of his letters to Anna, and even rough copies of her replies; but later on these so-called copies were much abridged, and many letters on both sides were not sent on at all.

Though selfish, and, superficially at least, infested with the self-indulgent vices of artificial society, there was a substratum of honesty and fairness in Raye's character. He had really a tender regard for the country girl, and it grew more tender than ever when he found her apparently capable of expressing the deepest sensibilities in the simplest words. He meditated, he wavered; and finally resolved to consult his sister, a maiden lady much older than himself, of lively sympathies and good intent. In making this confidence he showed her some of the letters.

"She seems fairly educated," Miss Raye observed, "and bright in ideas. She expresses herself with a taste that must be innate."

"Yes. She writes very prettily, doesn't she, thanks to these elementary schools."

"One is drawn out towards her, in spite of one's self, poor thing!"

The upshot of the discussion was that though he had not been directly advised to do it, Raye wrote, in his real name, what he would never have decided to write on his own responsibility—namely, that he could not live without her, and would come down in the spring and shelve her looming difficulty by marrying her.

This bold acceptance of the situation was made known to Anna by Mrs. Harnham driving out immediately to the cottage on the Plain. Anna jumped for joy like a little child ; and poor, crude directions for answering appropriately were given to Edith Harnham, who on her return to the city carried them out with warm intensifications.

"Oh !" she groaned, as she threw down the pen. "Anna — poor good little fool — hasn't intelligence enough to appreciate him. How should she? While I—don't bear his child !"

It was now February. The correspondence had continued altogether for four months, and the next letter from Raye contained incidentally a statement of his position and prospects. He said that in offering to wed her he had at first contemplated the step of retiring from a profession which hitherto had brought him very slight emolument, and which, to speak plainly, he had thought might be difficult of practice after his union with her. But the unexpected mines of brightness and warmth that her letters had disclosed to be lurking in her sweet nature had led him to abandon that somewhat sad prospect. He felt sure that with her powers of development, after a little private training in the social forms of London under his supervision, and a little help from a governess if necessary, she would make as good a professional man's wife as could be desired, even if he should rise to the woolsack. Many a lord-chancellor's wife had been less intuitively a lady than she had shown herself to be in her lines to him.

"Oh, poor fellow, poor fellow!" mourned Edith Harnham.

Her distress now raged as high as her infatuation. It was she who had wrought him to this pitch—to a marriage which meant his ruin; yet she could not, in mercy to her maid, do anything to hinder his plan. Anna was coming to Melchester that week, but she could hardly show the girl this last reply from the young man; it told too much of the second individuality that had usurped the place of the first.

Anna came, and her mistress took her into her own room for privacy. Anna began by saying with some anxiety that she was very glad the wedding was so near.

"Oh, Anna!" replied Mrs. Harnham. "I think we must tell him all—that I have been doing your writing for you—lest he should not know it till after you become his wife, and it might lead to dissension and recriminations—"

"Oh, mis'ess, dear mis'ess—please don't tell him now!" cried Anna, in distress. "If you were to do it, perhaps he would not marry me, and what should I do then? It would be terrible what would come to me! And I am getting on with my writing, too. I have brought with me the copybook you were so good as to give me, and I practise every day, and though it is so, so hard, I shall do it well at last, I believe, if I keep on trying."

Edith looked at the copybook. The copies had been set by herself, and such progress as the girl had made was in the way of grotesque fac-simile of her mistress's hand. But even if Edith's flowing caligraphy were reproduced the inspiration would be another thing.

"You do it so beautifully," continued Anna, "and say all that I want to say so much better than I could say it, that I do hope you won't leave me in the lurch just now!"

"Very well," replied the other. "But I—but I thought I ought not to go on."

"Why?"

Her strong desire to confide her sentiments led Edith to answer truly:

"Because of its effect upon me."

"But it *can't* have any!"

"Why, child?"

"Because you are married already!" said Anna, with lucid simplicity.

"Of course it can't," said her mistress, hastily; yet glad, despite her conscience, that two or three outpourings still remained to her. "But you must concentrate your attention on writing your name as I write it here."

VI

Soon Raye wrote about the wedding. Having decided to make the best of what he feared was a piece of romantic folly, he had acquired more zest for the grand experiment. He wished the ceremony to be in London, for greater privacy. Edith Harnham would have preferred it at Melchester; Anna was passive. His reasoning prevailed, and Mrs. Harnham threw herself with mournful zeal into the preparations for Anna's departure. In a last desperate feeling that she must at every hazard be in at the death of her dream, and see once again the man who by a species of telepathy had exercised such an influence on her, she offered to go up with Anna and be with her through the ceremony—"to see the end of her," as her mistress put it with forced gayety; an offer which the girl gratefully accepted; for she had no other friend capable of playing the part of companion and witness, in the presence of a gentlemanly bridegroom, in such a way as not to hasten an opinion that he had made an irremediable social blunder.

It was a muddy morning in March when Raye alighted from a four-wheel cab at the door of a registry-office in the S. W. district of London, and carefully handed down Anna and her companion Mrs. Harnham. Anna looked attractive in the somewhat fashionable clothes which Mrs. Harnham had helped her to buy, though not quite so attractive as, an innocent child, she had appeared in her country gown on the back of the wooden horse at Melchester Fair.

Mrs. Harnham had come up this morning by an early train, and a young man—a friend of Raye's—having met them at the door, all four entered the registry-office together. Till an hour before this time Raye had never known the wine-merchant's wife, except at that first casual encounter, and in the flutter of the performance before them he had little opportunity for more than a brief acquaintance. The contract of marriage at a registry is soon got through; but somehow, during its progress, Raye discovered a strange and secret gravitation between himself and Anna's friend.

The formalities of the wedding—or rather ratification of a previous union—being concluded, the four went in one cab to Raye's lodgings, newly taken in a new suburb in preference to a house, the rent of which he could ill afford just then. Here Anna cut the little cake which Raye had bought at a pastry-cook's on his way home from Lincoln's Inn the night before. But she did not do much besides. Raye's friend was obliged to depart almost immediately, and when he had left the only ones virtually present were Edith and Raye, who exchanged ideas with much animation. The conversation was indeed theirs only, Anna being as a domestic animal who humbly heard but understood not. Raye seemed startled in awakening to this fact, and began to feel dissatisfied with her inadequacy.

At last, more disappointed than he cared to own, he said, "Mrs. Harnham, my darling is so flurried that she doesn't know what she is doing or saying. I see that after this event a little quietude will be necessary before she gives tongue to that tender philosophy which she used to treat me to in her letters."

They had planned to start early that afternoon for Knollsea, to spend the few opening days of their married life there, and as the hour for departure was drawing near Raye asked his wife if she would go to the writing-desk in the next room and scribble a little note to his sister, who had been unable to attend through indisposition, informing her that the ceremony was over, thanking her for her little present, and hoping to know her well now that she was the writer's sister as well as Charles's.

"Say it in the pretty poetical way you know so well how to adopt," he added, "for I want you particularly to win her, and both of you to be dear friends."

Anna looked uneasy, but departed to her task, Raye remaining to talk to their guest. Anna was a long while absent, and her husband suddenly rose and went to her.

He found her still bending over the writing-table, with tears brimming up in her eyes; and he looked down upon the sheet of note-paper with some interest, to discover with what tact she had expressed her good-will in the delicate circumstances. To his surprise she had progressed but a few lines, in the characters and spelling of a child of eight, and with the ideas of a goose.

"Anna," he said, staring; "what's this?"

"It only means—that I can't do it any better!" she answered, through her tears.

"Eh? Nonsense!"

"I can't!" she insisted, with miserable, sobbing hardihood. "I—I—didn't write those letters, Charles; I only told *her* what to write, and not always that! But I am learning, oh, so fast, my dear, dear husband! And you'll forgive me, won't you, for not telling you before?" She slid to her knees, abjectly clasped his waist, and laid her face against him.

He stood a few moments, raised her, abruptly turned, and shut the door upon her, rejoining Edith in the drawing-room. She saw that something untoward had been discovered, and their eyes remained fixed on each other.

"Do I guess rightly?" he asked, with wan quietude. "*You* were her scribe through all this?"

"It was necessary," said Edith.

"Did she dictate every word you ever wrote to me?"

"Not every word."

"In fact, very little?"

"Very little."

"You wrote a great part of those pages every week from your own conceptions, though in her name?"

"Yes."

"Perhaps you wrote many of the letters when you were alone, without communication with her?"

"I did."

He turned to the bookcase, and leaned with his

hand over his face; and Edith, seeing his distress, became white as a sheet.

"You have deceived me—ruined me!" he murmured.

"Oh, don't say it!" she cried in her anguish, jumping up and putting her hand on his shoulder. "I can't bear that!"

"Delighting me deceptively. Why did you do it—*why* did you?"

"I began doing it in kindness to her. How could I do otherwise than try to save such a simple girl from misery? But I admit that I continued it for pleasure to myself."

Raye looked up. "Why did it give you pleasure?" he asked.

"I must not tell," said she.

He continued to regard her, and saw that her lips suddenly began to quiver under his scrutiny, and her eyes to fill and droop. She started aside, and said that she must go to the station to catch the return train; could a cab be called immediately?

But Raye went up to her, and took her unresisting hand. "Well, to think of such a thing as this!" he said. "Why, you and I are friends—lovers—devoted lovers—by correspondence!"

"Yes; I suppose."

"More."

"More?"

"Plainly more. It is no use blinking that. Legally I have married her—God help us both!—in soul and spirit I have married you, and no other woman in the world!"

"Hush!"

"But I will not hush! Why should you try to disguise the full truth, when you have already owned half of it? Yes, it is between you and me that the bond is—not between me and her! Now I'll say no more. But, oh, my cruel one, I think I have one claim upon you!"

She did not say what, and he drew her towards him, and bent over her. "If it was all pure invention in those letters," he said, emphatically, "give me your cheek only. If you meant what you said, let it be lips. It is for the first and last time, remember!"

She put up her mouth, and he kissed her long. "You forgive me?" she said, crying.

"Yes."

"But you are ruined!"

"What matter!" he said, shrugging his shoulders. "It serves me right!"

She withdrew, wiped her eyes, entered and bade good-bye to Anna, who had not expected her to go so soon, and was still wrestling with the letter. Raye followed Edith down-stairs, and in three minutes she was in a hansom driving to the Waterloo station.

He went back to his wife. "Never mind the letter, Anna, to-day," he said, gently. "Put on your things; we, too, must be off shortly."

The simple girl, upheld by the sense that she was indeed married, showed her delight at finding that he was as kind as ever after the disclosure. She did not know that before his eyes he beheld as it were a galley, in which he, the fastidious urban, was chained to work for the remainder of his life, with her, the unlettered peasant chained to his side.

Edith travelled back to Melchester that day with a face that showed the very stupor of grief. The end of her impassioned dream had come. When at dusk she reached the Melchester station her husband was there to meet her, but in his perfunctoriness and her preoccupation they did not see each other, and she went out of the station alone.

She walked mechanically homeward without calling a fly. Entering, she could not bear the silence of the house, and went up in the dark to where Anna had slept, where she remained thinking awhile. She then returned to the drawing-room, and not knowing what she did, crouched down upon the floor.

"I have ruined him!" she kept repeating—"I have ruined him; because I would not deal treacherously towards her!"

In the course of half an hour a figure opened the door of the apartment.

"Ah—who's that?" she said, starting up, for it was dark.

"Your husband. Who should it be?" said the worthy merchant.

"Ah—my husband!—I forgot I had a husband!" she whispered to herself.

"I missed you at the station," he continued. "Did you see Anna safely tied up? I hope so, for 'twas time."

"Yes—Anna is married."

Simultaneously with Edith's journey home, Anna and her husband were sitting at the opposite windows of a second-class carriage which sped along to Knollsea. In his hand was a pocket-book full of creased sheets closely written over. Unfolding them one after another he read them in silence and sighed.

"What are you doing, dear Charles?" she said, timidly, from the other window, and drew nearer to him as if he were a god.

"Reading over all those sweet letters to me signed 'Anna,'" he replied, with dreary resignation.

Autumn, 1891.

TO PLEASE HIS WIFE

I

The interior of St. James's Church, in Havenpool Town, was slowly darkening under the close clouds of a winter afternoon. It was Sunday—service had just ended, the face of the parson in the pulpit was buried in his hands, and the congregation, with a cheerful sigh of release, were rising from their knees to depart.

For the moment the stillness was so complete that the surging of the sea could be heard outside the harbor-bar. Then it was broken by the footsteps of the clerk going towards the west door to open it in the usual manner for the exit of the assembly. Before, however, he had reached the doorway, the latch was lifted from without, and the dark figure of a man in a sailor's garb appeared against the light.

The clerk stepped aside, the sailor closed the door gently behind him, and advanced up the nave till he stood at the chancel-step. The parson looked up from the private little prayer which, after so many for the parish, he quite fairly took for himself, rose to his feet, and stared at the intruder.

"I beg your pardon, sir," said the sailor, addressing the minister in a voice distinctly audible to all the congregation. "I have come here to offer thanks for my narrow escape from shipwreck. I am given to understand that it is a proper thing to do, if you have no objection?"

The parson, after a moment's pause, said, hesitatingly, "I have no objection; certainly. It is usual to mention any such wish before service, so that the proper words may be used in the General Thanksgiving. But, if you wish, we can read from the form for use after a storm at sea."

"Aye, sure; I ain't particular," said the sailor.

The clerk thereupon directed the sailor to the page in the prayer-book where the collect of thanksgiving would be found, and the rector began reading it, the sailor kneeling where he stood, and repeating it after him word by word in a distinct voice. The people, who had remained agape and motionless at the proceeding, mechanically knelt down likewise; but they continued to regard the isolated form of the sailor who, in the precise middle of the chancel-step, remained fixed on his knees, facing the east, his hat beside him, his hands joined, and he quite unconscious of his appearance in their regard.

When his thanksgiving had come to an end, he arose; the people arose also, and all went out of church together. As soon as the sailor emerged, so that the remaining daylight fell upon his face, old inhabitants began to recognize him as no other than Shadrach Jolliffe, a young man who had not been seen at Havenpool for several years. A son of the town, his parents had died when he was quite young, on which account he had early gone to sea, in the Newfoundland trade.

He talked with this and that townsman as he walked, informing them that, since leaving his native place years before, he had become captain and owner of a small coasting-ketch, which had providentially been saved from the gale as well as himself. Presently he drew near to two girls who were going out of the church-yard in front of him; they had been sitting in the nave at his entry, and had watched his doings with deep interest, afterwards discussing him as they moved out of church together. One was a slight and gentle creature, the other a tall, large-framed, deliberative girl. Captain Jolliffe regarded the loose curls of their hair, their backs and shoulders, down to their heels, for some time.

"Who may them two maids be?" he whispered to his neighbor.

"The little one is Emily Hanning; the tall one, Joanna Phippard."

"Ah! I recollect 'em now, to be sure."

He advanced to their elbow, and genially stole a gaze at them.

"Emily, you don't know me?" said the sailor, turning his beaming brown eyes on her.

"I think I do, Mr. Jolliffe," said Emily, shyly.

The other girl looked straight at him with her dark eyes.

"The face of Miss Joanna I don't call to mind so well," he continued. "But I know her beginnings and kindred."

They walked and talked together, Jolliffe narrating particulars of his late narrow escape, till they reached the corner of Sloop Lane, in which Emily Hanning dwelt, when, with a nod and smile, she left them. Soon the sailor parted also from Joanna, and, having no especial errand or appointment, turned back towards Emily's house. She lived with her father, who called himself an accountant, the daughter, however, keeping a little stationery-shop as a supplemental provision for the gaps of his somewhat uncertain business. On entering, Jolliffe found father and daughter about to begin tea.

"Oh, I didn't know it was tea-time," he said. "Aye, I'll have a cup with much pleasure."

He remained to tea and long afterwards, telling more tales of his seafaring life. Several neighbors called to listen, and were asked to come in. Somehow, Emily Hanning lost her heart to the sailor that Sunday night, and in the course of a week or two there was a tender understanding between them.

One moonlight evening in the next month Shadrach was ascending out of the town by the long straight road eastward, to an elevated suburb where the more fashionable houses stood—if anything near this ancient port could be called fashionable—when he saw a figure before him whom, from her manner of glancing back, he took to be Emily; but, on coming up, he found she was Joanna Phippard. He gave a gallant greeting, and walked beside her.

"Go along," she said, "or Emily will be jealous!"

He seemed not to like the suggestion, and remained.

What was said and what was done on that walk never could be clearly recollected by Shadrach; but in some way or other Joanna contrived to wean him away from her gentler and younger rival. From that week onward, Jolliffe was seen more and more in the wake of Joanna Phippard and less in the company of Emily; and it was soon rumored about the quay that old Jolliffe's son, who had come home from sea, was going to be married to the former young woman, to the great disappointment of the latter.

Just after this report had gone about, Joanna dressed herself for a walk one morning, and started for Emily's house in the little cross-street. Intelligence of the deep sorrow of her friend on account of the loss of Shadrach had reached her ears also, and her conscience reproached her for winning him away.

Joanna was not altogether satisfied with the sailor.

She liked his attentions, and she coveted the dignity of matrimony; but she had never been deeply in love with Jolliffe. For one thing, she was ambitious, and socially his position was hardly so good as her own, and there was always the chance of an attractive woman mating considerably above her. It had long been in her mind that she would not strongly object to give him back again to Emily if her friend felt so very badly about him. To this end she had written a letter of renunciation to Shadrach, which letter she carried in her hand, intending to post it if personal observation of Emily convinced her that her friend was suffering.

Joanna entered Sloop Lane and stepped down into the stationery-shop, which was below the pavement level. Emily's father was never at home at this hour of the day, and it seemed as though Emily were not at home either, for the visitor could make nobody hear. Customers came so seldom hither that a five minutes' absence of the proprietor counted for little. Joanna waited in the little shop, where Emily had tastefully set out—as women can—articles in themselves of slight value, so as to obscure the meagreness of the stock-in-trade, till she saw a figure pausing without the window apparently absorbed in the contemplation of the sixpenny books, packets of paper, and prints hung on a string. It was Captain Shadrach Jolliffe, peering in to ascertain if Emily were there alone. Moved by an impulse of reluctance to meet him in a spot which breathed of Emily, she slipped through the door that communicated with the parlor at the back. Joanna had frequently done so before, for in her friendship with Emily she had the freedom of the house without ceremony.

Jolliffe entered the shop. Through the thin blind which screened the glass partition she could see that he was disappointed at not finding Emily there. He was about to go out again, when Emily's form darkened the doorway, hastening home from some errand. At sight of Jolliffe she started back as if she would have gone out again.

"Don't run away, Emily; don't!" said he. "What can make ye afraid?"

"I'm not afraid, Captain Jolliffe. Only—only I saw you all of a sudden, and—it made me jump!" Her voice showed that her heart had jumped even more than the rest of her.

"I just called as I was passing," he said.

"For some paper?" She hastened behind the counter.

"No, no, Emily; why do ye get behind there? Why not stay by me? You seem to hate me."

"I don't hate you. How can I?"

"Then come out, so that we can talk like Christians."

Emily obeyed with a fitful laugh, till she stood again beside him in the open part of the shop.

"There's a dear," he said.

"You mustn't say that, Captain Jolliffe; because the words belong to somebody else."

"Ah! I know what you mean. But, Emily, upon my life I didn't know till this morning that you cared one bit about me, or I should not have done as I have done. I have the best of feelings for Joanna, but I know that from the beginning she hasn't cared for me more than in a friendly way; and I see now the one I ought to have asked to be my wife. You know, Emily, when a man comes home from sea after a long voyage he's as blind as a bat—he can't see who's who in women. They are all alike to him, beautiful creatures, and he takes the first that comes easy, without thinking if she loves him, or if he might not soon love another better than her. From the first I inclined to you most, but you were so backward and shy that I thought you didn't want me to bother 'ee, and so I went to Joanna."

"Don't say any more, Mr. Jolliffe, don't!" said she, choking. "You are going to marry Joanna next month, and it is wrong to—to—"

"Oh, Emily, my darling!" he cried, and clasped her little figure in his arms before she was aware.

Joanna, behind the curtain, turned pale, tried to withdraw her eyes, but could not.

"It is only you I love as a man ought to love the woman he is going to marry; and I know this from what Joanna has said—that she will willingly let me off! She wants to marry higher, I know, and only said 'Yes' to me out of kindness. A fine, tall girl like her isn't the sort for a plain sailor's wife; you be the best suited for that."

He kissed her and kissed her again, her flexible form quivering in the agitation of his embrace.

"I wonder—are you sure—Joanna is going to break off with you? Oh, are you sure? Because—"

"I know she would not wish to make us miserable. She will release me."

"Oh, I hope—I hope she will! Don't stay any longer, Captain Jolliffe!"

He lingered, however, till a customer came for a penny stick of sealing-wax, and then he withdrew.

Green envy had overspread Joanna at the scene. She looked about for a way of escape. To get out without Emily's knowledge of her visit was indispensable. She crept from the parlor into the passage, and thence to the front door of the house, where she let herself noiselessly into the street.

The sight of that caress had reversed all her resolutions. She could not let Shadrach go. Reaching home, she burned the letter, and told her mother that if Captain Jolliffe called she was too unwell to see him.

Shadrach, however, did not call. He sent her a note expressing in simple language the state of his feelings; and asked to be allowed to take advantage of the hints she had given him that her affection, too, was little more than friendly, by cancelling the engagement.

Looking out upon the harbor and the island beyond, he waited and waited in his lodgings for an answer that did not come. The suspense grew to be so intolerable that after dark he went up the high street. He could not resist calling at Joanna's to learn his fate.

Her mother said her daughter was too unwell to see him, and to his questioning admitted that it was in consequence of a letter received from himself, which had distressed her deeply.

"You know what it was about, perhaps, Mrs. Phippard?" he said.

Mrs. Phippard owned that she did, adding that it put them in a very painful position. Thereupon Shadrach, fearing that he had been guilty of an enormity, explained that if his letter had pained Joanna it must be owing to a misunderstanding, since he had thought it would be a relief to her. If otherwise, he would hold himself bound by his word, and she was to think of the letter as never having been written.

Next morning he received an oral message from the young woman, asking him to fetch her home from a meeting that evening. This he did, and while walking from the Town-hall to her door, with her hand in his arm, she said:

"It is all the same as before between us, isn't it, Shadrach? Your letter was sent in mistake?"

"It is all the same as before," he answered, "if you say it must be."

"I wish it to be," she murmured, with hard lineaments, as she thought of Emily.

Shadrach was a religious and scrupulous man, who respected his word as his life. Shortly afterwards the wedding took place, Jolliffe having conveyed to Emily as gently as possible the error he had fallen into when estimating Joanna's mood as one of indifference.

II

A month after the marriage Joanna's mother died, and the couple were obliged to turn their attention to very practical matters. Now that she was left without a parent, Joanna could not bear the notion of her husband going to sea again; but the question was, What could he do at home? They finally decided to take on a grocer's shop in the high street, the goodwill and stock of which were waiting to be disposed of at that time. Shadrach knew nothing of shopkeeping, and Joanna very little, but they hoped to learn.

To the management of this grocery business they now devoted all their energies, and continued to conduct it for many succeeding years, without great success. Two sons were born to them, whom their mother loved to idolatry, although she had never passionately loved her husband; and she lavished upon them all her forethought and care. But the shop did not thrive, and the large dreams she had entertained of her sons' education and career became attenuated in the face of realities. Their schooling was of the plainest, but, being by the sea, they grew alert in all such nautical arts and enterprises as were attractive to their age.

The great interest of the Jolliffes' married life, outside their own immediate household, had lain in the marriage of Emily. By one of those odd chances which lead those that lurk in unexpected corners to be discovered, while the obvious are passed by, the gentle girl had been seen and loved by a thriving merchant of the town, a widower, some years older than herself, though still in the prime of life. At first Emily had declared that she never, never could marry any one; but Mr. Lester had quietly persevered, and had at last won her reluctant assent. Two children also were the fruits of this union, and, as they grew and prospered, Emily declared that she had never supposed that she could live to be so happy.

The worthy merchant's home, one of those large, substantial brick mansions frequently jammed up in old-fashioned towns, faced directly on the high street, nearly opposite to the grocery-shop of the Jolliffes, and it now became the pain of Joanna to behold the woman whose place she had usurped out of pure covetousness looking down from her position of comparative wealth upon the humble shop-window with its dusty sugar-loaves, heaps of raisins, and canisters of tea, over which it was her own lot to preside. The business having so dwindled, Joanna was obliged to serve in the shop herself, and it galled and mortified her that Emily Lester, sitting in her large drawing-room over the way, could witness her own dancings up and down behind the counter at the beck and call of wretched twopenny customers, whose patronage she was driven to welcome gladly; persons to whom she was compelled to be civil in the street, while Emily was bounding along with her children and her governess, and conversing with the genteelest people of the town and neighborhood. This was what she had gained by not letting Shadrach Jolliffe, whom she had so faintly loved, carry his affection elsewhere.

Shadrach was a good and honest man, and he had

been faithful to her in heart and in deed. Time had clipped the wings of his love for Emily in his devotion to the mother of his boys; he had quite lived down that impulsive earlier fancy, and Emily had become in his regard nothing more than a friend. It was the same with Emily's feelings for him. Possibly, had she found the least cause for jealousy, Joanna would almost have been better satisfied. It was in the absolute acquiescence of Emily and Shadrach in the results she herself had contrived that her discontent found nourishment.

Shadrach was not endowed with the narrow shrewdness necessary for developing a retail business in the face of many competitors. Did a customer inquire if the grocer could really recommend the wondrous substitute for eggs which a persevering bagman had forced into his stock, he would answer that "when you did not put eggs into a pudding it was difficult to taste them there"; and when he was asked if his "real Mocha coffee" was real Mocha, he would say, grimly, "as understood in small shops."

One summer day, when the big brick house opposite was reflecting the oppressive sun's heat into the shop, and nobody was present but husband and wife, Joanna looked across at Emily's door, where a wealthy visitor's carriage had drawn up. Traces of patronage had been visible in Emily's manner of late.

"Shadrach, the truth is, you are not a business-man," his wife sadly murmured. "You were not brought up to shopkeeping, and it is impossible for a man to make a fortune at an occupation he has jumped into, as you did into this."

Jolliffe agreed with her, in this as in everything else. "Not that I care a rope's end about making a fortune," he said, cheerfully. "I am happy enough, and we can rub on somehow."

She looked again at the great house through the screen of bottled pickles.

"Rub on—yes," she said, bitterly. "But see how well off Emily Lester is, who used to be so poor! Her boys will go to college, no doubt; and think of yours—obliged to go to the parish school."

Shadrach's thoughts had flown to Emily.

"Nobody," he said, good-humoredly, "ever did Emily a better turn than you did, Joanna, when you warned her off me and put an end to that little simpering nonsense between us, so as to leave it in her power to say 'Aye' to Lester when he came along."

This almost maddened her.

"Don't speak of by-gones!" she implored, in stern sadness. "But think, for the boys' and my sake, if not for your own, what are we to do to get richer?"

"Well," he said, becoming serious, "to tell the truth, I have always felt myself unfit for this business, though I've never liked to say so. I seem to want more room for sprawling; a more open space to strike out in than here among friends and neighbors. I could get rich as well as any man, if I tried my own way."

"I wish you would! What is your way?"

"To go to sea again."

She had been the very one to keep him at home, hating the semi-widowed existence of sailors' wives. But her ambition checked her instincts now, and she said:

"Do you think success really lies that way?"

"I am sure it lies in no other."

"Do you want to go, Shadrach?"

"Not for the pleasure of it, I can tell 'ee. There's no such pleasure at sea, Joanna, as I can find in my back parlor here. To speak honest, I have no love for the brine. I never had much. But if it comes to a question of a fortune for you and the lads, it is another thing. That's the only way to it for one born and bred a seafarer as I."

"Would it take long to earn?"

"Well, that depends; perhaps not."

The next morning Shadrach pulled from a chest of drawers the nautical jacket he had worn during the first months of his return, brushed out the moths, donned it, and walked down to the quay. The port still did a fair business in the Newfoundland trade, though not so much as formerly.

It was not long after this that he invested all he possessed in purchasing a part ownership in a brig, of which he was appointed captain. A few months were passed in coast trading, during which interval Shadrach wore off the land-rust that had accumulated upon him in his grocery phase; and in the spring the brig sailed for Newfoundland.

Joanna lived on at home with her sons, who were now growing up into strong lads, and occupying themselves in various ways about the harbor and quay.

"Never mind, let them work a little," their fond mother said to herself. "Our necessities compel it now, but when Shadrach comes home they will be only seventeen and eighteen, and they shall be removed from the port, and their education thoroughly taken in hand by a tutor; and with the money they'll have they will perhaps be as near to gentlemen as Emmy Lester's precious two, with their algebra and their Latin!"

The date for Shadrach's return drew near and arrived, and he did not appear. Joanna was assured that there was no cause for anxiety, sailing-ships being so uncertain in their coming; which assurance proved to be well-grounded, for late one wet evening, about a month after the calculated time, the ship was announced as at hand, and presently the slip-slop step of Shadrach as the sailor sounded in the passage, and he entered. The boys had gone out and had missed him, and Joanna was sitting alone.

As soon as the first emotion of reunion between the couple had passed, Jolliffe explained the delay as owing to a small speculative contract, which had produced good results.

"I was determined not to disappoint 'ee," he said; "and I think you'll own that I haven't!"

With this he pulled out an enormous canvas bag, full and rotund as the money-bag of the giant whom Jack slew, untied it, and shook the contents out into her lap as she sat in her low chair by the fire. A mass of guineas (there were guineas on the earth in those days) fell into her lap with a sudden thud, weighing down her gown to the floor.

"There!" said Shadrach, complacently. "I told 'ee, dear, I'd do it; and have I done it or no?"

Somehow her face, after the first excitement of possession, did not retain its glory.

"It is a lot of gold, indeed," she said. "And—is this *all?*"

"All? Why, dear Joanna, do you know you can count to three hundred in that heap? It is a fortune!"

"Yes—yes. A fortune—judged by sea; but judged by land—"

However, she banished considerations of the money for the nonce. Soon the boys came in, and next Sunday Shadrach returned thanks to God—this time by the more ordinary channel of the italics in the General Thanksgiving. But a few days after, when the question of investing the money arose, he remarked that she did not seem so satisfied as he had hoped.

"Well, you see, Shadrach," she answered, "*we* count by hundreds; *they* count by thousands" (nodding towards the other side of the street). "They have set up a carriage and pair since you left."

"Oh! have they?"

"My dear Shadrach, you don't know how the world moves. However, we'll do the best we can with it. But they are rich, and we are poor still!"

The greater part of a year was desultorily spent. She moved sadly about the house and shop, and the boys were still occupying themselves in and around the harbor.

"Joanna," he said, one day, "I see by your movements that it is not enough."

"It is not enough," said she. "My boys will have to live by steering the ships that the Lesters own; and I was once above her!"

Jolliffe was not an argumentative man, and he only murmured that he thought he would make another voyage. He meditated for several days, and coming home from the quay one afternoon said, suddenly:

"I could do it for 'ee, dear, in one more trip, for certain, if—if—"

"Do what, Shadrach?"

"Enable 'ee to count by thousands instead of hundreds."

"If what?"

"If I might take the boys."

She turned pale.

"Don't say that, Shadrach," she answered, hastily.

"Why?"

"I don't like to hear it. There's danger at sea. I want them to be something genteel, and no danger to them. I couldn't let them risk their lives at sea. Oh, I couldn't ever, ever!"

"Very well, dear, it sha'n't be done."

Next day, after a silence, she asked a question:

"If they were to go with you it would make a great deal of difference, I suppose, to the profit?"

"'Twould treble what I should get from the venture single-handed. Under my eye they would be as good as two more of myself."

Later on she said: "Tell me more about this."

"Well, the boys are almost as clever as master-mariners in handling a craft, upon my life! There isn't a more cranky place in the South Seas than about the sand-banks of this harbor, and they've practised here from their infancy. And they are so steady. I couldn't get their steadiness and their trustworthiness in half a dozen men twice their age."

"And is it *very* dangerous at sea; now, too, there are rumors of war?" she asked, uneasily.

"Oh, well, there be risks. Still—"

The idea grew and magnified, and the mother's heart was crushed and stifled by it. Emmy was growing *too* patronizing; it could not be borne. Shadrach's wife could not help nagging him about their comparative poverty. The young men, amiable as their father, when spoken to on the subject of a voyage of enterprise, were quite willing to embark; and though they, like their father, had no great love for the sea, they became quite enthusiastic when the proposal was detailed.

Everything now hung upon their mother's assent. She withheld it long, but at last gave the word: the young men might accompany their father. Shadrach was unusually cheerful about it. Heaven had preserved him hitherto, and he had uttered his thanks. God would not forsake those who were faithful to him.

All that the Jolliffes possessed in the world was put into the enterprise. The grocery stock was pared down to the least that possibly could afford a bare sustenance to Joanna during the absence, which was to last through the usual "New-f'nland spell." How she would endure the weary time she hardly knew, for the boys had been with her formerly; but she nerved herself for the trial.

The ship was laden with boots and shoes, ready-made clothing, fishing-tackle, butter, cheese, cordage, sail-cloth, and many other commodities; and was to bring back oil, furs, skins, fish, cranberries, and what else came to hand. But much trading to other ports was to be undertaken between the voyages out and homeward, and thereby much money made.

III

The brig sailed on a Monday morning in spring; but Joanna did not witness its departure. She could not bear the sight that she had been the means of bringing about. Knowing this, her husband told her overnight that they were to sail some time before noon next day; hence when, awakening at five the next morning, she heard them bustling about down-stairs, she did not hasten to descend, but lay trying to nerve herself for the parting, imagining they would leave about nine, as her husband had done on his previous voyage. When she did descend she beheld words chalked upon the sloping face of the bureau; but no husband or sons. In the hastily-scrawled lines Shadrach said they had gone off thus not to pain her by a leave-taking; and the sons had chalked under his words: "Good-bye, mother."

She rushed to the quay and looked down the harbor towards the blue rim of the sea, but she could only see the masts and bulging sails of the *Joanna;* no human figures. "'Tis I have sent them!" she said, wildly, and burst into tears. In the house the chalked "Good-bye" nearly broke her heart. But when she had re-entered the front-room and looked across at Emily's, a gleam of triumph lit her thin face at her anticipated release from the thraldom of subservience.

To do Emily Lester justice, her assumption of superiority was mainly a figment of Joanna's brain. That the circumstances of the merchant's wife were more luxurious than Joanna's, the former could not conceal; though whenever the two met, which was not very often now, Emily endeavored to subdue the difference by every means in her power.

The first summer lapsed away, and Joanna meagrely maintained herself by the shop, which now consisted of little more than a window and a counter. Emily was, in truth, her only large customer; and Mrs. Lester's kindly readiness to buy anything and everything without questioning the quality had a sting of bitterness in it, for it was the uncritical attitude of a patron, and almost of a donor. The long, dreary winter moved on; the face of the bureau had been turned to the wall to protect the chalked words of farewell, for Joanna could never bring herself to rub them out, and she often glanced at them with wet eyes. Emily's handsome boys came home for the Christmas holidays; the university was talked of for them; and still Joanna subsisted, as it were, with held breath, like a person submerged. Only one summer more, and the spell would end. Towards the end of the time Emily called on her quondam friend. She had heard that Joanna began to feel anxious; she had received no letter from husband or sons for some months. Emily's silks rustled arrogantly when, in response to Joanna's almost dumb invitation, she squeezed through the opening of the counter and into the parlor behind the shop.

"*You* are all success, and *I* am all the other way!" said Joanna.

"But why do you think so?" said Emily. "They are to bring back a fortune, I hear."

"Ah! will they come? The doubt is more than a woman can bear. All three in one ship — think of that! And I have not heard of them for months!"

"But the time is not up. You should not meet misfortune half-way."

"Nothing will repay me for the grief of their absence."

"Then why did you let them go? You were doing fairly well."

"I *made* them go!" she said, turning vehemently upon Emily. "And I'll tell you why. I could not bear that we should be only muddling on, and you so rich and thriving. Now I have told you, and you may hate me if you will!"

"I shall never hate you, Joanna."

And she proved the truth of her words afterwards. The end of autumn came and the brig should have been in port, but nothing like the *Joanna* appeared in the channel between the sands. It was now really time to be uneasy. Joanna Jolliffe sat by the fire, and every gust of wind caused her a cold thrill. She had always feared and detested the sea; to her it was a treacherous, restless, slimy creature, glorying in the griefs of women. "Still," she said, "they *must* come!"

She recalled to her mind that Shadrach had said before starting that if they returned safe and sound, with success crowning their enterprise, he would go, as he had gone after his shipwreck, and kneel with his sons in the church and offer sincere thanks for their deliverance. She went to church regularly morning and afternoon, and sat in the most forward pew, nearest the chancel step. Her eyes were mostly fixed on that step, where Shadrach had knelt in the bloom of his young manhood; she knew to an inch the spot which his knees had pressed twenty winters before—his outline as he had knelt, his hat on the step beside him. God was good. Surely her husband must kneel there again—a son on each side, as he had said; George just here, Jim just there. By long watching the spot as she worshipped, it became as if she saw the three returned ones there kneeling; the two slim outlines of her boys, the more bulky form between them; their hands clasped, their heads shaped against the eastern wall. The fancy grew almost to an hallucination; she could never turn her worn eyes to the step without seeing them there.

Nevertheless, they did not come. Heaven was merciful, but it was not yet pleased to relieve her soul. This was her purgation for the sin of making them the slaves of her ambition. But it became more than purgation soon, and her mood approached despair. Months had passed since the brig had been due, but it had not returned.

Joanna was always hearing or seeing evidences of their arrival. When on the hill behind the port, whence a view of the open channel could be obtained, she felt sure that a little speck on the horizon, breaking the eternally level waste of waters southward, was the truck of the *Joanna's* main-mast. Or when in-doors, a shout or excitement of any kind at the corner of the Town Cellar, where the high street joined the quay, caused her to spring to her feet and cry, "'Tis they!"

But it was not. The visionary forms knelt every Sunday afternoon on the chancel step, but not the real. Her shop had, as it were, eaten itself hollow. In the apathy which had resulted from her loneliness and grief she had ceased to take in the smallest supplies, and thus had sent away her last customer.

In this strait Emily Lester tried by every means in her power to aid the afflicted woman, but she met with constant repulses.

"I don't like you! I can't bear to see you!" Joanna would whisper hoarsely, when Emily came to her and made advances.

"But I want to help and soothe you, Joanna," Emily would say.

"You are a lady, with a rich husband and fine sons. What can you want with a bereaved crone like me?"

"Joanna, I want this: I want you to come and live in my house, and not stay alone in this dismal place any longer."

"And suppose they come and don't find me at home? You wish to separate me and mine! No, I'll stay here. I don't like you, and I can't thank you, whatever kindness you do me!"

However, as time went on Joanna could not afford to pay the rent of the shop and house without an income. She was assured that all hope of the return of Shadrach and his sons was vain, and she reluctantly consented to accept the asylum of the Lesters' house. Here she was allotted a room of her own on the second floor, and went and came as she chose, without contact with the family. Her hair grayed and whitened, deep lines channelled her forehead, and her form grew gaunt and stooping. But she still expected the lost ones, and when she met Emily on the staircase she would say, morosely: "I know why you've got me here! They'll come, and be disappointed at not finding me at home, and perhaps go away again; and then you'll be revenged for my taking Shadrach away from 'ee!"

Emily Lester bore these reproaches from the grief-stricken soul. She was sure—all the people of Havenpool were sure—that Shadrach and his sons could not return. For years the vessel had been given up as lost.

Nevertheless, when awakened at night by any noise, Joanna would rise from bed and glance at the shop opposite by the light from the flickering lamp, to make sure it was not they.

It was a damp and dark December night, six years after the departure of the brig *Joanna*. The wind was from the sea, and brought up a fishy mist which mopped the face like moist flannel. Joanna had prayed her usual prayer for the absent ones with more fervor and confidence than she had felt for months, and had fallen asleep about eleven. It must have been between one and two when she suddenly started up. She had certainly heard steps in the street, and the voices of Shadrach and her sons calling at the door of the grocery-shop. She sprang out of bed, and, hardly knowing what clothing she dragged on herself, hastened down Emily's large and carpeted staircase, put the candle on the hall-table, unfastened the bolts and chain, and stepped into the street. The mist, blowing up the street from the quay, hindered her seeing the shop, although it was so near; but she had crossed to it in a moment. How was it? Nobody stood there. The wretched woman walked wildly up and down with her bare feet—there was not a soul. She returned and knocked with all her might at the door which had once been her own—they might have been admitted for the night, unwilling to disturb her till the morning. It was not till several minutes had elapsed that the young man who now kept the shop looked out of an upper window, and saw the skeleton of something human standing below half-dressed.

"Has anybody come?" asked the form.

"Oh, Mrs. Jolliffe, I didn't know it was you," said the young man, kindly, for he was aware how her baseless expectations moved her. "No, nobody has come."

June, 1891.

THE MELANCHOLY HUSSAR OF THE GERMAN LEGION

I

Here stretch the downs, high and breezy and green, absolutely unchanged since those eventful days. A plough has never disturbed the turf, and the sod that was uppermost then is uppermost now. Here stood the camp; here are distinct traces of the banks thrown up for the horses of the cavalry, and spots where the midden-heaps lay are still to be observed. At night, when I walk across the lonely place, it is impossible to avoid hearing, amid the scourings of the wind over the grass-bents and thistles, the old trumpet and bugle calls, the rattle of the halters; to help seeing rows of spectral tents and the impedimenta of the soldiery; from within the canvases come guttural syllables of foreign tongues, and broken songs of the fatherland; for they were mainly regiments of the King's German Legion that slept round the tent-poles hereabout at that time.

It was nearly ninety years ago. The British uniform of the period, with its immense epaulettes, queer cocked-hat, breeches, gaiters, ponderous cartridge-box, buckled shoes, and what not, would look strange and barbarous now. Ideas have changed; invention has followed invention. Soldiers were monumental objects then. A divinity still hedged kings here and there; and war was considered a glorious thing.

Secluded old manor-houses and hamlets lie in the ravines and hollows among these hills, where a stranger had hardly ever been seen till the king chose to take the baths yearly at the sea-side watering-place a few miles to the south; as a consequence of which battalions descended in a cloud upon the open country around. Is it necessary to add that the echoes of many characteristic tales, dating from that picturesque time, still linger about here in more or less fragmentary form, to be caught by the attentive ear? Some of them I have repeated; most of them I have forgotten; one I have never repeated, and assuredly can never forget.

Phyllis told me the story with her own lips. She was then an old lady of seventy-five, and her auditor a lad of fifteen. She enjoined silence as to her share in the incident till she should be "dead, buried, and forgotten." Her life was prolonged twelve years after the day of her narration, and she has now been dead nearly twenty. The oblivion which in her modesty and humility she courted for herself has only partially fallen on her, with the unfortunate result of inflicting an injustice upon her memory; since such fragments of her story as got abroad at the time, and have been kept alive ever since, are precisely those which are most unfavorable to her character.

It all began with the arrival of the York Hussars, one of the foreign regiments above alluded to. Before that day scarcely a soul had been seen near her father's house for weeks. When a noise like the brushing skirt of a visitor was heard on the door-step it proved to be a scudding leaf; when a carriage seemed to be nearing the door, it was her father grinding his sickle on the stone in the garden for his favorite relaxation of trimming the box-tree borders to the plots. A sound like luggage thrown down from the coach was a gun far away at sea; and what looked like a tall man by the gate at dusk was a yew bush cut into a quaint and attenuated shape. There is no such solitude in country places now as there was in those old days.

Yet all the while King George and his court were at his favorite sea-side resort, not more than five miles off.

The daughter's seclusion was great, but beyond the seclusion of the girl lay the seclusion of the father. If her social condition was twilight, his was darkness. Yet he enjoyed his darkness, while her twilight oppressed her. Dr. Grove had been a professional man whose taste for lonely meditation over metaphysical questions had diminished his practice till it no longer paid him to keep it going; after which he had relinquished it and hired at a nominal rent the small, dilapidated half-farm half-manor-house of this obscure inland nook, to make a sufficiency of an income which in a town would have been inadequate for their maintenance. He stayed in his garden the greater part of the day, growing more and more irritable with the lapse of time and the increasing perception that he had wasted his life in the pursuit of illusions. He saw his friends less and less frequently. Phyllis became so shy that if she met a stranger anywhere in her short rambles she felt ashamed at his gaze, walked awkwardly, and blushed to her shoulders.

Yet Phyllis was discovered even here by an admirer, and her hand most unexpectedly asked in marriage.

The king, as aforesaid, was at the neighboring town, where he had taken up his abode at Gloucester Lodge;

and his presence in the town naturally brought many county people thither. Among these idlers — many of whom professed to have connections and interests with the court—was one Humphrey Gould, a bachelor; a personage neither young nor old; neither good-looking nor positively plain. Too steady-going to be "a buck" (as fast and unmarried men were then called), he was an approximately fashionable man of a mild type. This bachelor of thirty found his way to the village on the down; beheld Phyllis; made her father's acquaintance in order to make hers, and by some means or other she sufficiently inflamed his heart to lead him in that direction almost daily, till he became engaged to marry her.

As he was of an old local family, some of whose members were held in respect in the county, Phyllis, in bringing him to her feet, had accomplished what was considered a brilliant move for one in her constrained position. How she had done it was not quite known to Phyllis herself. In those days unequal marriages were regarded rather as a violation of the laws of nature than as a mere infringement of convention, the more modern view, and hence when Phyllis, of the watering-place *bourgeoisie,* was chosen by such a gentlemanly fellow, it was as if she were going to be taken to heaven, though perhaps the uninformed would have seen no great difference in the respective positions of the pair, the said Gould being as poor as a crow.

This pecuniary condition was his excuse—probably a true one — for postponing their union, and as the winter drew nearer, and the king departed for the season, Mr. Humphrey Gould set out for Bath, promising to return to Phyllis in a few weeks. The winter arrived, the date of his promise passed, yet Gould postponed his coming, on the ground that he could not very easily leave his father in the city of their sojourn, the elder having no other relative near him. Phyllis, though lonely in the extreme, was content. The man who had asked her in marriage was a desirable husband for her in many ways; her father highly approved of his suit; but this neglect of her was awkward, if not painful, for Phyllis. Love him in the true sense of the word she assured me she never did, but she had a genuine regard for him; admired a certain methodical and dogged way in which he sometimes took his pleasure; valued his knowledge of what the court was doing, had done, or was about to do; and she was not without a feeling of pride that he had chosen her when he might have exercised a more ambitious choice.

But he did not come, and the spring developed. His letters were regular though formal; and it is not to be wondered that the uncertainty of her position, linked with the fact that there was not much passion in her thoughts of Humphrey, bred an indescribable dreariness in the heart of Phyllis Grove. The spring was soon summer, and the summer brought the king; but still no Humphrey Gould. All this while the engagement by letter was maintained intact.

At this point of time a golden radiance flashed in upon the lives of people here, and charged all youthful thought with emotional interest. This radiance was the York Hussars.

II

The present generation has probably but a very dim notion of the celebrated York Hussars of ninety years ago. They were one of the regiments of the King's German Legion, and (though they somewhat degenerated later on) their brilliant uniforms, their splendid horses, and, above all, their foreign air and mustaches (rare appendages then), drew crowds of admirers of both sexes wherever they went. These with other regiments had come to encamp on the downs and pastures, because of the presence of the king in the neighboring town.

The spot was high and airy, and the view extensive, commanding the Isle of Portland in front, and reaching to St. Aldhelm's Head eastward, and almost to the Start on the west.

Phyllis, though not precisely a girl of the village, was as interested as any of them in this military investment. Her father's home stood somewhat apart, and on the highest point of ground to which the lane ascended, so that it was almost level with the top of the church-tower in the lower part of the parish. Immediately from the outside of the garden-wall the grass spread away to a great distance, and it was crossed by a path which came close to the wall. Ever since her childhood it had been Phyllis's pleasure to clamber up this fence and sit on the top—a feat not so difficult as it may seem, the walls in this district being built of rubble, without mortar, so that there were plenty of crevices for small toes.

She was sitting up here one day, listlessly surveying the pasture without, when her attention was arrested by a solitary figure walking along the path. It was one of the renowned German Hussars, and he moved onward with his eyes on the ground, and with the manner of one who wished to escape company. His head would probably have been bent like his eyes but for his stiff neck-gear. On nearer view she perceived that his face was marked with deep sadness. Without observing her, he advanced by the foot-path till it brought him almost immediately under the wall.

Phyllis was much surprised to see a fine, tall soldier in such a mood as this. Her theory of the military, and of the York Hussars in particular (derived entirely from hearsay, for she had never talked to a soldier in her life), was that their hearts were as gay as their accoutrements.

At this moment the Hussar lifted his eyes and noticed her on her perch, the white muslin neckerchief which covered her shoulders and neck where left bare by her low gown, and her white raiment in general, showing conspicuously in the bright sunlight of this summer day. He blushed a little at the suddenness of the encounter, and without halting a moment from his pace passed on.

All that day the foreigner's face haunted Phyllis; its aspect was so striking, so handsome, and his eyes were so blue and sad and abstracted. It was perhaps only natural that on some following day at the same hour she should look over that wall again, and wait till he had passed a second time. On this occasion he was reading a letter, and at the sight of her his manner was that of one who had half expected or hoped to discover her. He almost stopped, smiled, and made a courteous salute. The end of the meeting was that they exchanged a few words. She asked him what he was reading, and he readily informed her that he was reperusing letters from his mother in Germany; he did not get them often, he said, and was forced to read the old ones a great many times. This was all that passed at the present interview, but others of the same kind followed.

Phyllis used to say that his English, though not good, was quite intelligible to her, so that their acquaintance was never hindered by difficulties of speech. Whenever the subject became too delicate, subtle, or tender, for such words of English as were at his command, the eyes no doubt helped out the tongue, and—though this was later on—the lips helped out the eyes. In short, this acquaintance, unguardedly made, and rash enough on her part, developed and ripened. Like Desdemona, she pitied him, and learned his history,

His name was Matthäus Tina, and Saarbrück his native town, where his mother was still living. His age was twenty-two, and he had already risen to the grade of corporal, though he had not long been in the army. Phyllis used to assert that no such refined or well-educated young man could have been found in the ranks of the purely English regiments, some of these foreign soldiers having rather the graceful manner and presence of our native officers than of our rank and file.

She by degrees learned from her foreign friend a circumstance about himself and his comrades which Phyllis would least have expected of the York Hussars. So far from being as gay as its uniform, the regiment was pervaded by a dreadful melancholy, a chronic homesickness, which depressed many of the men to such an extent that they could hardly attend to their drill. The worst sufferers were the younger soldiers who had not been over here long. They hated England and English life; they took no interest whatever in King George and his island kingdom, and they only wished to be out of it and never to see it any more. Their bodies were here, but their hearts and minds were always far away in their dear fatherland, of which—brave men and stoical as they were in many ways—they would speak with tears in their eyes. One of the worst of the sufferers from this home-woe, as he called it in his own tongue, was Matthäus Tina, whose dreamy musing nature felt the gloom of exile still more intensely from the fact that he had left a lonely mother at home with nobody to cheer her.

Though Phyllis, touched by all this, and interested in his history, did not disdain her soldier acquaintance, she declined (according to her own account, at least) to permit the young man to overstep the line of mere friendship for a long while—as long, indeed, as she considered herself likely to become the possession of another; though it is probable that she had lost her heart to Matthäus before she was herself aware. The stone wall of necessity made anything like intimacy difficult; and he had never ventured to come, or to ask to come, inside the garden, so that all their conversation had been overtly conducted across this boundary.

III

But news reached the village from a friend of Phyllis's father concerning Mr. Humphrey Gould, her remarkably cool and patient betrothed. This gentleman had been heard to say in Bath that he considered his overtures to Miss Phyllis Grove to have reached only the stage of a half-understanding; and in view of his enforced absence on his father's account, who was too great an invalid now to attend to his affairs, he thought it best that there should be no definite promise as yet on either side. He was not sure, indeed, that he might not cast his eyes elsewhere.

This account—though only a piece of hearsay, and as such entitled to no absolute credit—tallied so well with the infrequency of his letters and their lack of warmth, that Phyllis did not doubt its truth for one moment; and from that hour she felt herself free to bestow her heart as she should choose. Not so her father; he declared the whole story to be a fabrication. He had known Mr. Gould's family from his boyhood; and if there was one proverb which expressed the matrimonial aspect of that family well, it was "Love me little, love me long." Humphrey was an honorable man, who would not think of treating his engagement so lightly. "Do you wait in patience," he said; "all will be right enough in time."

From these words Phyllis at first imagined that her father was in correspondence with Mr. Gould, and her heart sank within her; for in spite of her original intentions she had been relieved to hear that her engagement had come to nothing. But she presently learned that her father had heard no more of Humphrey Gould than she herself had done; while he would not write and address her affianced directly on the subject, lest it should be deemed an imputation on that bachelor's honor.

"You want an excuse for encouraging one or other of those foreign fellows to flatter you with his unmeaning attentions," her father exclaimed, his mood having of late been a very unkind one towards her. "I see more than I say. Don't you ever set foot outside that garden-fence without my permission. If you want to see the camp I'll take you myself some Sunday afternoon."

Phyllis had not the smallest intention of disobeying him as to her actions, but she assumed herself to be independent with respect to her feelings. She no longer checked her fancy for the Hussar, though she was far from regarding him as her lover in the serious sense in which an Englishman might have been regarded as such. The young foreign soldier was almost an ideal being to her, with none of the appurtenances of an ordinary house-dweller; one who had descended she knew not whence, and would disappear she knew not whither; the subject of a fascinating dream — no more.

They met continually now—mostly at dusk—during the brief interval between the going down of the sun and the minute at which the last trumpet-call summoned him to his tent. Perhaps her manner had become less restrained latterly; at any rate that of the Hussar was so; he had grown more tender every day, and at parting after these hurried interviews, she reached down her hand from the top of the wall that he might press it. One evening he held it so long that she exclaimed "The wall is white, and somebody in the field may see your shape against it!"

He lingered so long that night that it was with the greatest difficulty that he could run across the intervening stretch of ground and enter the camp in time. On the next occasion of his awaiting her she did not appear in her usual place at the usual hour. His disappointment was unspeakably keen; he remained staring blankly at the wall, like a man in a trance. The trumpets and tattoo sounded, and still he did not go.

She had been delayed purely by an accident. When she arrived she was anxious because of the lateness of the hour, having heard the sounds denoting the closing of the camp as well as he. She implored him to leave immediately.

"No," he said, gloomily. "I shall not go in yet—the moment you come—I have thought of your coming all day."

"But you may be disgraced at being after time?"

"I don't mind that. I should have disappeared from the world some time ago if it had not been for two persons—my beloved, here, and my mother in Saarbrück. I hate the army. I care more for a minute of your company than for all the promotion in the world."

Thus he stayed and talked to her, and told her interesting details of his native place, and incidents of his childhood, till she was in a simmer of distress at his recklessness in remaining. It was only because she insisted on bidding him good-night and leaving the wall that he returned to his quarters.

The next time that she saw him he was without the stripes that had adorned his sleeve. He had been broken to the level of private for his lateness that night; and as Phyllis considered herself to be the cause of his disgrace her sorrow was deep. But the position was now reversed; it was his turn to cheer her.

"Don't grieve, meine Liebliche!" he said. "I have got a remedy for whatever comes. First, even supposing I regain my stripes, would your father allow you to marry a non-commissioned officer in the York Hussars?"

She flushed. This practical step had not been in her mind in relation to such an unrealistic person as he was, and a moment's reflection was enough for it. "My father would not—certainly would not," she answered, unflinchingly. "It cannot be thought of! My dear friend, please do forget me; I fear I am ruining you and your prospects!"

"Not at all," said he. "You are giving this country of yours just sufficient interest to me to make me care to keep alive in it. If my dear land were here also, and my old parent with you, I could be happy as I am, and would do my best as a soldier. But it is not so. And now listen. This is my plan. That you go with me to my own country, and be my wife there, and live there with my mother and me. I am not a Hanoverian, as you know, though I entered the army as such; my country is by the Saar, and is at peace with France, and if I were once in it I should be free."

"But how get there?" she asked. Phyllis had been

rather amazed than shocked at his proposition. Her position in her father's house was growing irksome and painful in the extreme; his parental affection seemed to be quite dried up. She was not a native of the village, like all the joyous girls around her; and in some way Matthäus Tina had infected her with his own passionate longing for his country and mother and home.

"But how?" she repeated, finding that he did not answer. "Will you buy your discharge?"

"Ah, no," he said. "That's impossible, in these times. No; I came here against my will; why should I not escape? Now is the time, as we shall soon be leaving here, and I might see you no more. This is my scheme. I will ask you to meet me on the highway two miles off, on some calm night next week that may be appointed. There will be nothing unbecoming in it, or to cause you shame; you will not fly alone with me, for I will bring with me my devoted young friend Christoph, an Alsatian, who has lately joined the regiment, and who has agreed to assist in this enterprise. We shall have come from yonder harbor, where we shall have examined the boats, and found one suited to our purpose. Christoph has already a chart of the Channel, and we will then go to the harbor, and at midnight cut the boat from her moorings, and row away round the point out of sight; and by the next morning we are on the coast of France, near Cherbourg. The rest is easy, for I have saved money for the land journey, and can get a change of clothes. I will write to my mother, who will meet us on the way."

He added details in reply to her inquiries, which left no doubt in Phyllis's mind of the feasibility of the undertaking. But its magnitude almost appalled her; and it is questionable if she would ever have gone further in the wild adventure if, on entering the house that night, her father had not accosted her in the most significant terms.

"How about the York Hussars?" he said.

"They are still at the camp; but they are soon going away, I believe."

"It is useless for you to attempt to cloak your actions in that way. You have been meeting one of those fellows; you have been seen walking with him—foreign barbarians, not much better than the French themselves! I have made up my mind—don't speak a word till I have done, please—I have made up my mind that you shall stay here no longer while they are on the spot. You shall go to your aunt's."

It was useless for her to protest that she had never taken a walk with any soldier or man under the sun except himself. Her protestations were feeble, too, for though he was not literally correct in his assertion, he was virtually only half in error.

The house of her father's sister was a prison to Phyllis. She had quite recently undergone experience of its gloom; and when her father went on to direct her to pack what would be necessary for her to take, her heart died within her. In after-years she never attempted to excuse her conduct during this week of agitation; but the result of her self-communing was that she decided to join in the scheme of her lover and his friend, and fly to the country which he had colored with such lovely hues in her imagination. She always said that the one feature in his proposal which overcame her hesitation was the obvious purity and straightforwardness of his intentions. He showed himself to be so virtuous and kind, he treated her with a respect to which she had never before been accustomed, and she was braced to the obvious risks of the voyage by her confidence in him.

IV

It was on a soft, dark evening of the following week that they engaged in the adventure. Tina was to meet her at a point in the highway at which the lane to the village branched off. Christoph was to go ahead of them to the harbor where the boat lay, row it round the Nothe—or Lookout as it was called in those days—and pick them up on the other side of the promontory, which they were to reach by crossing the harbor bridge on foot, and climbing over the Lookout hill.

As soon as her father had ascended to his room she left the house, and, bundle in hand, proceeded at a trot along the lane. At such an hour not a soul was afoot anywhere in the village, and she reached the junction of the lane with the highway unobserved. Here she took up her position in the obscurity formed by the angle of a fence, whence she could discern every one who approached along the turnpike-road without being herself seen.

She had not remained thus waiting for her lover longer than a minute—though from the tension of her nerves the lapse of even that short time was trying—when, instead of the expected footsteps, the stage-coach could be heard descending the hill. She knew that Tina would not show himself till the road was clear, and waited impatiently for the coach to pass. Nearing the corner where she was it slackened speed, and, instead of going by as usual, drew up within a few yards of her. A passenger alighted, and she heard his voice. It was Humphrey Gould's.

He had brought a friend with him, and luggage. The luggage was deposited on the grass, and the coach went on its route to the royal watering-place.

"I wonder where that young man is with the horse and trap?" said her former admirer to his companion. "I hope we sha'n't have to wait here long. I told him ten o'clock precisely."

"Have you got her present safe?"

"Phyllis's? Oh yes. It is in this trunk. I hope it will please her."

"Of course it will. What woman would not be pleased with such a handsome peace-offering?"

"Well—she deserves it. I've treated her rather badly. But she has been in my mind these last two days much more than I should care to confess to everybody. Ah, well; I'll say no more about that. It cannot be that she is so bad as they make out. I am quite sure that a girl of her good wit would know better than to get entangled with any of those Hanoverian soldiers. I won't believe it of her, and there's an end on't."

More words in the same strain were casually dropped as the two men waited; words which revealed to her, as by a sudden illumination, the enormity of her conduct. The conversation was at length cut off by the arrival of the man with the vehicle. The luggage was placed in it, and they mounted and were driven on in the direction from which she had just come.

Phyllis was so conscience-stricken that she was at first inclined to follow them; but a moment's reflection led her to feel that it would only be bare justice to Matthäus to wait till he arrived, and explain candidly that she had changed her mind—difficult as the struggle would be when she stood face to face with him. She bitterly reproached herself for having believed reports which represented Humphrey Gould as false to his engagement, when, from what she now heard from his own lips, she gathered that he had been living full of trust in her. But she knew well enough who had won her love. Without him her life seemed a dreary prospect, yet the more she looked at his proposal the more she feared to accept it—so wild as it was, so vague, so venturesome. She had promised Humphrey Gould, and it was only his assumed faithlessness which had led her to treat that promise as naught. His solicitude in bringing her these gifts touched her; her promise must be kept, and esteem must take the place of love. She would preserve her self-respect. She would stay at home, and marry him, and suffer.

Phyllis had thus braced herself to an exceptional fortitude when, a few minutes later, the outline of Matthäus Tina appeared behind a field-gate, over which he lightly leaped as she stepped forward. There was no evading it, he pressed her to his breast.

"It is the first and last time!" she wildly thought, as she stood encircled by his arms.

How Phyllis got through the terrible ordeal of that night she could never clearly recollect. She always attributed her success in carrying out her resolve to her lover's honor, for as soon as she declared to him in feeble words that she had changed her mind, and felt that she could not, dared not, fly with him, he forbore to urge her, grieved as he was at her decision. Unscrupulous pressure on his part, seeing how romantically she had become attached to him, would no doubt have turned the balance in his favor. But he did nothing to tempt her unduly or unfairly.

On her side, fearing for his safety, she begged him to remain. This, he declared, could not be. "I cannot break faith with my friend," said he. Had he stood alone he would have abandoned his plan. But Christoph, with the boat and compass and chart, was waiting on the shore; the tide would soon turn; his mother had been warned of his coming; go he must.

Many precious minutes were lost while he tarried, unable to tear himself away. Phyllis held to her resolve, though it cost her many a bitter pang. At last they parted, and he went down the hill. Before his footsteps had quite died away, she felt a desire to behold at least his outline once more, and running noiselessly after him, regained view of his diminishing figure. For one moment she was sufficiently excited to be on the point of rushing forward and linking her fate with his. But she could not. The courage which at the critical instant failed Cleopatra of Egypt could scarcely be expected of Phyllis Grove.

A dark shape, similar to his own, joined him in the highway. It was Christoph, his friend. She could see no more; they had hastened on in the direction of the harbor four miles ahead. With a feeling akin to despair she turned and slowly pursued her way homeward.

Tattoo sounded in the camp; but there was no camp for her now. It was as dead as the camp of the Assyrians after the passage of the Destroying Angel.

She noiselessly entered the house, seeing nobody, and went to bed. Grief, which kept her awake at first, ultimately wrapped her in a heavy sleep. The next morning her father met her at the foot of the stairs.

"Mr. Gould is come!" he said, triumphantly.

Humphrey was staying at the inn, and had already called to inquire for her. He had brought her a present of a very handsome looking-glass in a frame of *repoussé* silverwork, which her father held in his hand. He had promised to call again in the course of an hour, to ask Phyllis to walk with him.

Pretty mirrors were rarer in country-houses at that day than they are now, and the one before her won Phyllis's admiration. She looked into it, saw how heavy her eyes were, and endeavored to brighten them. She was in that wretched state of mind which leads a woman to move mechanically onward in what she conceives to be her allotted path. Mr. Humphrey had, in his undemonstrative way, been adhering all along to the old understanding; it was for her to do the same, and to say not a word of her own lapse. She put on her bonnet and tippet, and when he arrived at the hour named she was at the door awaiting him.

V

Phyllis thanked him for his beautiful gift; but the talking was soon entirely on Humphrey's side as they walked along. He told her of the latest movements of the world of fashion—a subject which she willingly discussed to the exclusion of anything more personal—and his measured language helped to still her disquieted heart and brain. Had not her own sadness been what it was she must have observed his embarrassment. At last he abruptly changed the subject.

"I am glad you are pleased with my little present," he said. "The truth is that I brought it to propitiate 'ee, and to get you to help me out of a mighty difficulty."

It was inconceivable to Phyllis that this independent bachelor, whom she admired in some respects, could have a difficulty.

"Phyllis, I'll tell you my secret at once; for I have a monstrous secret to confide before I can ask your counsel. The case is, then, that I am married: yes, I have privately married a dear young belle; and if you knew her, and I hope you will, you would say everything in her praise. But she is not quite the one that my father would have chosen for me—you know the paternal idea as well as I—and I have kept it secret. There will be a terrible noise, no doubt; but I think that with your help I may get over it. If you would only do me this good turn—when I have told my father, I mean—say that you never could have married me, you know, or something of that sort; 'pon my life it will help to smooth the way mightily. I am so anxious to win him round to my point of view, and not to cause any estrangement."

What Phyllis replied she scarcely knew, or how she counselled him as to his unexpected situation. Yet the relief that his announcement brought her was perceptible. To have confided her trouble in return was what her aching heart longed to do; and had Humphrey been a woman she would instantly have poured out her tale. But to him she feared to confess; and there was a real reason for silence, till a sufficient time had elapsed to allow her lover and his comrade to get out of harm's way.

As soon as she reached home again she sought a solitary place, and spent the time in half regretting that she had not gone away, and in dreaming over the meetings with Matthäus Tina from their beginning to their end. In his own country, among his own countrywomen, he would possibly soon forget her, even to her very name.

Her listlessness was such that she did not go out of the house for several days. There came a morning which broke in fog and mist, behind which the dawn could be discerned in greenish gray, and the outlines of the tents, and the rows of horses at the ropes. The smoke from the canteen fires drooped heavily.

The spot at the bottom of the garden where she had been accustomed to climb the wall to meet Matthäus was the only inch of English ground in which she took any interest; and in spite of the disagreeable haze prevailing, she walked out there till she reached the well-known corner. Every blade of grass was weighted with little liquid globes, and slugs and snails had crept out upon the plots. She could hear the usual faint noises from the camp, and in the other direction the trot of farmers on the road to the town, for it was market-day. She observed that her frequent visits to this corner had quite trodden down the grass in the angle of the wall, and left marks of garden soil on the stepping-stones by which she had mounted to look over the top. Seldom having gone there till dusk, she had not considered that her traces might be visible by day. Perhaps it was these which had revealed her trysts to her father.

While she paused in melancholy regard, she fancied that the customary sounds from the tents were changing their character. Indifferent as Phyllis was to camp doings now, she mounted by the steps to the old place. What she beheld at first awed and perplexed her; then she stood rigid, her fingers hooked to the wall, her eyes staring out of her head, and her face as if hardened to stone.

On the open green stretching before her all the regiments in the camp were drawn up in line, in the mid-front of which two empty coffins lay on the ground. The unwonted sounds which she had noticed came from an advancing procession. It consisted of the band of the York Hussars playing a dead march; next two soldiers of that regiment in a mourning-coach, guarded on each side, and accompanied by two priests. Behind came a crowd of rustics who had been attracted by the event. The melancholy procession marched along the front of the line, returned to the centre, and halted beside the coffins, where the two condemned men were blindfolded, and each placed kneeling on his coffin ; a few minutes' pause was now given, while they prayed.

A firing party of twenty-four men stood ready with levelled carbines. The commanding officer, who had his sword drawn, waved it through some cuts of the sword-exercise till he reached the downward stroke, whereat the firing party discharged their volley. The two victims fell, one upon his face across his coffin, the other backward.

As the volley resounded there arose a shriek from the wall of Dr. Grove's garden, and some one fell down inside ; but nobody among the spectators without noticed it at the time. The two executed hussars were Matthäus Tina and his friend Christoph. The soldiers on guard placed the bodies in the coffins almost instantly ; but the colonel of the regiment, an Englishman, rode up and exclaimed, in a stern voice, "Turn them out—as an example to the men !"

The coffins were lifted endwise, and the dead Germans flung out upon their faces on the grass. Then all the regiments wheeled in sections and marched past the spot in slow time. When the survey was over the corpses were again coffined and borne away.

Meanwhile Dr. Grove, attracted by the noise of the volley, had rushed out into his garden, where he saw his wretched daughter lying motionless against the wall. She was taken in-doors, but it was long before she recovered consciousness, and for weeks they despaired of her reason.

It transpired that the luckless deserters from the York Hussars had cut the boat from her moorings in the adjacent harbor, according to their plan, and, with two other comrades, who were smarting under ill-treatment from their colonel, had sailed in safety across the Channel ; but mistaking their bearings, they steered into Jersey, thinking that island the

French coast. Here they were perceived to be deserters, and delivered up to the authorities. Matthäus and Christoph interceded for the other two at the court-martial, saying that it was entirely by the former's representations that these were induced to go. Their sentence was accordingly commuted to flogging, the death punishment being reserved for their leaders.

The visitor to the old Georgian watering-place who may care to ramble to the neighboring village under the hills and examine the register of burials, will there find two entries in these words:

"*Matth: Tina (Corpl.) in His Majesty's Regmt. of York Hussars, and Shot for Desertion, was Buried June 30th, 1801, aged 22 years. Born in the town of Sarsbruk, Germany.*

"*Christoph Bless, belonging to His Majesty's Regmt. of York Hussars, who was Shot for Desertion, was Buried June 30th, 1801, aged 22 years. Born at Lothaargen, Alsatia.*"

Their graves were dug at the back of the little church, near the wall. There is no memorial to mark the spot, but Phyllis pointed it out to me. While she lived she used to keep their mounds neat; but now they are overgrown with nettles, and sunk nearly flat. The older villagers, however, who know of the episode from their parents, still recollect the place where the soldiers lie. Phyllis lies near.

October, 1889.

THE FIDDLER OF THE REELS

"TALKING of Exhibitions, World's Fairs, and what not," said the old gentleman, "I would not go round the corner to see a dozen of them nowadays. The only exhibition that ever made, or ever will make, any impression upon my imagination was the first of the series, the parent of them all, and now a thing of old times—the Great Exhibition of 1851, in Hyde Park, London. None of the younger generation can realize the sense of novelty it produced in us who were then in our prime. A noun substantive went so far as to become an adjective in honor of the occasion. It was 'exhibition' hat, 'exhibition' razor-strop, 'exhibition' watch; nay, even 'exhibition' weather, 'exhibition' spirits, sweethearts, babies, wives—for the time.

"For South Wessex, the year formed in many ways an extraordinary chronological frontier or transit-line, at which there occurred what one might call a precipice in Time. As in a geological 'fault,' we had presented to us a sudden bringing of ancient and modern into absolute contact, such as probably in no other single year since the Conquest was ever witnessed in this part of the country."

These observations led us onward to talk of the different personages, gentle and simple, who lived and moved within our narrow and peaceful horizon at that time; and of three people in particular, whose queer little history was oddly touched at points by the Exhibition, more concerned with it than that of anybody else who dwelt in those outlying shades of the world, Stickleford, Mellstock, and Egdon. First in prominence among these three came Wat Ollamoor—if that were his real name.

He was a woman's man—supremely so—and externally very little else. To men he was not attractive; perhaps a little repulsive at times. Musician, dandy, and company-man in practice; veterinary surgeon in theory, he lodged awhile in Mellstock village, coming from nobody knew where; though some said his first appearance in this neighborhood had been as fiddle-player in a show at Greenhill Fair.

Many a worthy villager envied him his power over unsophisticated maidenhood—a power which seemed sometimes to have a touch of the weird and wizardly in it. Personally he was not ill-favored, though rather un-English, his complexion being a rich olive, his rank hair dark and rather clammy—made still clammier by secret ointments, which, when he came fresh to a party, caused him to smell like "boys'-love" (southernwood) steeped in lamp-oil. On occasion he wore curls—a double row—running almost horizontally around his head. But as these were sometimes noticeably absent, it was concluded that they were not altogether of Nature's making. By girls whose love for him had turned to hatred he had been nicknamed "Mop," from this abundance of hair, which was long enough to rest upon his shoulders; as time passed, the name more and more prevailed.

His fiddling, possibly, had the most to do with the fascination he exercised, for, to speak fairly, it could claim for itself a most peculiar and personal quality, like that in a moving preacher. There were tones in it which bred the immediate conviction that indolence and averseness to systematic application were all that lay between "Mop" and the career of a second Paganini.

While playing he invariably closed his eyes; using no notes, and, as it were, allowing the violin to wander on at will into the most plaintive passages ever heard by rustic man. There was a certain lingual character in the supplicatory expressions he produced, which would wellnigh have drawn an ache from the heart of a gate-post. He could make any child in the parish, who was at all sensitive to music, burst into tears in a few minutes by simply fiddling one of the old dance-tunes he almost entirely affected—country jigs, reels, and "Favorite Quick-Steps" of the last century—some mutilated remains of which even now reappear as nameless phantoms in new quadrilles and gallops, where they are recognized only by the curious, or by such old-fashioned and far-between people as have been thrown with men like Wat Ollamoor in their early life.

His date was a little later than that of the old Mellstock choir-band, which comprised the Dewys, Mail, and the rest—in fact, he did not rise above the horizon thereabout till those well-known musicians were disbanded as ecclesiastical functionaries. In their honest love of thoroughness they despised the new man's style. Theophilus Dewy (Reuben the tranter's younger brother) used to say there was no "plumness" in it—no bowing, no solidity—it was all fantastical. And probably this was true. Anyhow, Mop had, very obviously, never bowed a note of church-music from his birth; he never once sat in the gallery of Mellstock church, where the others had tuned their venerable psalmody so many hundreds of times; had never, in all likelihood, entered a church at all. All were devil's tunes in his repertory. "He could no more play the 'Wold Hundredth' to his true time than he could play the brazen serpent," the tranter would say. (The brazen serpent was supposed in Mellstock to be a musical instrument particularly hard to blow.)

Occasionally Mop could produce the aforesaid moving effect upon the souls of grown-up persons, especially young women of fragile and responsive organization. Such a one was Car'line Aspent. Though she was already engaged to be married before she met him, Car'line, of them all, was the most influenced by Mop Ollamoor's heart-stealing melodies, to her discomfort, nay, positive pain and ultimate injury. She was a pretty, invocating, weak-mouthed girl, whose chief defect as a companion with her sex was a tendency to peevishness now and then. At this time she was not a resident in Mellstock parish, where Mop lodged, but lived some miles off at Stickleford, farther down the river.

How and where she first made acquaintance with him and his fiddling is not truly known, but the story was that it either began or was developed on one spring evening, when, in passing through Lower Mellstock, she chanced to pause on the bridge near his house to rest herself, and languidly leaned over the parapet. Mop was standing on his door-step, as was his custom, spinning the insidious thread of semi- and demi-semi-quavers from the E string of his fiddle for the benefit of passers-by, and laughing as the tears rolled down the cheeks of the little children hanging around him. Car'line pretended to be engrossed with the rippling of the stream under the arches, but in reality she was listening, as he knew. Presently the aching of the heart seized her simultaneously with a wild desire to glide airily in the mazes of an infinite dance. To shake off the fascination she resolved to go on, although it would be necessary to pass him as he played. On stealthily glancing ahead at the performer, she found to her relief that his eyes were closed in abandonment to instrumentation, and she strode on boldly. But when closer her step grew timid, her tread convulsed itself more and more accordantly with the time of the melody, till she very nearly danced along. Gaining another glance at him when immediately opposite, she saw that *one* of his eyes was open, quizzing her as he smiled at her emotional state. Her gait could not divest itself of its compelled capers till she had gone a long way past the house; and Car'line was unable to shake off the strange infatuation for hours.

After that day, whenever there was to be in the neighborhood a dance to which she could get an invitation, and where Mop Ollamoor was to be the musician, Car'line contrived to be present, though it sometimes involved a walk of several miles; for he did not play so often in Stickleford as elsewhere.

The next evidences of his influence over her were singular enough, and it would require a neurologist to fully explain them. She would be sitting quietly, any evening after dark, in the house of her father, the parish-clerk, which stood in the middle of Stickleford village street, this being the high-road between Lower Mellstock and Moreford, six miles eastward. Here, without a moment's warning, and in the midst of a general conversation between her father, sister, and the young man before alluded to, who devotedly wooed her in ignorance of her infatuation, she would start from her seat in the chimney-corner as if she had received a galvanic shock, and spring convulsively towards the ceiling; then she would burst into tears, and it was not till some half-hour had passed that she grew calm as usual. Her father, knowing her hysterical tendencies, was always excessively anxious about this trait in his youngest girl, and feared the attack to be a species of epileptic fit. Not so her sister Julia. Julia had found out what was the cause. At the moment before the jumping, only an exceptionally sensitive ear situated in the chimney-nook could have caught from down the flue the beat of a man's footstep along the highway without. But it was in that foot-fall, for which she had been waiting, that the origin of Car'line's involuntary springing lay. The pedestrian was Mop Ollamoor, as the girl well knew; but his business that way was not to visit her; he sought another woman, whom he spoke of as his Intended, and who lived at Moreford, two miles farther on. On one, and only one, occasion did it happen that Car'line could not control her utterance; it was when her sister alone chanced to be present. "Oh—oh—oh—!" she cried. "He's going to *her*, and not coming to *me!*"

To do the fiddler justice, he had not at first thought greatly of, or spoken much to, this girl of impressionable mould. But he had soon found out her secret, and could not resist a little by-play with her too easily hurt heart, as an interlude between his more serious performances at Moreford. The two became well acquainted, though only by stealth, hardly a soul in Stickleford except her sister, and her lover Ned Hipcroft, being aware of the attachment. Her father disapproved of her coldness to Ned; her sister, too, hoped she might get over this nervous passion for a man of whom so little was known. The ultimate result was that Car'line's manly and simple wooer Edward found his suit becoming practically hopeless. He was a respectable mechanic, in a far sounder position than Mop the nominal horse-doctor; but when, before leaving her, Ned put his flat and final question, would she marry him, then and there, now or never, it was with little expectation of obtaining more than the negative she gave him. Though her father supported him and her sister supported him, he could not play the fiddle so as to draw your soul out of your body like a spider's thread, as Mop did, till you felt as limp as withy-wind and yearned for something to cling to. Indeed, Hipcroft had not the slightest ear for music; could not sing two notes in tune, much less play them.

The No he had expected and got from her, in spite of a preliminary encouragement, gave Ned a new start in life. It had been uttered in such a tone of sad entreaty that he resolved to persecute her no more; she should not even be distressed by a sight of his form in the distant perspective of the street and lane. He left the place, and his natural course was to London.

The railway to South Wessex was in process of construction, but it was not as yet opened for traffic; and Hipcroft reached the capital by a six days' trudge on foot, as many a better man had done before him. He was one of the last of the artisan class who used that now extinct method of travel to the great centres of labor, so customary then from time immemorial.

In London he lived and worked regularly at his trade. More fortunate than many, his disinterested willingness recommended him from the first. During the ensuing four years he was never out of employment. He neither advanced nor receded in the modern sense; he improved as a workman, but he did not shift one jot in social position. About his love for Car'line he maintained a rigid silence. No doubt he often thought of her; but being always occupied, and having no relations at Stickleford, he held no communication with that part of the country, and showed no desire to return. In his quiet lodging in Lambeth he moved about after working-hours with the facility of a woman, doing his own cooking, attending to his stocking-heels, and shaping himself by degrees to a life-long bachelorhood. For this conduct one is bound to advance the canonical reason that time could not efface from his heart the image of little Car'line Aspent—and it may be in part true; but there was also the inference that his was a nature not greatly dependent upon the ministrations of the other sex for its comforts.

The fourth year of his residence as a mechanic in London was the year of the Hyde-Park Exhibition already mentioned, and at the construction of this huge glass-house, then unexampled in the world's history, he worked daily. It was an era of great hope and activity among the nations and industries. Though Hipcroft was, in his small way, a central man in the movement, he plodded on with his usual outward placidity. Yet for him, too, the year was destined to have its surprises, for when the bustle of getting the building ready for the opening day was past, the ceremonies had been witnessed, and people were flocking thither from all parts of the globe, he received a letter from Car'line. Till that day the silence of four years between himself and Stickleford had never been broken.

She informed her old lover, in an uncertain penmanship which suggested a trembling hand, of the trouble she had been put to in ascertaining his address, and then broached the subject which had prompted her to write. Four years ago, she said, with the greatest delicacy of which she was capable, she had been so foolish as to refuse him. Her wilful wrongheadedness had since been a grief to her many times, and of late particularly. As for Mr. Ollamoor, he had been absent almost as long as Ned—she did not know where. She would gladly marry Ned now if he were to ask her again, and be a tender little wife to him till her life's end.

A tide of warm feeling must have surged through Ned Hipcroft's frame on receipt of this news, if we may judge by the issue. Unquestionably he loved her still, even if not to the exclusion of every other happiness. This from his Car'line, she who had been dead to him these many years, alive to him again as of old, was in itself a pleasant, gratifying thing. Ned had grown so resigned to, or satisfied with, his lonely lot, that he probably would not have shown much jubilation at anything. Still, a certain ardor of preoccupation, after his first surprise, revealed how deeply her confession of faith in him had stirred him. Measured and methodical in his ways, he did not answer the letter that day, nor the next, nor the next. He was having "a good think." When he did answer it, there was a great deal of sound reasoning mixed in with the unmistakable tenderness of his reply; but the tenderness itself was sufficient to reveal that he was pleased with her straightforward frankness; that the anchorage she had once obtained in his heart was renewable, if it had not been continuously firm.

He told her—and as he wrote his lips twitched humorously over the few gentle words of raillery he indited among the rest of his sentences—that it was all very well for her to come round at this time of day. Why wouldn't she have him when he wanted her? She had no doubt learned that he was not married, but suppose his affections had since been fixed on another? She ought to beg his pardon. Still, he was not the man to forget her. But, considering how he had been used, and what he had suffered, she could not quite expect him to go down to Stickleford and fetch her. But if she would come to him, and say she was sorry, as was only fair; why, yes, he would marry her, knowing what a good little woman she was to the core. He added that the request for her to come to him was a less one to make than it would have been when he first left Stickleford, or even a few months ago; for the new railway into South Wessex was now open, and there had just begun to be run wonderfully contrived special trains, called excursion-trains, on account of the Great Exhibition; so that she could come up easily alone.

She said in her reply how good it was of him to treat her so generously, after her hot-and-cold treatment of him; that though she felt frightened at the magnitude of the journey, and was never as yet in a railway-train, having only seen one pass at a distance, she embraced his offer with all her heart; and would, indeed, own to him how sorry she was, and beg his pardon, and try to be a good wife always, and make up for lost time.

The remaining details of when and where were soon settled, Car'line informing him, for her ready identification in the crowd, that she would be wearing "my new sprigged-laylock cotton gown," and Ned gayly responding that, having married her the morning after her arrival, he would make a day of it by taking her to the Exhibition. One early summer afternoon, accordingly, he came from his place of work, and hastened towards Waterloo Station to meet her. It was as wet and chilly as an English June day can occasionally be, but as he waited on the platform in the drizzle he glowed inwardly, and seemed to have something to live for again.

The "excursion-train"—an absolutely new departure in the history of travel — was still a novelty on the Wessex line, and probably everywhere. Crowds of people had flocked to all the stations on the way up to witness the unwonted sight of so long a train's passage, even where they did not take advantage of the opportunity it offered. The seats for the humbler class of travellers in these early experiments in steam-locomotion were open trucks, without any protection whatever from the wind and rain; and damp weather having set in with the afternoon, the unfortunate occupants of these vehicles were, on the train drawing up at the London terminus, found to be in a pitiable condition from their long journey; blue-faced, stiff-necked, sneezing, rain-beaten, chilled to the marrow, many of the men being hatless; in fact, they resembled people who had been out all night in an open boat on a rough sea, rather than inland excursionists for pleasure. The women had in some degree protected themselves by turning up the skirts of their gowns over their heads, but as by this arrangement they were additionally exposed about the hips, they were all more or less in a sorry plight.

In the bustle and crush of alighting forms of both sexes which followed the entry of the huge concatenation into the station, Ned Hipcroft soon discerned the slim little figure his eye was in search of in the sprigged lilac, as described. She came up to him with a frightened smile—still pretty, though so damp, weather-beaten, and shivering from long exposure to the wind.

"Oh, Ned!" she sputtered, "I—I—" He clasped her in his arms and kissed her, whereupon she burst into a flood of tears.

"You are wet, my poor dear! I hope you'll not get cold," he said. And surveying her and her multifarious surrounding packages, he noticed that by the hand she led a toddling child—a little girl of three or so—

whose hood was as clammy and tender face as blue as those of the other travellers.

"Who is this—somebody you know?" asked Ned, curiously.

"Yes, Ned. She's mine."

"Yours?"

"Yes—my own!"

"Your own child?"

"Yes!"

"Well—as God's in—"

"Ned, I didn't name it in my letter, because, you see, it would have been so hard to explain. I thought that when we met I could tell you how she happened to be born, so much better than in writing. I hope you'll excuse it this once, dear Ned, and not scold me, now I've come so many, many miles!"

"This means Mr. Mop Ollamoor, I reckon!" said Hipcroft, gazing palely at them from the distance of the yard or two to which he had withdrawn with a start.

Car'line gasped. "But he's been gone away for years!" she supplicated. "And I never had a young man before! And I was so onlucky to be catched the first time, though some of the girls down there go on like anything!"

Ned remained in silence, pondering.

"You'll forgive me, dear Ned?" she added, beginning to sob outright. "I haven't taken 'ee in after all, because you can pack us back again, if you want to; though 'tis hundreds o' miles, and so wet, and night a-coming on, and I with no money!"

"What the devil can I do?" Hipcroft groaned.

A more pitiable picture than the pair of helpless creatures presented was never seen on a rainy day, as they stood on the great, gaunt, puddled platform, a whiff of drizzle blowing under the roof upon them now and then; the pretty attire in which they had started from Stickleford in the early morning bemuddled and sodden, weariness on their faces, and fear of him in their eyes; for the child began to look as if she thought she too had done some wrong, remaining in an appalled silence till the tears rolled down her chubby cheeks.

"What's the matter, my little maid?" said Ned, mechanically.

"I do want to go home!" she let out, in tones that told of a bursting heart. "And my totties be cold, an' I sha'n't have no bread-an'-butter no more!"

"I don't know what to say to it all!" declared Ned, his own eye moist as he turned and walked a few steps with his head down; then regarded them again point-blank. From the child escaped troubled breaths and silently welling tears.

"Want some bread-and-butter, do 'ee?" he said, with factitious hardness.

"Ye-e-s!"

"Well, I dare say I can get 'ee a bit. Naturally, you must want some. And you, too, for that matter, Car'line."

"I do feel a little hungered. But I can keep it off," she murmured.

"Folk shouldn't do that," he said, gruffly. . . . "There, come along!" He caught up the child as he added, "You must bide here to-night, anyhow, I s'pose! What can you do otherwise? I'll get 'ee some tea and victuals; and as for this job, I'm sure I don't know what to say. This is the way out."

They pursued their way, without speaking, to Ned's lodgings, which were not far off. There he dried them and made them comfortable, and prepared tea; they thankfully sat down. The ready-made household of which he suddenly found himself the head imparted a cosey aspect to his room, and a paternal one to himself. Presently he turned to the child and kissed her now blooming cheeks; and, looking wistfully at Car'line, kissed her also.

"I don't see how I can send 'ee back all them miles," he growled, "now you've come all the way o' purpose to join me. But you must trust me, Car'line, and show you've real faith in me. Well, do you feel better now, my little woman?"

The child nodded, her mouth being otherwise occupied.

"I did trust you, Ned, in coming; and I shall always!"

Thus, without any definite agreement to forgive her, he tacitly acquiesced in the fate that Heaven had sent him; and on the day of their marriage (which was not quite so soon as he had expected it could be, on account of the time necessary for banns) he took her to the Exhibition when they came back from church, as he had promised. While standing near a large mirror in one of the courts devoted to furniture, Car'line started, for in the glass appeared the reflection of a form exactly resembling Mop Ollamoor's—so exactly that it seemed impossible to believe anybody but that artist in person to be the original. On passing round the objects which hemmed in Ned, her, and the child from a direct view, no Mop was to be seen. Whether he were really in London or not at that time was never known; and Car'line always stoutly denied that her readiness to go and meet Ned in town arose from any rumor that Mop had also gone thither; which denial there was no reasonable ground for doubting.

And then the year glided away, and the Exhibition folded itself up and became a thing of the past. The park trees that had been enclosed for six months were again exposed to the winds and storms, and the sod grew green anew. Ned found that Car'line resolved herself into a very good wife and companion, though she had made herself what is called cheap to him; but in that she was like another domestic article, a cheap teapot, which often brews better tea than a dear one. One autumn Hipcroft found himself with but little work to do, and a prospect of less for the winter. Both being country born and bred, they fancied they would like to live again in their natural atmosphere. It was accordingly decided between them that they should leave the pent-up London lodging, and that Ned should seek out employment near his native place, his wife and her daughter staying with Car'line's father during the search for occupation and an abode of their own.

Tinglings of pleasure pervaded Car'line's spasmodic little frame as she journeyed down with Ned to the place she had left two or three years before in silence and under a cloud. To return to where she had once been despised, a smiling London wife with a distinct London accent, was a triumph which the world did not witness every day.

The train did not stop at the petty road-side station that lay nearest to Stickleford, and the trio went on to Casterbridge. Ned thought it a good opportunity to make a few preliminary inquiries for employment at workshops in the borough where he had been known; and feeling cold from her journey, and it being dry underfoot and only dusk as yet, with a moon on the point of rising, Car'line and her little girl walked on towards Stickleford, leaving Ned to follow at a quicker pace, and pick her up at a certain half-way house, widely known as an inn.

The woman and child pursued the well-remembered way comfortably enough, though they were both becoming wearied. In the course of three miles they had passed Heedless William's Pond, the familiar landmark by Bloom's End, and were drawing near the Quiet Woman Inn, a lone road-side hostel on the lower verge of the Egdon Heath, since and for many years abolished. In stepping up towards it Car'line heard more voices within than had formerly been customary at such an hour, and she learned that an auction of fat stock had been held near the spot that afternoon. The child would be the better for a rest as well as herself, she thought, and she entered.

The guests and customers overflowed into the passage, and Car'line had no sooner crossed the threshold than a man whom she remembered by sight came forward with a glass and mug in his hands towards a friend leaning against the wall; but, seeing her, very gallantly offered her a drink of the liquor, which was gin-and-beer hot, pouring her out a tumblerful and saying, in a moment or two: "Surely, 'tis little Car'-line Aspent that was—down at Stickleford?"

She assented, and, though she did not exactly want this beverage, she drank it since it was offered, and her entertainer begged her to come in farther and sit down. Once within the room she found that all the persons present were seated close against the walls, and there being a chair vacant she did the same. An explanation of their position occurred the next moment. In the opposite corner stood Mop, rosining his bow and looking just the same as ever. The company had cleared the middle of the room for dancing, and they were about to dance again. As she wore a veil to keep off the wind she did not think he had recognized her, or could possibly guess the identity of the child; and to her satisfied surprise she found that she could confront him quite calmly—mistress of herself in the dignity her London life had given her. Before she had quite emptied her glass the dance was called, the dancers formed in two lines, the music sounded, and the figure began.

Then matters changed for Car'line. A tremor quickened itself to life in her, and her hand so shook that she could hardly set down her glass. It was not the dance nor the dancers, but the notes of that old violin which thrilled the London wife, these having still all the witchery that she had so well known of yore, and under which she had used to lose her power of independent will. How it all came back! There was the fiddling figure against the wall; the large, oily, mop-like head of him, and beneath the mop the face with closed eyes.

After the first moments of paralyzed reverie the familiar tune in the familiar rendering made her laugh and shed tears simultaneously. Then a man at the bottom of the dance, whose partner had dropped away, stretched out his hand and beckoned to her to take the place. She did not want to dance; she entreated by signs to be left where she was, but she was entreating of the tune and its player rather than of the dancing man. The saltatory tendency which the fiddler and his cunning instrument had ever been able to start in her was seizing Car'line just as it had done in earlier years, possibly assisted by the gin-and-beer hot. Tired as she was she grasped her little girl by the hand, and, plunging in at the bottom of the figure, whirled about with the rest. She found that her companions were mostly people of the neighboring hamlets and farms —Bloom's End, Mellstock, Lewgate, and elsewhere; and by degrees she was recognized as she convulsively danced on, wishing that Mop would cease and let her heart rest from the aching he caused, and her feet also.

After long and many minutes the dance ended, when

she was urged to fortify herself with more gin-and-beer; which she did, feeling very weak and overpowered with hysteric emotion. She refrained from unveiling, to keep Mop in ignorance of her presence, if possible. Several of the guests having left, Car'line hastily wiped her lips and also turned to go; but, according to the account of some who remained, at that very moment a five-handed reel was proposed, in which two or three begged her to join.

She declined on the plea of being tired and having to walk to Stickleford, when Mop began aggressively tweedling "My Fancy Lad," in D major, as the air to which the reel was to be footed. He must have recognized her, though she did not know it, for it was the strain of all seductive strains which she was least able to resist—the one he had played when she was leaning over the bridge at the date of their first acquaintance. Car'line stepped despairingly into the middle of the room with the other four.

Reels were resorted to hereabouts at this time by the more robust spirits for the reduction of superfluous energy which the ordinary figure-dances were not powerful enough to exhaust. As everybody knows, or does not know, the five reelers stood in the form of a cross, the reel being performed by each line of three alternately, the persons who successively came to the middle place dancing in both directions. Car'line soon found herself in this place, the axis of the whole performance, and could not get out of it, the tune turning into the first part without giving her opportunity. And now she began to suspect that Mop did know her, and was doing this on purpose, though whenever she stole a glance at him his closed eyes betokened obliviousness to everything outside his own brain. She continued to wend her way through the figure of eight that was formed by her course, the fiddler introducing into his notes the wild and agonizing sweetness of a living voice in one too highly wrought; its pathos running high and running low in endless variation, projecting through her nerves excruciating spasms—a sort of blissful torture. The room swam, the tune was endless; and in about a quarter of an hour the only other woman in the figure dropped out exhausted, and sank panting on a bench.

The reel instantly resolved itself into a four-handed one. Car'line would have given anything to leave off; but she had, or fancied she had, no power, while Mop played such tunes; and thus another ten minutes slipped by, a haze of dust now clouding the candles, the floor being of stone, sanded. Then another dancer fell out—one of the men—and went into the passage, in a frantic search for liquor. To turn the figure into a three-handed reel was the work of a second, Mop modulating at the same time into "The Fairy Dance," as better suited to the contracted movement, and no less one of those foods of love which, as manufactured by his bow, had always intoxicated her.

In a reel for three there was no rest whatever, and four or five minutes were enough to make her remaining two partners, now thoroughly blown, stamp their last bar, and, like their predecessors, limp off into the next room to get something to drink. Car'line, half-stifled inside her veil, was left dancing alone, the apartment now being empty of everybody save herself, Mop, and their little girl.

She flung up the veil, and cast her eyes upon him, as if imploring him to withdraw himself and his acoustic magnetism from the atmosphere. Mop opened one of his own orbs, as though for the first time, fixed it peeringly upon her, and smiling dreamily, threw into his strains the reserve of expression which he could not afford to waste on a big and noisy dance.

Crowds of little chromatic subtleties, capable of drawing tears from a statue, proceeded straightway from the ancient fiddle, as if it were dying of the emotion which had been pent up within it ever since its banishment from some Italian city where it first took shape and sound. There was that in the look of Mop's one dark eye which said: "You cannot leave off, dear, whether you would or no," and it bred in her a paroxysm of desperation that defied him to tire her down.

She thus continued to dance alone, defiantly as she thought, but in truth slavishly and abjectly, subject to every wave of the melody, and probed by the gimlet-like gaze of her fascinator's open eye; keeping up at the same time a feeble smile in his face, as a feint to signify it was still her own pleasure which led her on. A terrified embarrassment as to what she could say to him if she were to leave off, had its unrecognized share in keeping her going. The child, who was beginning to be distressed by the strange situation, came up and said: "Stop, mother, stop, and let's go home!" as she seized Car'line's hand.

Suddenly Car'line sank staggering to the floor; and rolling over on her face, prone she remained. Mop's fiddle thereupon emitted an elfin shriek of finality; stepping quickly down from the nine-gallon beer-cask which had formed his rostrum, he went to the little girl, who disconsolately bent over her mother.

The guests who had gone into the backroom for liquor and change of air, hearing something unusual, trooped back hitherward, where they endeavored to revive poor, weak Car'line by blowing her with the bellows and opening the window. Ned, her husband, who had been detained in Casterbridge, as aforesaid, came along the road at this juncture, and hearing excited voices through the open window, and, to his great surprise, the mention of his wife's name, he entered amid the rest upon the scene. Car'line was now in convulsions, weeping violently, and for a long time nothing could be done with her. While he was sending for a cart to take her onward to Stickleford, Hipcroft anxiously inquired how it had all happened; and then the assembly explained that a fiddler formerly known in the locality had lately revisited his old haunts, and had taken upon himself without invitation to play that evening at the inn.

Ned demanded the fiddler's name, and they said Ollamoor.

"Ah!" exclaimed Ned, looking round him. "Where is he, and where—where's my little girl?"

Ollamoor had disappeared, and so had the child. Hipcroft was in ordinary a quiet and tractable fellow, but a determination which was to be feared settled in his face now. "Blast him!" he cried. "I'll beat his skull in for'n, if I swing for it to-morrow!"

He had rushed to the poker which lay on the hearth, and hastened down the passage, the people following. Outside the house, on the other side of the highway, a mass of dark heath-land rose sullenly upward to its not easily accessible interior, a ravined plateau, whereon jutted into the sky, at the distance of a couple of miles, the fir-woods of Mistover backed by the Yalbury coppices—a place of Dantesque gloom at this hour, which would have afforded secure hiding for a battery of artillery, much less a man and a child.

Some other men plunged thitherward with him, and more went along the road. They were gone about twenty minutes altogether, returning without result to the inn. Ned sat down in the settle, and clasped his forehead with his hands.

"Well—what a fool the man is, and hev been all these years, if he thinks the child his, as a' do seem to!" they whispered. "And everybody else knowing otherwise!"

"No, I don't think 'tis mine!" cried Ned, hoarsely, as he looked up from his hands. "But she is mine, all the same! Ha'n't I nussed her? Ha'n't I fed her and teached her? Ha'n't I played wi' her? Oh, little Carry—gone with that rogue—gone!"

"You ha'n't lost your mis'ess, anyhow," they said to console him. "She's throwed up the sperrits, and she is feeling better, and she's more to 'ee than a child that isn't yours."

"She isn't! She's not so particular much to me, especially now she's lost the little maid! But Carry's everything!"

"Well, ver' like you'll find her to-morrow."

"Ah—but shall I? Yet he *can't* hurt her—surely he can't! Well—how's Car'line now? I am ready. Is the cart here?"

She was lifted into the vehicle, and they sadly lumbered on towards Stickleford. Next day she was calmer; but the fits were still upon her; and her will seemed shattered. For the child she appeared to show singularly little anxiety, though Ned was nearly distracted. It was nevertheless quite expected that the impish Mop would restore the lost one after a freak of a day or two; but time went on, and neither he nor she could be heard of, and Hipcroft murmured that perhaps he was exercising upon her some unholy musical charm, as he had done upon Car'line herself. Weeks passed, and still they could obtain no clew either to the fiddler's whereabouts or the girl's; and how he could have induced her to go with him remained a mystery.

Then Ned, who had obtained only temporary employment in the neighborhood, took a sudden hatred towards his native district, and a rumor reaching his ears through the police that a somewhat similar man and child had been seen at a fair near London, he playing a violin, she dancing on stilts, a new interest in the capital took possession of Hipcroft with an intensity which would scarcely allow him time to pack before returning thither. He did not, however, find the lost one, though he made it the entire business of his over-hours to stand about in by-streets in the hope of discovering her, and would start up in the night, saying, "That rascal's torturing her to maintain him!" To which his wife would answer, peevishly, "Don't 'ee raft yourself so, Ned! You prevent my getting a bit o' rest! He won't hurt her!" and fall asleep again.

That Carry and her father had emigrated to America was the general opinion; Mop, no doubt, finding the girl a highly desirable companion when he had trained her to keep him by her earnings as a dancer. There, for that matter, they may be performing in some capacity now, though he must be an old scamp verging on threescore-and-ten, and she a woman of four-and-forty.

May, 1893.

A TRADITION OF 1804

THE widely discussed possibility of an invasion of England through a Channel tunnel has more than once recalled old Solomon Selby's story to my mind.

The occasion on which I numbered myself among his audience was one evening when he was sitting in the yawning chimney-corner of the inn-kitchen, with some others who had gathered there, awaiting the cessation of the rain. Withdrawing the stem of his pipe from the dental notch in which it habitually rested, he leaned back in the recess behind him and smiled into the fire. The smile was neither mirthful nor sad, not precisely humorous nor altogether thoughtful. We who knew him recognized it in a moment: it was his narrative smile. Breaking off our few desultory remarks, we drew up closer, and he thus began:

"My father, as you mid know, was a shepherd all his life, and lived out by the Cove, four miles yonder, where I was born and lived likewise, till I moved here shortly afore I wer married. The cottage that first knew me stood on the top of the down, near the sea; there was no house within a mile and a half of it; it was built o' purpose for the farm-shepherd, and had no other use. They tell me that it is now pulled down, but that you can see where it stood by the mounds of earth and a few broken bricks that are still lying about. It was a bleak and dreary place in winter-time, but in summer it was well enough, though the garden never came to much, because we could not get up a good shelter for the vegetables and currant bushes, and where there is much wind they don't thrive.

"Of all them years of my growing up the ones that bide clearest in my mind were eighteen hundred and three, four, and five. This was for two reasons: I had just then grown to an age when a child's eyes and ears take in and note down everything about him, and there was more at that date to bear in mind than there ever has been since with me. It was, as I need hardly tell ye, the time after the first peace, when Bonaparte was scheming his descent upon England. He had crossed the great Alp mountains, fought in Egypt, drubbed the Turks, the Austrians, and the Proossians, and now thought he'd have a slap at us. On the other side of the Channel, scarce out of sight and hail of a man standing on our English shore, the French army of a hundred and sixty thousand men and fifteen thousand horses had been brought together from all parts, and were drilling every day. Bonaparte had been three years a-making his preparations; and to ferry these soldiers and cannon and horses across he had contrived a couple of thousand flat-bottomed boats. These boats were small things, but wonderfully built. A good few of 'em were so made as to have a little stable on board each for the two horses that were to haul the cannon carried at the stern. To get in order all these, and other things required, he had assembled there five or six thousand fellows that worked at trades—carpenters, blacksmiths, wheelwrights, saddlers, and what not. Oh, 'twas a curious time!

"Every morning neighbor Boney would muster his

multitude of soldiers on the beach, draw 'em up in line, practise 'em in the manœuvre of embarking, horses and all, till they could do it without a single hitch. My father drove a flock of ewes up into Sussex that year, and as he went along the drover's track over the high downs thereabout he could see this drilling actually going on—the accoutrements of the rank and file glittering in the sun like silver. It was thought and always said by my uncle Job, sergeant of foot (who used to know all about these matters), that Bonaparte meant to cross with oars on a calm night. The grand query with us was, Where would my gentleman land? Many of the common people thought it would be at Dover; others, who knew how unlikely it was that any skilful general would make a business of landing just where he was expected, said he'd go either east into the river Thames, or west'ard to some convenient place, most likely one of the little bays inside the Isle of Portland, between the Beal and St. Alban's Head—and for choice the three-quarter-round Cove, screened from every mortal eye, that seemed made o' purpose, out by where we lived, and which I've climmed up with two tubs of brandy across my shoulders on scores o' dark nights in my younger days. Some had heard that a part o' the French fleet would sail right round Scotland, and come up the Channel to a suitable haven. However, there was much doubt upon the matter; and no wonder, for after-years proved that Bonaparte himself could hardly make up his mind upon that great and very particular point—where to land. His uncertainty came about in this wise: that he could get no news as to where and how our troops lay in waiting, and that his knowledge of possible places where flat-bottomed boats might be quietly run ashore, and the men they brought marshalled in order, was dim to the last degree. Being flat-bottomed, they didn't require a harbor for unshipping their cargo of men, but a good shelving beach away from sight, and with a fair open road towards London. How the question posed that great Corsican tyrant (as we used to call him), what pains he took to settle it, and, above all, what a risk he ran on one particular night in trying to do so, were known only to one man here and there; and certainly to no maker of newspapers or printer of books, or my account o't would not have had so many heads shaken over it as it has by gentry who only believe what they see in printed lines.

"The flocks my father had charge of fed all about the downs near our house, overlooking the sea and shore each way for miles. In winter and early spring father was up a deal at nights, watching and tending the lambing. Often he'd go to bed early, and turn out at twelve or one; and, on the other hand, he'd sometimes stay up till twelve or one, and then turn in to bed. As soon as I was old enough I used to help him, mostly in the way of keeping an eye upon the ewes while he was gone home to rest. This is what I was doing in a particular month in either the year four or five—I can't certainly fix which, but it was long before I was took away from the sheep-keeping to be bound prentice to a trade. Every night at that time I was at the fold, about half a mile, or it may be a little more, from our cottage, and no living thing at all with me but the ewes and young lambs. Afeard? No; I was never afeard of being alone at these times; for I had been reared in such an out-step place that the lack o' human beings at night made me less fearful than the sight of 'em. Directly I saw a man's shape after dark in a lonely place I was frightened out of my senses.

"One day in that month we were surprised by a visit from my uncle Job, the sergeant in the Sixty-first foot, then in camp on the downs above King George's watering-place, several miles to the west yonder. Uncle Job dropped in about dusk, and went up with my father to the fold for an hour or two. Then he came home, had a drop to drink from the tub of sperrits that the smugglers kept us in for housing their liquor when they'd made a run, and for burning 'em off when there was danger. After that he stretched himself out on the settle to sleep. I went to bed: at one o'clock father came home, and waking me to go and take his place, according to custom, went to bed himself. On my way out of the house I passed Uncle Job on the settle. He opened his eyes, and upon my telling him where I was going he said it was a shame that such a youngster as I should go up there all alone; and when he had fastened up his stock and waist-belt he set off along with me, taking a drop from the sperrit-tub in a little flat bottle that stood in the corner cupboard.

"By-and-by we drew up to the fold, saw that all was right, and then, to keep ourselves warm, curled up in a heap of straw that lay inside the thatched hurdles we had set up to break the stroke of the wind when there was any. To-night, however, there was none. It was one of those very still nights when, if you stand on the high hills anywhere within two or three miles of the sea, you can hear the rise and fall of the tide along the shore, coming and going every few moments like a sort of great snore of the sleeping world. Over the lower ground there was a bit of a mist, but on the hill where we lay the air was clear, and the moon, then in her last quarter, flung a fairly good light on the grass and scattered straw.

"While we lay there Uncle Job amused me by telling me strange stories of the wars he had served in and the wounds he had got. He had already fought the French in the Low Countries, and hoped to fight 'em again. His stories lasted so long that at last I was hardly sure that I was not a soldier myself, and had seen such service as he told of. The wonders of his tales quite bewildered my mind, till I fell asleep and dreamed of battle, smoke, and flying soldiers, all of a kind with the doings he had been bringing up to me.

"How long my nap lasted I am not prepared to say. But some faint sounds over and above the rustle of the ewes in the straw, the bleat of the lambs, and the tinkle of the sheep-bell brought me to my waking senses. Uncle Job was still beside me; but he too had fallen asleep. I looked out from the straw, and saw what it was that had aroused me. Two men, in boat cloaks, cocked hats, and swords, stood by the hurdles about twenty yards off.

"I turned my ear thitherward to catch what they were saying, but though I heard every word o't, not one did I understand. They spoke in a tongue that was not ours — in French, as I afterwards found. But if I could not gain the meaning of a word, I was shrewd boy enough to find out a deal of the talkers' business. By the light o' the moon I could see that one of 'em carried a roll of paper in his hand, while every moment he spoke quick to his comrade, and pointed right and left with the other hand to spots along the shore. There was no doubt that he was explaining to the second gentleman the shapes and features of the coast. What happened soon after made this still clearer to me.

"All this time I had not waked Uncle Job, but now I began to be afeard that they might light upon us, because uncle breathed so heavily through 's nose. I put my mouth to his ear and whispered, 'Uncle Job.'

"'What is it, my boy?' he said, just as if he hadn't been asleep at all.

"'Hush!' says I. 'Two French generals—'

"'French?' says he.

"'Yes,' says I. 'Come to see where to land their army!'

"I pointed 'em out; but I could say no more, for the pair were coming at that moment much nearer to where we lay. As soon as they got as near as eight or ten yards, the officer with a roll in his hand stooped down to a slanting hurdle, unfastened his roll upon it, and spread it out. Then suddenly he sprung a dark-lantern open on the paper, and showed it to be a map.

"'What be they looking at?' I whispered to Uncle Job.

"'A chart of the Channel,' says the sergeant (knowing about such things).

"The other French officer now stooped likewise, and over the map they had a long consultation, as they pointed here and there on the paper, and then hither and thither at places along the shore beneath us. I noticed that the manner of one officer was very respectful towards the other, who seemed much his superior, the second in rank calling him by a sort of title that I did not know the sense of. The head one, on the other hand, was quite familiar with his friend, and more than once clapped him on the shoulder.

"Uncle Job had watched as well as I, but though the map had been in the lantern-light, their faces had always been in shade. But when they rose from stooping over the chart, the light flashed upward, and fell smart upon one of 'em's features. No sooner had this happened than Uncle Job gasped, and sank down as if he'd been in a fit.

"'What is it—what is it, Uncle Job?' said I.

"'O good God!' says he, under the straw.

"'What?' says I.

"'Boney!' he groaned out.

"'Who?' says I.

"'Bonaparty,' he said. 'The Corsican ogre. O that I had got but my new-flinted firelock, that there man should die! But I haven't got my new-flinted firelock, and that there man must live. So lie low, as you value your life!'

"I did lie low, as you mid suppose. But I couldn't help peeping. And then I too, lad as I was, knew that it was the face of Bonaparte. Not know Boney? I should think I did know Boney. I should have known him by half the light o' that lantern. If I had seen a picture of his features once, I had seen it a hundred times. There was his bullet head, his short neck, his round yaller cheeks and chin, his gloomy face, and his great, glowing eyes. He took off his hat to blow himself a bit, and there was the forelock in the middle of his forehead, as in all the draughts of him. In moving, his cloak fell a little open, and I could see for a moment his white-fronted jacket and one of his epaulets.

"But none of this lasted long. In a minute he and his general had rolled up the map, shut the lantern, and turned to go down towards the shore.

"Then Uncle Job came to himself a bit. 'Slipped across in the night-time to see how to put his men ashore,' he said. 'The like o' that man's coolness eyes will never again see! Nephew, I must act in this, and immediate, or England's lost!'

"When they were over the brow, we crope out, and went some little way to look after them. Half-way down they were joined by two others, and six or seven minutes brought them to the shore. Then, from behind a rock, a boat came out into the weak moonlight of the Cove, and they jumped in; it put off instantly, and vanished in a few minutes between the two rocks that stand at the mouth of the Cove as we all know. We climmed back to where we had been before, and I could see, a little way out, a larger vessel, though still not very large. The little boat drew up alongside, was made fast at the stern as I suppose, for the largest sailed away, and we saw no more.

"My uncle Job told his officers as soon as he got back to camp; but what they thought of it I never heard—neither did he. Boney's army never came, and a good job for me; for the Cove below my father's house was where he meant to land, as this secret visit showed. We coast-folk should have been cut down one and all, and I should not have sat here to tell this tale."

We who listened to old Selby that night have been familiar with his simple gravestone for these ten years past. Thanks to the incredulity of the age, his tale has been seldom repeated. But if anything short of the direct testimony of his own eyes could persuade an auditor that Bonaparte had examined these shores for himself with a view to a practicable landing-place, it would have been Solomon Selby's manner of narrating the adventure which befell him on the down.

Christmas, 1882.

A FEW CRUSTED CHARACTERS

A FEW CRUSTED CHARACTERS

It is a Saturday afternoon of blue-and-yellow autumn-time, and the scene is the high street of a well-known market-town. A large carrier's van stands in the quadrangular fore-court of the White Hart Inn, upon the sides of its spacious tilt being painted, in weather-beaten letters: "Burthen, Carrier to Longpuddle." These vans, so numerous hereabout, are a respectable, if somewhat lumbering, class of conveyance, much resorted to by decent travellers not overstocked with money, the better among them roughly corresponding to the old French *diligences*.

The present one is timed to leave the town at four in the afternoon precisely, and it is now half-past three by the clock in the turret at the top of the street. In a few seconds errand-boys from the shops begin to arrive with packages which they fling into the vehicle, and turn away whistling, and care for the packages no more. At twenty minutes to four an elderly woman places her basket upon the shafts, slowly mounts, takes up a seat inside, and folds her hands and her lips. She has secured her corner for the journey, though there is as yet no sign of a horse being put in, nor of a carrier. At the three-quarters, two other women arrive, in whom the first recognizes the postmistress of Upper Longpuddle and the registrar's wife, they recognizing her as the aged groceress of the same village. At five minutes to the hour there approach Mr. Profitt, the school-master, in a soft felt hat, and Christopher Twink, the master-thatcher; and as the hour strikes there rapidly drop in the parish-clerk and his wife, the seedsman and his aged father, the registrar; also Mr. Day, the world-ignored local landscape-painter, an elderly man who resides in his native place, and has never sold a picture outside it, though his pretensions to art have been nobly supported by his fellow-villagers, whose confidence in his genius has been as remarkable as the outer neglect of it, leading them to buy his paintings so extensively (at the price of a few shillings each, it is true) that every dwelling in the parish exhibits three or four of those admired productions on its walls.

Burthen, the carrier, is by this time seen bustling round the vehicle; the horses are put in, the proprietor arranges the reins and springs up into his seat as if he were used to it—which he is.

"Is everybody here?" he asks, preparatorily, over his shoulder to the passengers within.

As those who were not there did not reply in the negative the muster was assumed to be complete, and after a few hitches and hinderances the van with its human freight was got under way. It jogged on at an easy pace till it reached the bridge which formed the last outpost of the town. The carrier pulled up suddenly

"Bless my soul!" he said, "I've forgot the curate!"

All who could do so gazed from the little back window of the van, but the curate was not in sight.

"Now I wonder where that there man is?" continued the carrier.

"Poor man, he ought to have a living at his time of life."

"And he ought to be punctual," said the carrier. "'Four o'clock sharp is my time for starting,' I said to 'en. And he said, 'I'll be there.' Now he's not here; and as a serious old Church minister he ought to be as good as his word. Perhaps Mr. Flaxton knows, being in the same line of life?" He turned to the parish-clerk.

"I was talking an immense deal with him, that's true, half an hour ago," replied that ecclesiastic, as one of whom it was no erroneous supposition that he should be on intimate terms with another of the cloth. "But he didn't say he would be late."

The discussion was cut off by the appearance round the corner of the van of rays from the curate's spectacles, followed hastily by his face and a few white whiskers, and the swinging tails of his long gaunt coat. Nobody reproached him, seeing how he was reproaching himself; and he entered breathlessly and took his seat.

"Now be we all here?" said the carrier again. They started a second time, and moved on till they were about three hundred yards out of the town, and had nearly reached the second bridge, behind which, as every native remembers, the road takes a turn and travellers by this highway disappear finally from the view of gazing burghers.

"Well, as I'm alive!" cried the postmistress from the interior of the conveyance, peering through the little square back window along the road townward.

"What?" said the carrier.

"A man hailing us!"

Another sudden stoppage. "Somebody else?" the carrier asked.

"Aye, sure!" All waited silently, while those who could gaze out did so.

"Now, who can that be?" Burthen continued. "I

just put it to ye, neighbors, can any man keep time with such hinderances? Bain't we full a'ready? Who in the world can the man be?"

"He's a sort of gentleman," said the school-master, his position commanding the road more comfortably than that of his comrades.

The stranger, who had been holding up his umbrella to attract their notice, was walking forward leisurely enough, now that he found, by their stopping, that it had been secured. His clothes were decidedly not of a local cut, though it was difficult to point out any particular mark of difference. In his left hand he carried a small leather travelling-bag. As soon as he had overtaken the van he glanced at the inscription on its side, as if to assure himself that he had hailed the right conveyance, and asked if they had room.

The carrier replied that though they were pretty well laden he supposed they could carry one more, whereupon the stranger mounted, and took the seat cleared for him within. And then the horses made another move, this time for good, and swung along with their burden of fourteen souls all told.

"You bain't one of these parts, sir?" said the carrier. "I could tell that as far as I could see 'ee."

"Yes, I am one of these parts," said the stranger.

"Oh? H'm."

The silence which followed seemed to imply a doubt of the truth of the new-comer's assertion. "I was speaking of Upper Longpuddle more particular," continued the carrier, hardily, "and I think I know most faces of that valley."

"I was born at Longpuddle, and nursed at Longpuddle, and my father and grandfather before me," said the passenger, quietly.

"Why, to be sure," said the aged groceress in the background, "it isn't John Lackland's son—never—

it can't be—he who went to foreign parts five-and-thirty years ago with his wife and family? Yet—what do I hear?—that's his father's voice!"

"That's the man," replied the stranger. "John Lackland was my father, and I am John Lackland's son. Five-and-thirty years ago, when I was a boy of eleven, my parents emigrated across the seas, taking me and my sister with them. Kytes's boy Tony was the one who drove us and our belongings to Casterbridge on the morning we left; and his was the last Longpuddle face I saw. We sailed the same week across the ocean, and there we've been ever since, and there I've left those I went with—all three."

"Alive or dead?"

"Dead," he replied in a low voice. "And I have come back to the old place, having nourished a thought—not a definite intention, but just a thought—that I should like to return here in a year or two, to spend the remainder of my days."

"Married man, Mr. Lackland?"

"No."

"And have the world used 'ee well, sir—or rather John, knowing 'ee as a child? In these rich new countries that we hear of so much, you've got rich with the rest?"

"I am not very rich," Mr. Lackland said. "Even in new countries, you know, there are failures. The race is not always to the swift, nor the battle to the strong; and even if it sometimes is, you may be neither swift nor strong. However, that's enough about me. Now, having answered your inquiries, you must answer mine; for, being in London, I have come down here entirely to discover what Longpuddle is looking like, and who are living there. That was why I preferred a seat in your van to hiring a carriage for driving across."

"Well, as for Longpuddle, we rub on there much as usual. Old figures have dropped out o' their frames, so to speak it, and new ones have been put in their places. You mentioned Tony Kytes as having been the one to drive your family and your goods to Casterbridge in his father's wagon when you left. Tony is, I believe, living still, but not at Longpuddle. He went away and settled at Lewgate, near Mellstock, after his marriage. Ah, Tony was a sort o' man!"

"His character had hardly come out when I knew him."

"No. But 'twas well enough, as far as that goes—except as to women. I shall never forget his courting—never!"

The returned villager waited silently, and the carrier went on:

TONY KYTES, THE ARCH-DECEIVER

"I SHALL never forget Tony's face. 'Twas a little, round, firm, tight face, with a seam here and there left by the small-pox, but not enough to hurt his looks in a woman's eye, though he'd had it badish when he was a boy. So very serious looking and unsmiling 'a was, that young man, that it really seemed as if he couldn't laugh at all without great pain to his conscience. He looked very hard at a small speck in your eye when talking to 'ee. And there was no more sign of a whisker or beard on Tony Kytes's face than on the palm of my hand. He used to sing 'The Tailor's Breeches' with a religious manner, as if it were a hymn:

"'O the petticoats went off, and the breeches they went on;'

and all the rest of the scandalous stuff. He was quite the women's favorite, and in return for their likings he loved 'em in shoals.

"But in course of time Tony got fixed down to one in particular, Milly Richards—a nice, light, small, tender little thing; and it was soon said that they were engaged to be married. One Saturday he had been to market to do business for his father, and was driving home the wagon in the afternoon. When he reached the foot of the very hill we shall be going over in ten minutes, who should he see waiting for him at the top but Unity Sallet, a handsome girl, one of the young women he'd been very tender towards before he'd got engaged to Milly.

"As soon as Tony came up to her she said, 'My dear Tony, will you give me a lift home?'

"'That I will, darling,' said Tony. 'You don't suppose I could refuse 'ee?'

"She smiled a smile, and up she hopped, and on drove Tony.

"'Tony,' she says, in a sort of tender chide, 'why did ye desert me for that other one? In what is she better than I? I should have made 'ee a finer wife, and a more loving one, too. 'Tisn't girls that are so easily won at first that are the best. Think how long we've known each other—ever since we were children almost—now haven't we, Tony?'

"'Yes, that we have,' says Tony, a-struck with the truth o't.

"'And you've never seen anything in me to complain of, have ye, Tony? Now tell the truth to me.'

"'I never have, upon my life,' says Tony.

"'And—can you say I'm not pretty, Tony? Now look at me!'

"He let his eyes light upon her for a long while. 'I really can't,' says he. 'In fact, I never knowed you was so pretty before!'

"'Prettier than she?'

"What Tony would have said to that nobody knows, for before he could speak, what should he see ahead, over the hedge past the turning, but a feather he knew well—the feather in Milly's hat—she to whom he had been thinking of putting the question as to giving out the banns that very week.

"'Unity,' says he, as mild as he could, 'here's Milly coming. Now I shall catch it mightily if she sees 'ee riding here with me; and if you get down she'll be turning the corner in a moment, and, seeing 'ee in the road, she'll know we've been coming on together. Now, dearest Unity, will ye, to avoid all unpleasantness, which I know ye can't bear any more than I, will ye lie down in the back part of the wagon, and let me cover you over with the tarpaulin till Milly has passed? It will all be done in a minute. Do!—and I'll think over what we've said; and perhaps I shall put a loving question to you after all, instead of to Milly. 'Tisn't true that it is all settled between her and me.'

"Well, Unity Sallet agreed, and lay down at the back end of the wagon, and Tony covered her over, so that the wagon seemed to be empty but for the loose tarpaulin; and then he drove on to meet Milly.

"'My dear Tony!' cries Milly, looking up with a little pout at him as he came near. 'How long you've been coming home! Just as if I didn't live at Upper Longpuddle at all! And I've come to meet you as you asked me to do, and to ride back with you, and talk over our future home—since you asked me, and I promised. But I shouldn't have come else, Mr. Tony!'

"'Ay, my dear, I did ask ye—to be sure I did, now I think of it—but I had quite forgot it. To ride back with me, did you say, dear Milly?'

"'Well, of course! What can I do else? Surely you don't want me to walk, now I've come all this way?'

"'Oh no, no! I was thinking you might be going on to town to meet your mother. I saw her there—and she looked as if she might be expecting 'ee.'

"'Oh no; she's just home. She came across the fields, and so got back before you.'

"'Ah! I didn't know that,' says Tony. And there was no help for it but to take her up beside him.

"They talked on very pleasantly, and looked at the trees and beasts and birds and insects, and at the ploughmen at work in the fields, till presently who should they see looking out of the upper window of a house that stood beside the road they were following but Hannah Jolliver, another young beauty of the place at that time, and the very first woman that Tony had fallen in love with — before Milly and before Unity, in fact—the one that he had almost arranged to marry instead of Milly. She was a much more dashing girl than Milly Richards, though he'd not thought much of her of late. The house Hannah was looking from was her aunt's.

"'My dear Milly—my coming wife, as I may call 'ee,' says Tony in his modest way, and not so loud that Unity could overhear 'I see a young woman looking out of window who I think may accost me. The fact is, Milly, she had a notion that I was wishing to marry her, and since she's discovered I've promised another, and prettier than she, I'm rather afeared of her temper if she sees us together. Now, Milly, would you do me a favor—my coming wife, as I may say?'

"'Certainly, dearest Tony,' says she.

"'Then would ye creep under the tarpaulin just here in the front of the wagon, and hide there out of sight till we've passed the house? She hasn't seen us yet. You see, we ought to live in peace and good-will since 'tis almost Christmas, and 'twill prevent angry passions rising, which we always should do.'

"'I don't mind, to oblige you, Tony,' Milly said; and though she didn't care much about doing it, she crept under, and crouched down just behind the seat, Unity being snug at the other end. So they drove on till they got near the road-side cottage. Hannah had soon seen him coming, and waited at the window, looking down upon him. She tossed her head a little disdainful and smiled off-hand.

"'Well, aren't you going to be civil enough to ask

me to ride home with you?' she says, seeing that he was for driving past with a nod and a smile.

"'Ah, to be sure! What was I thinking of?' said Tony, in a flutter. 'But you seem as if you was staying at your aunt's?'

"'No, I am not,' she said. 'Don't you see I have my bonnet and jacket on? I have only called to see her on my way home. How can you be so stupid, Tony?'

"'In that case—ah—of course you must come along wi' me,' says Tony, feeling a dim sort of sweat rising up inside his clothes. And he reined in the horse, and waited till she'd come down-stairs, and then helped her up beside him. He drove on again, his face as long as a face that was a round one by nature well could be.

"Hannah looked round sideways into his eyes. 'This is nice, isn't it, Tony?' she says. 'I like riding with you.'

"Tony looked back into her eyes. 'And I with you,' he said, after a while. In short, having considered her, he warmed up, and the more he looked at her the more he liked her, till he couldn't for the life of him think why he had ever said a word about marriage to Milly or Unity while Hannah Jolliver was in question. So they sat a little closer and closer, their feet upon the foot-board and their shoulders touching, and Tony thought over and over again how handsome Hannah was. He spoke tenderer and tenderer, and called her 'dear Hannah' in a whisper at last.

"'You've settled it with Milly by this time, I suppose,' said she.

"'N—no, not exactly.'

"'What? How low you talk, Tony.'

"'Yes—I've a kind of hoarseness. I said, not exactly.'

"'I suppose you mean to?'

"'Well, as to that—' His eyes rested on her face, and hers on his. He wondered how he could have been such a fool as not to follow up Hannah. 'My sweet Hannah!' he bursts out, taking her hand, not being really able to help it, and forgetting Milly and Unity and all the world besides. 'Settled it? I don't think I have!'

"'Hark!' says Hannah.

"'What?' says Tony, letting go her hand.

"'Surely I heard a sort of little screaming squeak under that tar-cloth? Why, you've been carrying corn, and there's mice in this wagon, I declare!' She began to haul up the tails of her gown.

"'Oh no; 'tis the axle,' said Tony, in an assuring way. 'It do go like that sometimes in dry weather.'

"'Perhaps it was. . . . Well, now, to be quite honest, dear Tony, do you like her better than me? Because—because, although I've held off so independent, I'll own at last that I do like 'ee, Tony, to tell the truth; and I wouldn't say no if you asked me—you know what.'

"Tony was so won over by this pretty offering mood of a girl who had been quite the reverse (Hannah had a backward way with her at times, if you can mind) that he just glanced behind, and then whispered very soft, 'I haven't quite promised her, and I think I can get out of it, and ask you that question you speak of.'

"'Throw over Milly?—all to marry me! How delightful!' broke out Hannah, quite loud, clapping her hands.

"At this there was a real squeak—an angry, spiteful squeak, and afterwards a long moan, as if something had broke its heart, and a movement of the wagon cloth.

"'Something's there!' said Hannah, starting up.

"'It's nothing, really,' says Tony, in a soothing voice, and praying inwardly for a way out of this. 'I wouldn't tell 'ee at first, because I wouldn't frighten 'ee. But, Hannah, I've really a couple of ferrets in a bag under there, for rabbiting, and they quarrel sometimes. I don't wish it knowed, as 'twould be called poaching. Oh, they can't get out, bless ye!—you are quite safe. And—and—what a fine day it is, isn't it, Hannah, for this time of year? Be you going to market next Saturday? How is your aunt now?' And so on, says Tony, to keep her from talking any more about love in Milly's hearing.

"But he found his work cut out for him, and wondering again how he should get out of this ticklish business, he looked about for a chance. Nearing home he saw his father in a field not far off, holding up his hand as if he wished to speak to Tony.

"'Would you mind taking the reins a moment, Hannah,' he said, much relieved, 'while I go and find out what father wants?'

"She consented, and away he hastened into the field, only too glad to get breathing-time. He found that his father was looking at him with rather a stern eye.

"'Come, come, Tony,' says old Mr. Kytes, as soon as his son was alongside him, 'this won't do, you know.'

"'What?' says Tony.

"'Why, if you mean to marry Milly Richards, do it, and there's an end o't. But don't go driving about the country with Jolliver's daughter and making a scandal. I won't have such things done.'

"'I only asked her—that is, she asked me—to ride home.'

"'She? Why, now, if it had been Milly, 'twould have been quite proper; but you and Hannah Jolliver going about by yourselves—'

"'Milly's there, too, father.'

"'Milly? Where?'

"'Under the tarpaulin! Yes; the truth is, father, I've got rather into a nunny-watch, I'm afeard! Unity Sallet is there, too—yes, under the other end of the tarpaulin. All three are in that wagon, and what to do with 'em I know no more than the dead. The best plan is, as I'm thinking, to speak out loud and plain to one of 'em before the rest, and that will settle it; not but what 'twill cause 'em to kick up a bit of a miff, for certain. Now, which would you marry, father, if you was in my place?'

"'Whichever of 'em did *not* ask to ride with thee.'

"'That was Milly, I'm bound to say, as she only mounted by my invitation. But Milly—'

"'Then stick to Milly, she's the best. . . . But look at that!'

"His father pointed towards the wagon. 'She can't hold that horse in. You shouldn't have left the reins in her hands. Run on and take the horse's head, or there'll be some accident to them maids!'

"Tony's horse, in fact, in spite of Hannah's tugging at the reins, had started on his way at a brisk walking pace, being very anxious to get back to the stable, for he had had a long day out. Without another word, Tony rushed away from his father to overtake the horse.

"Now, of all things that could have happened to wean him from Milly, there was nothing so powerful as his father's recommending her. No; it could not be Milly, after all. Hannah must be the one, since he could not marry all three. This he thought while running after the wagon. But queer things were happening inside it.

"It was, of course, Milly who had screamed under the tarpaulin, being obliged to let off her bitter rage and shame in that way at what Tony was saying, and never daring to show, for very pride and dread o' being laughed at, that she was in hiding. She became more and more restless, and in twisting herself about, what did she see but another woman's foot and white stocking close to her head. It quite frightened her, not knowing that Unity Sallet was in the wagon likewise. But after the fright was over she determined to get to the bottom of all this, and she crept and crept along the bed of the wagon, under the cloth, like a snake, when lo and behold she came face to face with Unity.

"'Well, if this isn't disgraceful!' says Milly, in a raging whisper, to Unity.

"''Tis,' says Unity, 'to see you hiding in a young man's wagon like this, and no great character belonging to either of ye!'

"'Mind what you are saying!' replied Milly, getting louder. 'I am engaged to be married to him, and haven't I a right to be here? What right have you, I should like to know? What has he been promising you? A pretty lot of nonsense, I expect! But what Tony says to other women is all mere wind, and no concern to me!'

"'Don't you be too sure!' says Unity. 'He's going to have Hannah, and not you, nor me either; I could hear that.'

"Now, at these strange voices sounding from under the cloth Hannah was thunderstruck a'most into a swound; and it was just at this time that the horse moved on. Hannah tugged away wildly, not knowing what she was doing; and as the quarrel rose louder and louder Hannah got so horrified that she let go the reins altogether. The horse went on at his own pace, and coming to the corner where we turn round to drop down the hill to Lower Longpuddle he turned too quick, the off-wheels went up the bank, the wagon rose sideways till it was quite on edge upon the near axles, and out rolled the three maidens into the road in a heap.

"When Tony came up, frightened and breathless, he was relieved enough to see that neither of his darlings was hurt, beyond a few scratches from the brambles of the hedge. But he was rather alarmed when he heard how they were going on at one another.

"'Don't ye quarrel, my dears—don't ye!' says he, taking off his hat out of respect to 'em. And then he would have kissed them all round, as fair and square as a man could, but they were in too much of a taking to let him, and screeched and sobbed till they was quite spent.

"'Now, I'll speak out honest, because I ought to,' says Tony, as soon as he could get heard. 'And this is the truth,' says he: 'I've asked Hannah to be mine, and she is willing, and we are going to put up the banns next—'

"Tony had not noticed that Hannah's father was coming up behind, nor had he noticed that Hannah's face was beginning to bleed from the scratch of a bramble. Hannah had seen her father, and had run to him, crying worse than ever.

"'My daughter is *not* willing, sir,' says Mr. Jolliver, hot and strong. 'Be you willing, Hannah? I ask ye to have spirit enough to refuse him, if yer virtue is left to 'ee and you run no risk?'

"'She's as sound as a bell for me, that I'll swear!' says Tony, flaring up. 'And so's the others, come to that, though you may think it an onusual thing!'

"'I have spirit, and I do refuse him!' says Hannah, partly because her father was there, and partly, too, in a tantrum because of the discovery and the scratch on her face. 'Little did I think when I was so soft with him just now that I was talking to such a false deceiver!'

"'What, you won't have me, Hannah?' says Tony, his jaw hanging down like a dead man's.

"'Never; I would sooner marry no—nobody at all!' she gasped out, though with her heart in her throat, for she would not have refused Tony if he had asked her quietly, and her father had not been there, and her face had not been scratched by the bramble. And having said that, away she walked upon her father's arm, thinking and hoping he would ask her again.

"Tony didn't know what to say next. Milly was sobbing her heart out; but as his father had strongly recommended her he couldn't feel inclined that way. So he turned to Unity.

"'Well, will you, Unity dear, be mine?' he says.

"'Take her leavings? Not I!' says Unity. 'I'd scorn it!' And away walks Unity Sallet likewise, though she looked back when she'd gone some way, to see if he was following her.

"So there at last were left Milly and Tony by themselves, she crying in watery streams, and Tony looking like a tree struck by lightning.

"'Well, Milly,' he says at last, going up to her, 'it do seem as if fate had ordained that it should be you and I, or nobody. And what must be must be, I suppose. Hey, Milly?'

"'If you like, Tony. You didn't really mean what you said to them?'

"'Not a word of it,' declares Tony, bringing down his fist upon his palm.

"And then he kissed her, and put the wagon to rights, and they mounted together; and their banns were put up the very next Sunday. I was not able to go to their wedding, but it was a rare party they had, by all account. Everybody in Longpuddle was there almost; you among the rest, I think, Mr. Flaxton?" The speaker turned to the parish-clerk.

"I was," said Mr. Flaxton. 'And that party was the cause of a very curious change in some other people's affairs; I mean in Steve Hardcome's and his cousin James's."

"Ah! the Hardcomes," said the stranger. "How familiar that name is to me! What of them?"

The clerk cleared his throat and began:

THE HISTORY OF THE HARDCOMES

"Yes, Tony's was the very best wedding-randy that ever I was at; and I've been at a good many, as you may suppose"—turning to the newly-arrived one—"having, as a Church officer, the privilege to attend all christening, wedding, and funeral parties—such being our Wessex custom.

"'Twas on a frosty night in Christmas week, and among the folk invited were the said Hardcomes o' Climmerston—Steve and James—first cousins, both of them small farmers, just entering into business on their own account. With them came, as a matter of course, their intended wives, two young women of the neighborhood, both very pretty and sprightly maidens, and numbers of friends from Abbot's-Cernel and Weatherbury and Mellstock and I don't know where—a regular houseful.

"The kitchen was cleared of furniture for dancing, and the old folk played at 'Put' and 'All-fours' in the parlor, though at last they gave that up to join in the dance. The top of the figure was by the large front window of the room, and there were so many couples that the lower part of the figure reached through the door at the back, and into the darkness of the out-house; in fact, you couldn't see the end of the row at all, and 'twas never known exactly how long that dance was, the lowest couples being lost among the fagots and brushwood in the out-house.

"When we had danced a few hours, and the crowns of we taller men were swelling into lumps with bumping the beams of the ceiling, the first fiddler laid down his fiddle-bow, and said he should play no more, for he wished to dance. And in another hour the second fiddler laid down his, and said he wanted to dance, too; so there was only the third fiddler left, and he was a' old, aged man, very weak in the wrist. However, he managed to keep up a feeble tweedle-dee; but there being no chair in the room, and his knees being as weak as his wrists, he was obliged to sit upon as much of the little corner-table as projected beyond the corner cupboard fixed over it, which was not a very wide seat for a man advanced in years.

"Among those who danced most continually were the two engaged couples, as was natural to their situation. Each pair was very well matched, and very unlike the other. James Hardcome's intended was called Emily Darth, and both she and James were gentle, nice-minded, in-door people, fond of a quiet life. Steve and his chosen, named Olive Pawle, were different; they were of a more bustling nature, fond of racketing about and seeing what was going on in the world. The two couples had arranged to get married on the same day, and that not long thence; Tony's wedding being a sort of stimulant, as is often the case; I've noticed it professionally many times.

"They danced with such a will as only young people in that stage of courtship can dance; and it happened that as the evening wore on James had for his partner Stephen's plighted one, Olive, at the same time that Stephen was dancing with James's Emily. It was noticed that in spite o' the exchange the young men seemed to enjoy the dance no less than before. By-and-by they were treading another tune in the same changed order as we had noticed earlier, and though at first each one had held the other's mistress strictly at half-arm's length, lest there should be shown any objection to too close quarters by the lady's proper man, as time passed there was a little more closeness between 'em; and presently a little more closeness still.

"The later it got the more did each of the two cousins dance with the wrong young girl, and the tighter did he hold her to his side as he whirled her round; and, what was very remarkable, neither seemed to mind what the other was doing. The party began to draw towards its end, and I saw no more that night, being one of the first to leave, on account of my serious calling. But I learned the rest of it from those that knew.

"After finishing a particularly warming dance with the changed partners, as I've mentioned, the two young men looked at one another, and in a moment or two went out into the porch together.

"'James,' says Steve, 'what were you thinking of when you were dancing with my Olive?'

"'Well,' said James, 'perhaps what you were thinking of when you were dancing with my Emily.'

"'I was thinking,' said Steve, with some hesitation, 'that I wouldn't mind changing for good and all!'

"'It was what I was feeling likewise,' said James.

"'I willingly agree to it, if you think we could manage it.'

"'So do I. But what would the girls say?'

"''Tis my belief,' said Steve, 'that they wouldn't particularly object. Your Emily clung as close to me as if she already belonged to me, dear girl.'

"'And your Olive to me,' says James. 'I could feel her heart beating like a clock.'

"Well, they agreed to put it to the girls when they were all four walking home together. And they did so. When they parted that night the exchange was decided on—all having been done under the hot excitement of that evening's dancing. Thus it happened that on the following Sunday morning, when the people were sitting in church with mouths wide open to hear the names published as they had expected, there was no small amazement to hear them coupled the wrong way, as it seemed. The congregation whispered, and thought the parson had made a mistake, till they discovered that his reading of the names was verily the true way. As they had decided, so they were married, each one to the other's original property.

"Well, the two couples lived on for a year or two ordinarily enough, till the time came when these young people began to grow a little less warm to their respective spouses, as is the rule of married life; and the two cousins wondered more and more in their hearts what had made 'em so mad at the last moment to marry crosswise as they did, when they might have married straight, as was planned by nature, and as they had fallen in love. 'Twas Tony's party that had done it, plain enough, and they half wished they had never gone there. James, being a quiet, fireside, perusing man, felt at times a wide gap between himself and Olive, his wife, who loved riding and driving and out-door jaunts to a degree; while Steve, who was always knocking about hither and thither, had a very domestic wife, who worked samplers, and made hearth-rugs, scarcely ever wished to cross the threshold, and only drove out with him to please him.

"However, they said very little about this mismating to any of their acquaintances, though sometimes Steve would look at James's wife and sigh, and James would look at Steve's wife and do the same. Indeed, at last the two men were frank enough towards each other not to mind mentioning it quietly to themselves, in a long-faced, sorry-smiling, whimsical sort of way, and would shake their heads together over their foolishness in upsetting a well-considered choice on the strength of an hour's fancy in the whirl and wildness of a dance. Still, they were sensible and honest young fellows enough, and did their best to make shift with their lot as they had arranged it, and not to repine at what could not now be altered or mended.

"So things remained till one fine summer day they went for their yearly little outing together, as they had made it their custom to do for a long while past. This year they chose Budmouth-Regis as the place to spend their holiday in; and off they went in their best clothes at nine o'clock in the morning.

"When they had reached Budmouth-Regis they walked two and two along the shore—their new boots going squeakity-squash upon the clammy velvet sands. I can seem to see 'em now! Then they looked at the ships in the harbor; and then went up to the Look-out; and then had dinner at an inn; and then again walked two and two, squeakity-squash, upon the velvet sands. As evening drew on they sat on one of the public seats upon the Esplanade, and listened to the band; and then they said "What shall we do next?"

"'Of all things,' said Olive (Mrs. James Hardcome, that is), 'I should like to row in the bay! We could listen to the music from the water as well as from here, and have the fun of rowing besides.'

"'The very thing; so should I,' says Stephen, his tastes being always like hers.

Here the clerk turned to the curate.

"But you, sir, know the rest of the strange particulars of that strange evening of their lives better than anybody else, having had much of it from their own lips, which I had not; and perhaps you'll oblige the gentleman?"

"Certainly, if it is wished," said the curate. And he took up the clerk's tale:

"Stephen's wife hated the sea, except from land, and couldn't bear the thought of going into a boat. James, too, disliked the water, and said that for his part he would much sooner stay on and listen to the band in the seat they occupied, though he did not wish to stand in his wife's way if she desired a row. The end of the discussion was that James and his cousin's wife Emily agreed to remain where they were sitting and enjoy the music, while they watched the other two hire a boat just beneath, and take their water excursion of half an hour or so, till they should choose to come back and join the sitters on the Esplanade, when they would all start homeward together.

"Nothing could have pleased the other two restless ones better than this arrangement; and Emily and James watched them go down to the boatman below and choose one of the little yellow skiffs, and walk carefully out upon the little plank that was laid on trestles to enable them to get alongside the craft. They saw Stephen hand Olive in, and take his seat facing her; when they were settled they waved their hands to the couple watching them, and then Stephen took the pair of sculls and pulled off to the tune beat by the band, she steering through the other boats skimming about, for the sea was as smooth as glass that evening, and pleasure-seekers were rowing everywhere.

"'How pretty they look moving on, don't they?' said Emily to James (as I've been assured). 'They both enjoy it equally. In everything their likings are the same.'

"'That's true,' said James.

"'They would have made a handsome pair if they had married,' said she.

"'Yes,' said he. ''Tis a pity we should have parted 'em.'

"'Don't talk of that, James,' said she. 'For better or for worse we decided to do as we did, and there's an end of it.'

"They sat on after that without speaking, side by side, and the band played as before; the people strolled up and down, and Stephen and Olive shrank smaller and smaller as they shot straight out to sea. The two on shore used to relate how they saw Stephen stop rowing a moment, and take off his coat to get at his work better; but James's wife sat quite still in the stern, holding the tiller-ropes by which she steered the boat. When they had got very small indeed she turned her head to shore.

"'She is waving her handkerchief to us,' said Stephen's wife, who thereupon pulled out her own, and waved it as a return signal.

"The boat's course had been a little awry while Mrs. James neglected her steering to wave her handkerchief to her husband and Mrs. Stephen; but now the light skiff went straight onward again, and they could soon see nothing more of the two figures it contained than Olive's light mantle and Stephen's white shirt-sleeves behind.

"The two on the shore talked on. ''Twas very curious—our changing partners at Tony Kytes's wedding,' Emily declared. 'Tony was of a fickle nature by all account, and it really seemed as if his character had infected us that night. Which of you two was it that first proposed not to marry as we were engaged?'

"'H'm—I can't remember at this moment,' says

James. 'We talked it over, you know, and no sooner said than done.'

"''Twas the dancing,' said she. 'People get quite crazy sometimes in a dance.'

"'They do,' he owned.

"'James—do you think they care for one another still?' asks Mrs. Stephen.

"James Hardcome mused, and admitted that perhaps a little tender feeling might flicker up in their hearts for a moment now and then. 'Still, nothing of any account,' he said.

"'I sometimes think that Olive is in Steve's mind a good deal,' murmurs Mrs. Stephen; 'particularly when she pleases his fancy by riding past our window at a gallop on one of the draught-horses. . . . I never could do anything of that sort; I could never get over my fear of a horse.'

"'And I am no horseman, though I pretend to be on her account,' murmured James Hardcome. 'But isn't it almost time for them to turn and sweep round to the shore, as the other boating folk have done? I wonder what Olive means by steering away straight to the horizon like that? She has hardly swerved from a direct line seaward since they started.'

"'No doubt they are talking, and don't think of where they are going,' suggests Stephen's wife.

"'Perhaps so,' said James. 'I didn't know Steve could row like that.'

"'Oh yes,' says she. 'He often comes here on business, and generally has a pull round the bay.'

"'I can hardly see the boat or them,' says James again; 'and it is getting dark.'

"The heedless pair afloat now formed a mere speck in the films of the coming night, which thickened apace, till it completely swallowed up their distant shapes. They had disappeared while still following the same straight course away from the world of land-livers, as if they were intending to drop over the sea-edge into space, and never return to earth again.

"The two on the shore continued to sit on, punctually abiding by their agreement to remain on the same spot till the others returned. The Esplanade lamps were lit one by one, the bandsmen folded up their stands and departed, the yachts in the bay hung out their riding lights, and the little boats came back to shore one after another, their hirers walking on to the sands by the plank they had climbed to go afloat; but among these Stephen and Olive did not appear.

"'What a time they are!' said Emily. 'I am getting quite chilly. I did not expect to have to sit so long in the evening air.'

"Thereupon James Hardcome said that he did not require his overcoat, and insisted on lending it to her.

"He wrapped it round Emily's shoulders.

"'Thank you, James,' she said. 'How cold Olive must be in that thin jacket!'

"He said he was thinking so, too. 'Well, they are sure to be quite close at hand by this time, though we can't see 'em. The boats are not all in yet. Some of the rowers are fond of paddling along the shore to finish out their hour of hiring.'

"'Shall we walk by the edge of the water,' said she, 'to see if we can discover them?'

"He assented, reminding her that they must not lose sight of the seat, lest the belated pair should return and miss them, and be vexed that they had not kept the appointment.

"They walked a sentry beat up and down the sands immediately opposite the seat; and still the others did not come. James Hardcome at last went to the boatman, thinking that after all his wife and cousin might have come in under shadow of the dusk without being perceived, and might have forgotten the appointment at the bench.

"'All in?' asked James.

"'All but one boat,' said the lessor. 'I can't think where that couple is keeping to. They might run foul of something or other in the dark.'

"Again Stephen's wife and Olive's husband waited, with more and more anxiety. But no little yellow boat returned. Was it possible they could have landed farther down the Esplanade?

"'It may have been done to escape paying,' said the boat-owner. 'But they didn't look like people who would do that.'

"James Hardcome knew that he could found no hope on such a reason as that. But now, remembering what had been casually discussed between Steve and himself about their wives from time to time, he admitted for the first time the possibility that their old tenderness had been revived by their face-to-face position more strongly than either had anticipated at starting—the excursion having been so obviously undertaken for the pleasure of the performance only—and that they had landed at some steps he knew of farther down towards the pier, to be longer alone together.

"Still he disliked to harbor the thought, and would not mention its existence to his companion. He merely said to her, 'Let us walk farther on.'

"They did so, and lingered between the boat-stage and the pier till Stephen Hardcome's wife was uneasy, and was obliged to accept James's offered arm. Thus the night advanced. Emily was presently so worn out by fatigue that James felt it necessary to conduct her home; there was, too, a remote chance that the truants had landed in the harbor on the other side of the town, or elsewhere, and hastened home in some unexpected way, in the belief that their spouses would not have waited so long.

"However, he left a direction in the town that a lookout should be kept, though this was arranged privately, the bare possibility of an elopement being enough to make him reticent; and, full of misgivings, the two remaining ones hastened to catch the last train out of Budmouth-Regis; and when they got to Casterbridge drove back to Upper Longpuddle."

"Along this very road as we do now," remarked the parish-clerk.

"To be sure—along this very road," said the curate. "However, Stephen and Olive were not at their homes; neither had entered the village since leaving it in the morning. Emily and James Hardcome went to their respective dwellings to snatch a hasty night's rest, and at daylight the next morning they drove again to Casterbridge and entered the Budmouth train.

"Nothing had been heard of the couple there during this brief absence. In the course of a few hours some young men testified to having seen such a man and woman rowing in a frail hired craft, the head of the boat kept straight to sea; they had sat looking in each other's face as if they were in a dream, with no consciousness of what they were doing, or whither they were steering. It was not till late that day that more tidings reached James's ears. The boat had been found drifting bottom upward a long way from land. In the evening the sea rose somewhat, and a cry spread through the town that two bodies were cast ashore in Lullstead Bay, several miles to the eastward. They were brought to Budmouth, and inspection revealed them to be the missing pair. It was said that they had been found tightly locked in each other's arms, his lips upon hers, their features still wrapt in the same calm and dream-like repose which had been observed in their demeanor as they had glided along.

"Neither James nor Emily questioned the original motives of the unfortunate man and woman in putting to sea. They were both above suspicion as to intention. Whatever their mutual feelings might have led them on to, underhand behavior was foreign to the nature of either. Conjecture pictured that they might have fallen into tender reverie while gazing each into a pair of eyes that had formerly flashed for him and her alone, and, unwilling to avow what their mutual sentiments were, they had continued thus, oblivious of time and space, till darkness suddenly overtook them far from land. But nothing was truly known. It had been their destiny to die thus. The two halves, intended by Nature to make the perfect whole, had failed in that result during their lives, though 'in their death they were not divided.' Their bodies were brought home, and buried on one day. I remember that, on looking round the church-yard while reading the service, I observed nearly all the parish at their funeral."

"It was so, sir," said the clerk.

"The remaining two," continued the curate (whose voice had grown husky while relating the lovers' sad fate), "were a more thoughtful and far-seeing, though less romantic, couple than the first. They were now mutually bereft of a companion, and found themselves by this accident in a position to fulfil their destiny according to Nature's plan and their own original and calmly-formed intention. James Hardcome took Emily to wife in the course of a year and a half; and the marriage proved in every respect a happy one. I solemnized the service, Hardcome having told me, when he came to give notice of the proposed wedding, the story of his first wife's loss almost word for word as I have told it to you."

"And are they living in Longpuddle still?" asked the new-comer.

"Oh no, sir," interposed the clerk. "James has been dead these dozen years, and his mis'ess about six or seven. They had no children. William Privett used to be their odd man till he died."

"Ah—William Privett! He, dead too?—dear me!" said the other. "All passed away!"

"Yes, sir. William was much older than I. He'd ha' been over eighty if he had lived till now."

"There was something very strange about William's death—very strange indeed!" sighed a melancholy man in the back of the van. It was the seedsman's father, who had hitherto kept silence.

"And what might that have been?" asked Mr. Lackland.

THE SUPERSTITIOUS MAN'S STORY

"William, as you may know, was a curious, silent man; you could feel when he came near ye; and if he was in the house or anywhere behind your back without your seeing him, there seemed to be something clammy in the air, as if a cellar door was opened close by your elbow. Well, one Sunday, at a time that William was in very good health to all appearance, the bell that was ringing for church went very heavy all of a sudden; the sexton, who told me o't, said he'd not known the bell go so heavy in his hand for years—it was just as if the gudgeons wanted oiling. That was on the Sunday, as I say. During the week after, it chanced that William's wife was staying up late one night to finish her ironing, she doing the washing for Mr. and Mrs. Hardcome. Her husband had finished his supper and gone to bed as usual some hour or two before. While she ironed she heard him coming downstairs; he stopped to put on his boots at the stair-foot, where he always left them, and then came on into the living-room where she was ironing, passing through it towards the door, this being the only way from the staircase to the outside of the house. No word was said on either side, William not being a man given to much speaking, and his wife being occupied with her work. He went out and closed the door behind him. As her husband had now and then gone out in this way at night before when unwell, or unable to sleep for want of a pipe, she took no particular notice, and continued at her ironing. This she finished shortly after, and as he had not come in she waited awhile for him, putting away the irons and things, and preparing the table for his breakfast in the morning. Still he did not return, but supposing him not far off, and wanting to get to bed herself, tired as she was, she left the door unbarred and went to the stairs, after writing on the back of the door with chalk: *Mind and do the door* (because he was a forgetful man).

"To her great surprise, I might say alarm, on reaching the foot of the stairs his boots were standing there as they always stood when he had gone to rest; going up to their chamber she found him in bed sleeping as sound as a rock. How he could have got back again without her seeing or hearing him was beyond her comprehension. It could only have been by passing behind her very quietly while she was bumping with the iron. But this notion did not satisfy her; it was surely impossible that she should not have seen him come in through a room so small. She could not unravel the mystery, and felt very queer and uncomfortable about it. However, she would not disturb him to question him then, and went to bed herself.

"He rose and left for his work very early the next morning, before she was awake, and she waited his return to breakfast with much anxiety for an explanation, for thinking over the matter by daylight made it seem only the more startling. When he came in to the meal he said, before she could put her question, "What's the meaning of them words chalked on the door?"

"She told him, and asked him about his going out the night before. William declared that he had never left the bedroom after entering it, having in fact undressed, lain down, and fallen asleep directly, never once waking till the clock struck five, and he rose up to go to his labor.

"Betty Privett was as certain in her own mind that he did go out as she was of her own existence, and was little less certain that he did not return. She felt too disturbed to argue with him, and let the subject drop as though she must have been mistaken. When she was walking down Longpuddle Street, later in the day, she met Jim Weedle's daughter Nancy, and said, 'Well, Nancy, you do look sleepy to-day!'

"'Yes, Mrs. Privett," says Nancy. "Now don't tell anybody, but I don't mind letting you know what the reason o't is. Last night being Old Midsummer Eve, some of us went to church porch, and didn't get home till near one.'

"'Did ye?' says Mrs. Privett. 'Old Midsummer yesterday, was it? Faith, I didn't think whe'r 'twas Midsummer or Michaelmas; I'd too much work to do.'

"'Yes. And we were frightened enough, I can tell 'ee, by what we saw.'

"'What did ye see?'

("You may not remember, sir, having gone off to foreign parts so young, that on Midsummer Night it is believed hereabout that the faint shapes of all the folk in the parish who are going to be at death's door within the year can be seen entering the church. Those who get over their illness come out again after a while; those that are doomed to die do not return.)

"'What did you see?' asked William's wife.

"'Well,' says Nancy, backwardly—'we needn't tell what we saw, or who we saw.'

"'You saw my husband,' says Betty Privett, in a quiet way.

"'Well, since you put it so,' says Nancy, hanging fire, 'we—thought we did see him; but it was darkish, and we was frightened, and of course it might not have been he.'

"'Nancy, you needn't mind letting it out, though

'tis kept back in kindness. And he didn't come out of church again ; I know it as well as you.'

"Nancy did not answer yes or no to that, and no more was said. But three days after, William Privett was mowing with John Chiles in Mr. Hardcome's meadow, and in the heat of the day they sat down to eat their bit o' lunch under a tree, and empty their flagon. Afterwards both of 'em fell asleep as they sat. John Chiles was the first to wake, and as he looked towards his fellow-mower he saw one of those great white miller's-souls as we call 'em—that is to say, a miller-moth—come from William's open mouth while he slept, and fly straight away. John thought it odd enough, as William had worked in a mill for several years when he was a boy. He then looked at the sun, and found by the place o't that they had slept a long while, and as William did not wake, John called to him and said it was high time to begin work again. He took no notice, and then John went up and shook him, and found he was dead.

"Now on that very day old Philip Hookhorn was down at Longpuddle Spring dipping up a pitcher of water ; and as he turned away, who should he see coming down to the spring on the other side but William, looking very pale and odd. This surprised Philip Hookhorn very much, for years before that time William's little son—his only child—had been drowned in that spring while at play there, and this had so preyed upon William's mind that he'd never been seen near the spring afterwards, and had been known to go half a mile out of his way to avoid the place. On inquiry, it was found that William in body could not have stood by the spring, being in the mead two miles off ; and it also came out that the time at which he was seen at the spring was the very time when he died."

"A rather melancholy story," observed the emigrant after a minute's silence.

"Yes, yes. Well, we must take ups and downs together," said the seedsman's father.

"You don't know, Mr. Lackland, I suppose, what a rum start that was between Andrey Satchel and Jane Vallens and the pa'son and clerk o' Scrimpton?" said the master-thatcher, a man with a spark of subdued liveliness in his eye, who had hitherto kept his attention mainly upon small objects a long way ahead, as he sat in front of the van with his feet outside. "Theirs was a queerer experience of a pa'son and clerk than some folks get, and may cheer 'ee up a little after this dampness that's been flung over yer soul.

The returned one replied that he knew nothing of the history, and should be happy to hear it, quite recollecting the personality of the man Satchel.

"Ah, no; this Andrey Satchel is the son of the Satchel that you knew; this one has not been married more than two or three years, and 'twas at the time o' the wedding that the accident happened that I could tell 'ee of, or anybody else here, for that matter."

"No, no; you must tell it, neighbor, if anybody," said several; a request in which Mr. Lackland joined, adding that the Satchel family was one he had known well before leaving home.

"I'll just mention, as you be a stranger," whispered the carrier to Lackland, "that Christopher's stories will bear pruning."

The emigrant nodded.

"Well, I can soon tell it," said the master-thatcher, schooling himself to a tone of actuality. "Though as it has more to do with the pa'son and clerk than with Andrey himself, it ought to be told by a better churchman than I."

ANDREY SATCHEL AND THE PARSON AND CLERK

"It all arose, you must know, from Andrey being fond of a drop of drink at that time—though he's a sober enough man now by all account, so much the better for him. Jane, his bride, you see, was somewhat older than Andrey; how much older I don't pretend to say; she was not one of our parish, and the register alone may be able to tell that. But, at any rate, her being a little ahead of her young man in mortal years, coupled with other bodily circumstances—"

("Ah, poor thing!" sighed the women.)

"—made her very anxious to get the thing done before he changed his mind; and 'twas with a joyful countenance (they say) that she, with Andrey and his brother and sister-in-law, marched off to church one November morning as soon as 'twas day a'most, to be made one with Andrey for the rest of her life. He had left our place long before it was light, and the folks that were up all waved their lanterns at him, and flung up their hats as he went.

"The church of her parish was a mile and more from the houses, and, as it was a wonderful fine day for the time of year, the plan was that as soon as they were married they would make out a holiday by driving straight off to Port Bredy, to see the ships and the sea and the sojers, instead of coming back to a meal at the house of the distant relation she lived wi', and moping about there all the afternoon.

"Well, some folks noticed that Andrey walked with rather wambling steps to church that morning; the truth o't was that his nearest neighbor's child had been christened the day before, and Andrey, having stood godfather, had stayed all night keeping up the christening, for he had said to himself, 'Not if I live to be a thousand shall I again be made a godfather one day and a husband the next and perhaps a father the next, and therefore I'll make the most of the blessing.' So that when he started from home in the morning he had not been in bed at all. The result was, as I say, that when he and his bride-to-be walked up the church to get married, the pa'son (who was a very strict man inside the church, whatever he was outside) looked hard at Andrey, and said, very sharp:

"'How's this, my man? You are in liquor. And so early, too. I'm ashamed of you!'

"'Well, that's true, sir,' says Andrey. 'But I can walk straight enough for practical purposes. I can walk a chalk-line,' he says (meaning no offence), 'as well as some other folk: and'— (getting hotter)—'I reckon that if you, Pa'son Billy Toogood, had kept up a christening all night so thoroughly as I have done, you wouldn't be able to stand at all; damn me if you would!'

"This answer made Pa'son Billy—as they used to call him—rather spitish, not to say hot, for he was a warm-tempered man if provoked, and he said, very decidedly: 'Well, I cannot marry you in this state; and I will not! Go home and get sober!' And he slapped the book together like a rat-trap.

"Then the bride burst out crying as if her heart would break, for very fear that she would lose Andrey after all her hard work to get him, and begged and implored the pa'son to go on with the ceremony. But no.

"'I won't be a party to your solemnizing matrimony with a tipsy man,' says Mr. Toogood. 'It is not right and decent. I am sorry for you, my young woman, but you'd better go home again. I wonder how you could think of bringing him here drunk like this.'

"'But if—if he don't come drunk he won't come at all, sir!' she says, through her sobs.

"'I can't help that,' says the pa'son; and plead as she might, it did not move him. Then she tried him another way.

"'Well, then, if you'll go home, sir, and leave us here, and come back to the church in an hour or two, I'll undertake to say that he shall be as sober as a judge,' she cries. 'We'll bide here, with your permission; for if he once goes out of this here church unmarried, all Van Amburgh's horses won't drag him back again!'

"'Very well,' says the pa'son. 'I'll give you two hours, and then I'll return.'

"'And please, sir, lock the door, so that we can't escape!' says she.

"'Yes,' says the pa'son.

"'And let nobody know that we are here.'

"The pa'son then took off his clane white surplice, and went away; and the others consulted upon the best means for keeping the matter a secret, which it was not a very hard thing to do, the place being so lonely, and the hour so early. The witnesses—Andrey's brother and brother's wife, neither one o' which cared about Andrey's marrying Jane, and had come rather against their will—said they couldn't wait two hours in that hole of a place, wishing to get home to Longpuddle before dinner-time. They were altogether so crusty that the clerk said there was no difficulty in their doing as they wished. They could go home as if their brother's wedding had actually taken place, and the married couple had gone onward for their day's pleasure jaunt to Port Bredy as intended. He, the clerk, and any casual passer-by would act as witnesses when the pa'son came back.

"This was agreed to, and away Andrey's relations went, nothing loath, and the clerk shut the church door and prepared to lock in the couple. The bride went up and whispered to him, with her eyes a-streaming still.

"'My dear good clerk,' she says, 'if we bide here in the church, folk may see us through the winders, and find out what has happened; and 'twould cause such a talk and scandal that I never should get over it; and perhaps, too, dear Andrey might try to get out and leave me! Will ye lock us up in the tower, my dear good clerk?' she says. 'I'll tole him in there if you will.'

"The clerk had no objection to do this to oblige the poor young woman, and they toled Andrey into the tower, and the clerk locked 'em both up straightway, and then went home, to return at the end of the two hours.

"Pa'son Toogood had not been long in his house after leaving the church when he saw a gentleman in pink and top-boots ride past his windows, and with a sudden flash of heat he called to mind that the hounds met that day just on the edge of his parish. The pa'son was one who dearly loved sport, and much he longed to be there.

"In short, except o' Sundays and at tide-times in the week, Pa'son Billy was the life o' the hunt. 'Tis true that he was poor, and that he rode all of a heap, and that his black mare was rat-tailed and old, and his tops older, and all over of one color, whity-brown, and full o' cracks. But he'd been in at the death of three thousand foxes. And—being a bachelor man—every time he went to bed in summer he used to open the bed at bottom and crawl up head-foremost, to mind en of the coming winter and the good sport he'd have, and the foxes going to earth. And whenever there was a christening at the squire's, and he had dinner there afterwards, as he always did, he never failed to christen the chiel over again in a bottle of port-wine.

"Now the clerk was the pa'son's groom and gardener and jineral manager, and had just got back to his work in the garden when he, too, saw the hunting man pass, and presently saw lots more of 'em, noblemen and gentry, and then he saw the hounds, the huntsman, Jim Treadhedge, the whipper-in, and I don't know who besides. The clerk loved going to cover as frantical as the pa'son, so much so that, whenever he saw or heard the pack, he could no more rule his feelings than if they were the winds of heaven. He might be bedding, or he might be sowing—all was forgot. So he throws down his spade and rushes in to the pa'son, who was by this time as frantical to go as he.

"'That there mare of yours, sir, do want exercise bad, very bad, this morning!' the clerk says, all of a tremble. 'Don't ye think I'd better trot her round the downs for an hour, sir?'

"'To be sure, she does want exercise badly. I'll trot her round myself,' says the pa'son.

"'Oh!—you'll trot her yerself? Well, there's the cob, sir. Really that cob is getting oncontrollable through biding in a stable so long! If you wouldn't mind my putting on the saddle—'

"'Very well. Take him out, certainly,' says the pa'son, never caring what the clerk did so long as he himself could get off immediately. So, scrambling into his riding-boots and breeches as quick as he could, he rode off towards the meet, intending to be back in an hour. No sooner was he gone than the clerk mounted the cob, and was off after him. When the pa'son got to the meet, he found a lot of friends, and was as jolly as he could be; the hounds found a'most as soon as they threw off, and there was great excitement. So, forgetting that he had meant to go back at once, away rides the pa'son with the rest o' the hunt, all across the fallow ground that lies between Lippet Wood and Green's Copse; and as he galloped he looked behind for a moment, and there was the clerk close to his heels.

"'Ha, ha, clerk—you here?' he says.

"'Yes, sir, here be I,' says t'other.

"'Fine exercise for the horses!'

"'Aye, sir—hee, hee!' says the clerk.

"So they went on and on, into Green's Copse, then across to Higher Jirton; then on across this very turnpike road to Climmerston Ridge, then away towards Yalbury Wood; up hill and down dale, like the very wind, the clerk close to the pa'son, and the pa'son not far from the hounds. Never was there a finer run knowed with that pack than they had that day; and neither pa'son nor clerk thought one word about the unmarried couple locked up in the church-tower waiting to get j'ined.

"'These hosses of yours, sir, will be much improved by this,' says the clerk as he rode along, just a neck behind the pa'son. ''Twas a happy thought of your reverent mind to bring 'em out to-day. Why, it may be frosty in a day or two, and then the poor things mid not be able to leave the stable for weeks.'

"'They may not, they may not, it is true. A merciful man is merciful to his beast,' says the pa'son.

"'Hee, hee!' says the clerk, glancing sly into the pa'son's eye.

"'Ha, ha!' says the pa'son, a-glancing back into the clerk's. 'Halloo!' he shouts, as he sees the fox break cover at that moment.

"'Halloo!' cries the clerk. 'There he goes! Why, dammy, there's two foxes—'

"'Hush, clerk, hush! Don't let me hear that word again! Remember our calling.'

"'True, sir, true. But really, good sport do carry away a man so that he's apt to forget his high persuasion!' And the next minute the corner of the clerk's eye shot again into the corner of the pa'son's, and the pa'son's back again to the clerk's. 'Hee, hee!' said the clerk.

"'Ha, ha!' said Pa'son Toogood.

"'Ah, sir,' says the clerk again, 'this is better than crying Amen to your Ever-and-ever on a winter's morning!'

"'Yes, indeed, clerk! To everything there's a season,' says Pa'son Toogood, quite pat, for he was a learned Christian man when he liked, and had chapter and ve'se at his tongue's end, as a pa'son should.

"At last, late in the day, the hunting came to an end by the fox running into a' old woman's cottage, under her table, and up the clock-case. The pa'son and clerk were among the first in at the death, their faces a-staring in at the old woman's winder, and the clock striking as he'd never been heard to strik' before. Then came the question of finding their way home.

"Neither the pa'son nor the clerk knowed how they were going to do this, for their beasts were wellnigh tired down to the ground. But they started back along as well as they could, though they were so done up that they could only drag along at a' amble, and not much of that at a time.

"'We shall never, never get there!' groaned Mr. Toogood, quite bowed down.

"'Never!' groans the clerk. ''Tis a judgment upon us for our iniquities!'

"'I fear it is,' murmurs the pa'son.

"Well, 'twas quite dark afore they entered the pa'sonage gate, having crept into the parish as quiet as if they'd stole a hammer, little wishing their congregation to know what they'd been up to all day long. And as they were so dog-tired, and so anxious about the horses, never once did they think of the unmarried couple. As soon as ever the horses had been stabled and fed, and the pa'son and clerk had had a bit and a sup theirselves, they went to bed.

"Next morning when Pa'son Toogood was at breakfast, thinking of the glorious sport he'd had the day before, the clerk came in a hurry to the door and asked to see him.

"'It has just come into my mind, sir, that we've forgot all about the couple that we was to have married yesterday!'

"The half-chawed victuals dropped from the pa'son's mouth as if he'd been shot. 'Bless my soul,' says he, 'so we have! How very awkward!'

"'It is, sir; very. Perhaps we've ruined the 'ooman!'

"'Ah—to be sure—I remember! She ought to have been married before.'

"'If anything has happened to her up in that there tower, and no doctor or nuss—'

("Ah—poor thing!" sighed the women.)

"'—'twill be a quarter-sessions matter for us, not to speak of the disgrace to the Church!'

"'Good God, clerk, don't drive me wild!' says the pa'son. 'Why the hell didn't I marry 'em, drunk or sober!' (Pa'sons used to cuss in them days like plain honest men.) 'Have you been to the church to see what happened to them, or inquired in the village?'

"'Not I, sir! It only came into my head a moment ago, and I always like to be second to you in Church matters. You could have knocked me down with a sparrer's feather when I thought o't, sir; I assure 'ee you could!'

"Well, the pa'son jumped up from his breakfast, and together they went off to the church.

"'It is not at all likely that they are there now,' says Mr. Toogood, as they went; 'and indeed I hope they are not. They be pretty sure to have 'scaped and gone home.'

"However, they opened the church-hatch, entered the church-yard, and, looking up at the tower, there they seed a little small white face at the belfry winder, and a little small hand waving. 'Twas the bride.

"'God my life, clerk,' says Mr. Toogood, 'I don't know how to face 'em!' And he sank down upon a tombstone. 'How I wish I hadn't been so cussed particular!'

"'Yes—'twas a pity we didn't finish it when we'd begun,' the clerk said. 'Still, since the feelings of your holy priestcraft wouldn't let ye, the couple must put up with it.'

"'True, clerk, true! Does she look as if anything premature had took place?'

"'I can't see her no lower down than her armpits, sir.'

"'Well—how do her face look?'

"'It do look mighty white!'

"'Well, we must know the worst! Dear me, how the small of my back do ache from that ride yesterday! . . . But to more godly business.'

"They went on into the church, and unlocked the tower stairs, and immediately poor Jane and Andrey busted out like starved mice from a cupboard, Andrey limp and sober enough now, and his bride pale and cold, but otherwise as usual.

"'What,' says the pa'son, with a great breath of relief, 'you haven't been here ever since?'

"'Yes, we have, sir!' says the bride, sinking down upon a seat in her weakness. "Not a morsel, wet or dry, have we had since! It was impossible to get out without help, and here we've stayed.'

"'But why didn't you shout, good souls?' said the pa'son.

"'She wouldn't let me,' says Andrey.

"'Because we were so ashamed at what had led to it,' sobs Jane. 'We felt that if it were noised abroad it would cling to us all our lives! Once or twice Andrey had a good mind to toll the bell, but then he said: "No; I'll starve first. I won't bring disgrace on my name and yours, my dear." And so we waited, and waited, and walked round and round; but never did you come till now!'

"'To my regret!' says the pa'son. 'Now, then, we will soon get it over.'

"'I—I should like some victuals,' said Andrey; ''twould gie me courage if it is only a crust o' bread and a' onion; for I am that leery that I can feel my stomach rubbing against my backbone.'

"'I think we had better get it done,' said the bride, a bit anxious in manner; 'since we are all here convenient, too.'

"Andrey gave way about the victuals, and the clerk called in a second witness who wouldn't be likely to gossip about it, and soon the knot was tied, and the bride looked smiling and calm forthwith, and Andrey limper than ever.

"'Now,' said Pa'son Toogood, 'you two must come to my house, and have a good lining put to your insides before you go a step farther.'

"They were very glad of the offer, and went out of the church-yard by one path while the pa'son and clerk went out by the other, and so did not attract notice, it being still early. They entered the rectory as if they'd just come back from their trip to Port Bredy; and then they knocked in the victuals and drink till they could hold no more.

"It was a long while before the story of what they had gone through was known, but it was talked of in time, and they themselves laugh over it now; though what Jane got for her pains was no great bargain after all. 'Tis true she saved her name."

"Was that the same Andrey who went to the squire's house as one of the Christmas fiddlers?" asked the seedsman.

"No, no," replied Mr. Profitt, the school-master. "It was his father did that. Aye, it was all owing to his being such a man for eating and drinking." Finding that he had the ear of the audience, the school-master continued without delay:

OLD ANDREY'S EXPERIENCE AS A MUSICIAN

"I WAS one of the choir-boys at that time, and we and the players were to appear at the manor-house as usual that Christmas week to play and sing in the hall to the squire's people and visitors (among 'em being the archdeacon, Lord and Lady Baxby, and I don't know who); afterwards going, as we always did, to have a good supper in the servants' hall. Andrew knew this was the custom, and meeting us when we we were starting to go, he said to us: 'Lord, how I should like to join in that meal of beef and turkey and plum-pudding and ale that you happy ones be going to just now! One more or less will make no difference to the squire. I am too old to pass as a singing boy, and too bearded to pass as a singing girl; can ye lend me a fiddle, neighbors, that I may come with ye as a bandsman?'

"Well, we didn't like to be hard upon him, and lent him an old one, though Andrew knew no more of music than the Cerne Giant; and armed with the instrument he walked up to the squire's house with the others of us at the time appointed, and went in boldly, his fiddle under his arm. He made himself as natural as he could in opening the music-books and moving the candles to the best points for throwing light upon the notes; and all went well till we had played and sung 'While shepherds watch,' and 'Star, arise,' and 'Hark the glad sound.' Then the squire's mother, a tall, gruff old lady, who was much interested in Church music, said quite unexpectedly to Andrew: 'My man, I see you don't play your instrument with the rest. How is that?'

"Every one of the choir was ready to sink into the earth with concern at the fix Andrew was in. We could see that he had fallen into a cold sweat, and how he would get out of it we did not know.

"'I've had a misfortune, mem,' he says, bowing as meek as a child. 'Coming along the road I fell down and broke my bow.'

"'Oh, I am sorry to hear that,' says she. 'Can't it be mended?'

"'Oh no, mem,' says Andrew. ''Twas broke all to splinters.'

"'I'll see what I can do for you,' says she.

"And then it seemed all over, and we played 'Rejoice, ye drowsy mortals all,' in D and two sharps. But no sooner had we got through it than she says to Andrew:

"'I've sent up into the attic, where we have some old musical instruments, and found a bow for you.' And she hands the bow to poor wretched Andrew, who didn't even know which end to take hold of. 'Now we shall have the full accompaniment,' says she.

"Andrew's face looked as if it were made of rotten apple as he stood in the circle of players in front of his book; for if there was one person in the parish that everybody was afraid of 'twas this hook-nosed old lady. However, by keeping a little behind the next man he managed to make pretence of beginning, sawing away with his bow without letting it touch the strings, so that it looked as if he were driving into the tune with heart and soul. 'Tis a question if he wouldn't have got through all right if one of the squire's visitors, no other than the archdeacon, hadn't noticed that he held the fiddle upside-down, the nut under his chin, and the tail-piece in his hand, and they began to crowd round him, thinking 'twas some new way of performing.

"This revealed everything; the squire's mother had Andrew turned out of the house as a vile impostor, and there was great interruption to the harmony of the proceedings, the squire declaring he should have notice to leave his cottage that day fortnight. However, when we got to the servants' hall there sat Andrew, who had been let in at the back door by the orders of the squire's wife, after being turned out at the front by the orders of the squire, and nothing more was heard about his leaving his cottage. But Andrew never performed in public as a musician after that night; and now he's dead and gone, poor man, as we all shall be."

"I had quite forgotten the old choir, with their fiddles and bass-viols," said the home-comer, musingly. "Are they still going on the same as of old?"

"Bless the man!" said Christopher Twink, the master-thatcher; "why, they've been done away with these twenty year. A young teetotaler plays the organ in church now, and plays it very well; though 'tis not quite such good music as in old times, because the organ is one of them that go with a winch, and the young teetotaler says he can't always throw the proper feeling into the tune without wellnigh working his arms off."

"Why did they make the change, then?"

"Well, partly because of fashion, partly because the old musicians got into a sort of scrape. A terrible scrape 'twas, too—wasn't it, John? I shall never forget it—never! They lost their character as officers of the church as complete as if they'd never had any character at all."

"That was very bad for them."

"Yes." The master-thatcher attentively regarded past times as if they lay about a mile off, and went on:

ABSENT-MINDEDNESS IN A PARISH CHOIR

"It happened on Sunday after Christmas—the last Sunday they ever played in Longpuddle church gallery, as it turned out, though they didn't know it then. As you may know, sir, the players formed a very good band—almost as good as the Mellstock parish players that were led by the Dewys ; and that's saying a great deal. There was Nicholas Puddingcome, the leader, with the first fiddle ; there was Timothy Thomas, the bass-viol man ; John Biles, the tenor fiddler ; Dan'l Hornhead, with the serpent ; Robert Dowdle, with the clarionet ; and Mr. Nicks, with the oboe—all sound and powerful musicians, and strong-winded men—they that blowed. For that reason they were very much in demand Christmas week for little reels and dancing-parties ; for they could turn a jig or a hornpipe out of hand as well as ever they could turn out a psalm, and perhaps better, not to speak irreverent. In short, one half-hour they could be playing a Christmas carol in the squire's hall to the ladies and gentlemen, and drinking tay and coffee with 'em as modest as saints ; and the next, at the Tinker's Arms, blazing away like wild horses with the 'Dashing White Sergeant' to nine couple of dancers and more, and swallowing rum-and-cider hot as flame.

"Well, this Christmas they'd been out to one rattling randy after another every night, and had got next to no sleep at all. Then came the Sunday after Christmas, their fatal day. 'Twas so mortal cold that year that they could hardly sit in the gallery ;

for though the congregation down in the body of the church had a stove to keep off the frost, the players in the gallery had nothing at all. So Nicholas said at morning service, when 'twas freezing an inch an hour, 'Please the Lord I won't stand this numbing weather no longer; this afternoon we'll have something in our insides to make us warm if it cost a king's ransom.'

"So he brought a gallon of hot brandy and beer, ready mixed, to church with him in the afternoon, and by keeping the jar well wrapped up in Timothy Thomas's bass-viol bag it kept drinkably warm till they wanted it, which was just a thimbleful in the Absolution, and another after the Creed, and the remainder at the beginning o' the sermon. When they'd had the last pull they felt quite comfortable and warm, and as the sermon went on—most unfortunately for 'em it was a long one that afternoon—they fell asleep, every man jack of 'em; and there they slept on as sound as rocks.

"'Twas a very dark afternoon, and by the end of the sermon all you could see of the inside of the church were the pa'son's two candles alongside of him in the pulpit, and his spaking face behind 'em. The sermon being ended at last, the pa'son gie'd out the Evening Hymn. But no choir set about sounding up the tune, and the people began to turn their heads to learn the reason why, and then Levi Limpet, a boy who sat in the gallery, nudged Timothy and Nicholas, and said, 'Begin! begin!'

"'Hey, what?' says Nicholas, starting up; and the church being so dark and his head so muddled he thought he was at the party they had played at all the night before, and away he went, bow and fiddle, at 'The Devil among the Tailors,' the favorite jig of our neighborhood at that time. The rest of the band, being in the same state of mind and nothing doubting, followed their leader with all their strength, according to custom. They poured out that there tune till the lower bass notes of 'The Devil among the Tailors' made the cobwebs in the roof shiver like ghosts; then Nicholas, seeing nobody moved, shouted out as he scraped (in his usual commanding way at dances when the folk didn't know the figures), 'Top couples cross hands! And when I make the fiddle squeak at the end, every man kiss his pardner under the mistletoe!'

"The boy Levi was so frightened that he bolted down the gallery stairs and out homeward like lightning. The pa'son's hair fairly stood on end when he heard the evil tune raging through the church; and thinking the choir had gone crazy, he held up his hand and said: 'Stop, stop, stop! Stop, stop! What's this?' But they didn't hear 'n for the noise of their own playing, and the more he called the louder they played.

"Then the folks came out of their pews, wondering down to the ground, and saying: 'What do they mean by such wickedness? We shall be consumed like Sodom and Gomorrah!'

"Then the squire came out of his pew lined wi' green baize, where lots of lords and ladies visiting at the house were worshipping along with him, and went and stood in front of the gallery, and shook his fist in the musicians' faces, saying, 'What! In this reverent edifice! What!'

"And at last they heard 'n through their playing, and stopped.

"'Never such an insulting, disgraceful thing—never!' says the squire, who couldn't rule his passion.

"'Never!' says the pa'son, who had come down and stood beside him.

"'Not if the angels of Heaven,' says the squire, (he was a wickedish man, the squire was, though now for once he happened to be on the Lord's side)—'not if the angels of Heaven come down,' he says, 'shall one of you villanous players ever sound a note in this church again; for the insult to me, and my family, and my visitors, and God Almighty, that you've a-perpetrated this afternoon!'

"Then the unfortunate church band came to their senses, and remembered where they were; and 'twas a sight to see Nicholas Puddingcome and Timothy Thomas and John Biles creep down the gallery stairs with their fiddles under their arms, and poor Dan'l Hornhead with his serpent, and Robert Dowdle with his clarionet, all looking as little as ninepins; and out they went. The pa'son might have forgi'ed 'em when he learned the truth o't, but the squire would not. That very week he sent for a barrel-organ that would play two-and-twenty new psalm tunes, so exact and particular that, however sinful inclined you was, you could play nothing but psalm tunes whatsomever. He had a really respectable man to turn the winch, as I said, and the old players played no more."

"And, of course, my old acquaintance, the annuitant, Mrs. Winter, who always seemed to have something on her mind, is dead and gone?" said the home-comer, after a long silence.

Nobody in the van seemed to recollect the name.

"Oh yes, she must be dead long since; she was seventy when I as a child knew her," he added.

"I can recollect Mrs. Winter very well, if nobody else can," said the aged groceress. "Yes, she's been dead these five-and-twenty year at least. You knew what it was upon her mind, sir, that gave her that hollow-eyed look, I suppose?"

"It had something to do with a son of hers, I think I once was told. But I was too young to know particulars."

The groceress sighed as she conjured up a vision of days long past. "Yes," she murmured, "it had all to do with a son." Finding that the van was still in a listening mood, she spoke on:

THE WINTERS AND THE PALMLEYS

"To go back to the beginning—if one must—there were two women in the parish when I was a child who were to a certain extent rivals in good looks. Never mind particulars, but in consequence of this they were at daggers-drawn, and they did not love each other any better when one of them tempted the other's lover away from her and married him. He was a young man of the name of Winter, and in due time they had a son.

"The other woman did not marry for many years; but when she was about thirty a quiet man named Palmley asked her to be his wife, and she accepted him. You don't mind when the Palmleys were Longpuddle folk, but I do well. She had a son also, who was, of course, nine or ten years younger than the son of the first. The child proved to be of rather weak intellect, though his mother loved him as the apple of her eye.

"This woman's husband died when the child was eight years old, and left his widow and boy in poverty. Her former rival, also a widow now, but fairly well provided for, offered for pity's sake to take the child as errand-boy, small as he was, her own son, Jack, being hard upon seventeen. Her poor neighbor could do no better than let the child go there. And to the richer woman's house little Palmley straightway went.

"Well, in some way or other—how, it was never exactly known—the thriving woman, Mrs. Winter, sent the little boy with a message to the next village one December day, much against his will. It was getting dark, and the child prayed to be allowed not to go, because he would be afraid coming home. But the mistress insisted, more out of thoughtlessness than cruelty, and the child went. On his way back he had to pass through Yalbury Wood, and something came out from behind a tree and frightened him into fits. The child was quite ruined by it; he became quite a drivelling idiot, and soon afterwards died.

"Then the other woman had nothing left to live for, and vowed vengeance against that rival who had first won away her lover, and now had been the cause of her bereavement. This last affliction was certainly not intended by her thriving acquaintance, though it must be owned that when it was done she seemed but little concerned. Whatever vengeance poor Mrs. Palmley felt, she had no opportunity of carrying it out, and time might have softened her feelings into forgetfulness of her supposed wrongs as she dragged on her lonely life. So matters stood when, a year after the death of the child, Mrs. Palmley's niece, who had been born and bred in the city of Exonbury, came to live with her.

"This young woman—Miss Harriet Palmley—was a proud and handsome girl, very well brought up, and more stylish and genteel than the people of our village, as was natural, considering where she came from. She regarded herself as much above Mrs. Winter and her son in position as Mrs. Winter and her son considered themselves above poor Mrs. Palmley. But love is an unceremonious thing, and what in the world should happen but that young Jack Winter must fall wofully and wildly in love with Harriet Palmley almost as soon as he saw her.

"She, being better educated than he, and caring

nothing for the village notion of his mother's superiority to her aunt, did not give him much encouragement. But Longpuddle being no very large world, the two could not help seeing a good deal of each other while she was staying there, and, disdainful young woman as she was, she did seem to take a little pleasure in his attentions and advances.

"One day, when they were picking apples together, he asked her to marry him. She had not expected anything so practical as that at so early a time, and was led by her surprise into a half-promise; at any rate, she did not absolutely refuse him, and accepted some little presents that he made her.

"But he saw that her view of him was rather as a simple village lad than as a young man to look up to, and he felt that he must do something bold to secure her. So he said one day, 'I am going away, to try to get into a better position than I can get here.' In two or three weeks he wished her good-bye, and went away to Monksbury to superintend a farm, with a view to start as a farmer himself; and from there he wrote regularly to her, as if their marriage were an understood thing.

"Now, Harriet liked the young man's presents and the admiration of his eyes, but on paper he was less attractive to her. Her mother had been a school-mistress, and Harriet had besides a natural aptitude for pen-and-ink work, in days when to be a ready writer was not such a common thing as it is now, and when actual handwriting was valued as an accomplishment in itself. Jack Winter's performances in the shape of love-letters quite jarred her city nerves and her finer taste, and when she answered one of them, in the lovely running hand that she took such pride in, she very strictly and loftily bade him to practise with a pen and spelling-book if he wished to please her,

Whether he listened to her request or not nobody knows, but his letters did not improve. He ventured to tell her in his clumsy way that if her heart were more warm towards him she would not be so nice about his handwriting and spelling; which indeed was true enough.

"Well, in Jack's absence the weak flame that had been set alight in Harriet's heart soon sank low, and at last went out altogether. He wrote and wrote, and begged and prayed her to give a reason for her coldness; and then she told him plainly that she was town born, and he was not sufficiently well educated to please her.

"Jack Winter's want of pen-and-ink training did not make him less thin-skinned than others; in fact, he was terribly tender and touchy about anything. This reason that she gave for finally throwing him over grieved him, shamed him, and mortified him more than can be told in these times, the pride of that day in being able to write with beautiful flourishes, and the sorrow at not being able to do so, raging so high. Jack replied to her with an angry note, and then she hit back with smart little stings, telling him how many words he had misspelled in his last letter, and declaring again that this alone was sufficient justification for any woman to put an end to an understanding with him. Her husband must be a better scholar.

"He bore her rejection of him in silence, but his suffering was sharp—all the sharper in being untold. She communicated with Jack no more; and as his reason for going out into the world had been only to provide a home worthy of her, he had no further object in planning such a home, now that she was lost to him. He therefore gave up the farming occupation by which he had hoped to make himself a master-farmer, and left the spot to return to his mother.

"As soon as he got back to Longpuddle he found that Harriet had already looked wi' favor upon another lover. He was a young road-contractor, and Jack could not but admit that his rival was, both in manners and scholarship, much ahead of him. Indeed, a more sensible match for the beauty who had been dropped into the village by fate could hardly have been found than this man, who could offer her so much better a chance than Jack could have done, with his uncertain future and narrow abilities for grappling with the world. The fact was so clear to him that he could hardly blame her.

"One day by accident Jack saw on a scrap of paper the handwriting of Harriet's new beloved. It was flowing like a stream, well spelled, the work of a man accustomed to the ink-bottle and the dictionary—of a man already called in the parish a good scholar. And then it struck all of a sudden into Jack's mind what a contrast the letters of this young man must make to his own miserable old letters, and how ridiculous they must make his lines appear. He groaned and wished he had never written to her, and wondered if she had ever kept his poor performances. Possibly she had kept them, for women are in the habit of doing that, he thought; and while they were in her hands there was always a chance of his honest, stupid love assurances to her being joked over by Harriet with her present lover, or by anybody who should accidentally uncover them.

"The nervous, moody young man could not bear the thought of it, and at length decided to ask her to return them, as was proper when engagements were broken off. He was some hours in framing, copying, and recopying the short note in which he made his request, and having finished it, he sent it to her house. His messenger came back with the answer, by word of mouth, that Miss Palmley bade him say she should not part with what was hers, and wondered at his boldness in troubling her.

"Jack was much affronted at this, and determined to go for his letters himself. He chose a time when he knew she was at home, and knocked and went in without much ceremony; for though Harriet was so high and mighty, Jack had small respect for her aunt, Mrs. Palmley, whose little child had been his boot-cleaner in earlier days. Harriet was in the room, this being the first time they had met since she had jilted him. He asked for his letters with a stern and bitter look at her.

"At first she said he might have them for all that she cared, and took them out of the bureau where she kept them. Then she glanced over the outside one of the packet, and, suddenly altering her mind, she told him shortly that his request was a silly one, and slipped the letters into her aunt's work-box, which stood open on the table, locking it, and saying with a bantering laugh that of course she thought it best to keep 'em, since they might be useful to produce as evidence that she had good cause for declining to marry him.

"He blazed up hot. 'Give me those letters!' he said. 'They are mine!'

"'No, they are not,' she replied; 'they are mine.'

"'Whos'ever they are I want them back,' says he. 'I don't want to be made sport of for my penmanship: you've another young man now! He has your confidence, and you pour all your tales into his ear. You'll be showing them to him!'

"'Perhaps,' said my lady Harriet, with calm coolness, like the heartless woman that she was.

"Her manner so maddened him that he made a step towards the work-box, but she snatched it up, locked it in the bureau, and turned upon him triumphant. For a moment he seemed to be going to wrench the key of the bureau out of her hand; but he stopped himself, and swung round upon his heel and went away.

"When he was out-of-doors alone, and it got night, he walked about restless, and stinging with the sense of being beaten at all points by her. He could not help fancying her telling her new lover or her acquaintances of this scene with himself, and laughing with them over those poor blotted, crooked lines of his that he had been so anxious to obtain. As the evening passed on he worked himself into a dogged resolution to have them back at any price, come what might.

"At the dead of night he came out of his mother's house by the back door, and creeping through the garden hedge went along the field adjoining till he reached the back of her aunt's dwelling. The moon struck bright and flat upon the walls, 'twas said, and every shiny leaf of the creepers was like a little looking-glass in the rays. From long acquaintance Jack knew the arrangement and position of everything in Mrs. Palmley's house as well as in his own mother's. The back window close to him was a casement with little leaded squares, as it is to this day, and was, as now, one of two lighting the sitting-room. The other, being in front, was closed up with shutters, but this back one had not even a blind, and the moonlight as it streamed in showed every article of the furniture to him outside. To the right of the room is the fireplace, as you may remember; to the left was the bureau at that time; inside the bureau was Harriet's work-box, as he supposed (though it was really her aunt's), and inside the work-box were his letters. Well, he took out his pocket-knife, and without noise lifted the leading of one of the panes, so that he could take out the glass, and putting his hand through the hole he unfastened the casement, and climbed in through the opening. All the household — that is to say, Mrs. Palmley, Harriet, and the little maid-servant—were asleep. Jack went straight to the bureau, so he said, hoping it might have been unfastened again — it not being kept locked in ordinary — but Harriet had never unfastened it since she secured her letters there the day before. Jack told afterwards how he thought of her asleep up-stairs, caring nothing for him, and of the way she had made sport of him and of his letters; and having advanced so far, he was not to be hindered now. By forcing the large blade of his knife under the flap of the bureau he burst the weak lock ; within was the rosewood work-box just as she had placed it in her hurry to keep it from him. There being no time to spare for getting the letters out of it then, he took it under his arm, shut the bureau, and made the best of his way out of the house, latching the casement behind him, and refixing the pane of glass in its place.

"Winter found his way back to his mother's as he had come, and being dog-tired, crept up-stairs to bed, hiding the box till he could destroy its contents. The next morning early he set about doing this, and carried it to the linhay at the back of his mother's dwelling. Here by the hearth he opened the box, and began burning one by one the letters that had cost him so much labor to write and shame to think of, meaning to return the box to Harriet, after repairing the slight damage he had caused it by opening it without a key, with a note—the last she would ever receive from him—telling her triumphantly that in refusing to return what he had asked for she had calculated too surely upon his submission to her whims.

"But on removing the last letter from the box he received a shock; for underneath it, at the very bottom, lay money—several golden guineas—'Doubtless Harriet's pocket-money,' he said to himself; though it was not, but Mrs. Palmley's. Before he had got over his qualms at this discovery he heard footsteps coming through the house-passage to where he was. In haste he pushed the box and what was in it under some brushwood which lay in the linhay; but Jack had been already seen. Two constables entered the out-house, and seized him as he knelt before the fire-place, securing the work-box and all it contained at the same moment. They had come to apprehend him on a charge of breaking into the dwelling-house of Mrs. Palmley on the night preceding; and almost before the lad knew what had happened to him they were leading him along the lane that connects that end of the village with this turnpike-road, and along they marched him between 'em all the way to Casterbridge jail.

"Jack's act amounted to night burglary—though he had never thought of it—and burglary was felony, and a capital offence in those days. His figure had been seen by some one against the bright wall as he came away from Mrs. Palmley's back window, and the box and money were found in his possession, while the evidence of the broken bureau lock and tinkered window-pane was more than enough for circumstantial detail. Whether his protestation that he went only for his letters, which he believed to be wrongfully kept from him, would have availed him anything if supported by other evidence I do not know; but the one person who could have borne it out was Harriet, and she acted entirely under the sway of her aunt. That aunt was deadly towards Jack Winter. Mrs. Palmley's time had come. Here was her revenge upon the woman who first won away her lover, and next ruined and deprived her of her one heart's treasure—her little son. When the assize week drew on, and Jack had to stand his trial, Harriet did not appear in the case at all, which was allowed to take its course, Mrs. Palmley testifying to the general facts of the burglary. Whether Harriet would have come forward if Jack had appealed to her is not known; possibly she would have done it for pity's sake; but Jack was too proud to ask a single favor of a girl who had jilted him, and he let her alone. The trial was a short one, and the death sentence was passed.

"The day o' young Jack's execution was a cold, dusty Saturday in March. He was so boyish and slim that they were obliged in mercy to hang him in the heaviest fetters kept in the jail, lest his heft should not break his neck, and they weighed so upon him that he could hardly drag himself up to the drop. At that time the gover'ment was not strict about burying the body of an executed person within the precincts of the prison, and at the earnest prayer of his poor mother his body was allowed to be brought home. All the parish waited at their cottage doors in the evening for its arrival; I remember how, as a very little girl, I stood by my mother's side. About eight o'clock, as we hearkened on our door-stones in the cold, bright starlight, we could hear the faint crackle of a wagon from the direction of the turnpike-road. The noise was lost as the wagon dropped into a hollow, then it was plain again as it lumbered down the next long incline, and presently it entered Longpuddle. The coffin was laid in the belfry for the night, and the next day, Sunday, between the services, we buried him. A funeral sermon was preached the same afternoon, the text chosen being, 'He was the only son of his mother, and she was a widow.' . . . Yes, they were cruel times!

"As for Harriet, she and her lover were married in due time; but by all account her life was no jocund one. She and her good-man found that they could not live comfortably at Longpuddle by reason of her connection with Jack's misfortunes, and they settled in a distant town, and were no more heard of by us; Mrs. Palmley, too, found it advisable to join 'em shortly after. The dark-eyed, gaunt old Mrs. Winter, remembered by the emigrant gentleman here, was, as you will have foreseen, the Mrs. Winter of this story; and I can well call to mind how lonely she was, how afraid the children were of her, and how she kept herself as a stranger among us, though she lived so long."

"Longpuddle has had her sad experiences as well as her sunny ones," said Mr. Lackland.

"Yes, yes. But I am thankful to say not many like that, though good and bad have lived among us."

"There was Georgy Crookhill—he was one of the shady sort, as I have reason to know," observed the registrar, with the manner of a man who would like to have his say also.

"I used to hear what he was as a boy at school."

"Well, as he began so he went on. It never got so far as a hanging matter with him, to be sure; but he had some narrow escapes of penal servitude, and once it was a case of the biter bit."

INCIDENT IN THE LIFE OF MR. GEORGE CROOKHILL

"One day," the registrar continued, "Georgy was ambling out of Melchester on a miserable screw, the fair being just over, when he saw in front of him a fine-looking young farmer riding out of the town in the same direction. He was mounted on a good, strong, handsome animal, worth fifty guineas if worth a crown. When they were going up Bissett Hill, Georgy made it his business to overtake the young farmer. They passed the time o' day to one another; Georgy spoke of the state of the roads, and jogged alongside the well-mounted stranger in very friendly conversation. The farmer had not been inclined to say much to Georgy at first, but by degrees he grew quite affable, too—as friendly as Georgy was towards him. He told Crookhill that he had been doing business at Melchester fair, and was going on as far as Shottsford-Forum that night, so as to reach Casterbridge market the next day. When they came to Woodyates Inn they stopped to bait their horses, and agreed to drink together; with this they got more friendly than ever, and on they went again. Before they had nearly reached Shottsford it came on to rain, and as they were now passing through the village of Trantridge, and it was quite dark, Georgy persuaded the young farmer to go no farther that night; the rain would most likely give them a chill. For his part he had heard that the little inn here was comfortable, and he meant to stay. At last the young farmer agreed to put up there also; and they dismounted and entered, and had a good supper together, and talked over their affairs like men who had known and proved each other a long time. When it was the hour for retiring they went up-stairs to a double-bedded room which Georgy Crookhill had asked the landlord to let them share, so sociable were they.

"Before they fell asleep they talked across the room about one thing and another, running from this to that till the conversation turned upon disguises, and changing clothes for particular ends. The farmer told Georgy that he had often heard tales of people doing it, but Crookhill professed to be very ignorant of all such tricks; and soon the young farmer sank into slumber.

"Early in the morning, while the tall young farmer was still asleep (I tell the story as 'twas told me), honest Georgy crept out of his bed by stealth, and dressed himself in the farmer's clothes, in the pockets of the said clothes being the farmer's money. Now though Georgy particularly wanted the farmer's nice clothes and nice horse, owing to a little transaction at the fair which made it desirable that he should not be too easily recognized, his desires had their bounds; he did not wish to take his young friend's money, at any rate more of it than was necessary for paying his bill. This he abstracted, and leaving the farmer's purse containing the rest on the bedroom table, went downstairs. The inn folks had not particularly noticed the faces of their customers, and the one or two who were up at this hour had no thought but that Georgy was the farmer; so when he had paid the bill very liberally, and said he must be off, no objection was made to his getting the farmer's horse saddled for himself; and he rode away upon it as if it were his own.

"About half an hour after the young farmer awoke, and looking across the room saw that his friend Georgy had gone away in clothes which didn't belong to him, and had kindly left for himself the seedy ones worn by Georgy. At this he sat up in a deep thought for some time, instead of hastening to give an alarm. 'The money, the money is gone,' he said to himself, 'and that's bad. But so are the clothes.'

"He then looked upon the table and saw that the money, or most of it, had been left behind.

"'Ha, ha, ha!' he cried, and began to dance about the room. 'Ha, ha, ha!' he said again, and made beautiful smiles to himself in the shaving-glass and in the brass candlestick; and then swung about his arms for all the world as if he were going through the sword exercise.

"When he had dressed himself in Georgy's clothes and gone down-stairs, he did not seem to mind at all that they took him for the other; and even when he saw that he had been left a bad horse for a good one, he was not inclined to cry out. They told him his friend had paid the bill, at which he seemed much pleased, and without waiting for breakfast he mounted Georgy's horse and rode away likewise, choosing the nearest by-lane in preference to the high-road, without knowing that Georgy had chosen that by-lane also.

"He had not trotted more than two miles in the personal character of Georgy Crookhill when, suddenly rounding a bend that the lane made thereabout, he came upon a man struggling in the hands of two village constables. It was his friend Georgy, the borrower of his clothes and horse. But so far was the young farmer from showing any alacrity in rushing forward to claim his property that he would have turned the poor beast he rode into the wood adjoining, if he had not been already perceived.

"'Help, help, help!' cried the constables. 'Assistance in the name of the Crown!'

"The young farmer could do nothing but ride forward. 'What's the matter?' he inquired, as coolly as he could.

"'A deserter—a deserter!' said they. 'One who's to be tried by court-martial and shot without parley. He deserted from the Dragoons at Cheltenham some days ago, and was tracked; but the search-party can't find him anywhere, and we told 'em if we met him we'd hand him on to 'em forthwith. The day after he left the barracks the rascal met a respectable farmer and made him drunk at an inn, and told him what a fine soldier he would make, and coaxed him to change clothes, to see how well a military uniform would become him. This the simple farmer did; when our deserter said that for a joke he would leave the room and go to the landlady, to see if she would know him in that dress. He never came back, and Farmer Jollice found himself in soldier's clothes, the money in his pockets gone, and, when he got to the stable, his horse gone too.'

"'A scoundrel!' says the young man in Georgy's clothes. 'And is this the wretched caitiff?' (pointing to Georgy).

"'No, no!' cries Georgy, as innocent as a babe of this matter of the soldier's desertion. 'He's the man! He was wearing Farmer Jollice's suit o' clothes, and he slept in the same room wi' me, and brought up the subject of changing clothes, which put it into my head to dress myself in his suit before he was awake. He's got on mine!'

"'D'ye hear the villain?' groans the tall young man to the constables. 'Trying to get out of his crime by charging the first innocent man with it that he sees! No, master soldier—that won't do!'

"'No, no! That won't do!' the constables chimed in. 'To have the impudence to say such as that, when we caught him in the act almost! But, thank God, we've got the handcuffs on him at last.'

"'We have, thank God,' said the tall young man. 'Well, I must move on. Good-luck to ye with your prisoner!' And off he went as fast as his poor jade would carry him.

"The constables then, with Georgy handcuffed between 'em, and leading the horse, marched off in the other direction, towards the village where they had been accosted by the escort of soldiers sent to bring the deserter back, Georgy groaning: 'I shall be shot, I shall be shot!' They had not gone more than a mile before they met them.

"'Hoi, there!' says the head constable.

"'Hoi, yerself!' says the corporal in charge.

"'We've got your man,' says the constable.

"'Where?' says the corporal.

"'Here, between us,' said the constable. 'Only you don't recognize him out o' uniform.'

"The corporal looked at Georgy hard enough; then shook his head and said he was not the absconder.

"'But the absconder changed clothes with Farmer Jollice, and took his horse; and this man has 'em, d'ye see!'

"''Tis not our man,' said the soldiers. 'He's a tall young fellow with a mole on his right cheek, and a military bearing, which this man decidedly has not.'

"'I told the servants of the Crown that 'twas the other!' pleaded Georgy. 'But they wouldn't believe me.'

"And so it became clear that the missing dragoon was the tall young farmer, and not Georgy Crookhill—a fact which Farmer Jollice himself corroborated when he arrived on the scene. As Georgy had only robbed the robber, his sentence was comparatively light. The deserter from the Dragoons was never traced; his double shift of clothing having been of the greatest advantage to him in getting off, though he left Georgy's horse behind him a few miles ahead, having found the poor creature more hinderance than aid."

The man from abroad seemed to be less interested in the questionable characters of Longpuddle and their strange adventures than in the ordinary inhabitants and the ordinary events, though his local fellow-travellers preferred the former as subjects of discussion. He now for the first time asked concerning young persons of the opposite sex—or rather those who had been young when he left his native land. His informants, adhering to their own opinion that the remarkable was better worth telling than the ordinary, would not allow him to dwell upon the simple chronicles of those who had merely come and gone. They asked him if he remembered Netty Sargent.

"Netty Sargent—I do, just remember her. She was a young woman living with her uncle when I left, if my childish recollection may be trusted."

"That was the maid. She was a oneyer, if you like, sir. Not any harm in her, you know, but up to everything. You ought to hear how she got the copyhold of her house extended. Oughtn't he, Mr. Day?"

"He ought," replied the world-ignored old painter.

"Tell him, Mr. Day. Nobody can do it better than you, and you know the legal part better than some of us."

Day apologized, and began:

NETTY SARGENT'S COPYHOLD

"She continued to live with her uncle, in the lonely house by the copse, just as at the time you knew her; a tall, spry young woman. Ah, how well one can remember her black hair and dancing eyes at that time, and her sly way of screwing up her mouth when she meant to tease ye! Well, she was hardly out of short frocks before the chaps were after her, and by long and by late she was courted by a young man whom perhaps you did not know—Jasper Cliff was his name—and, though she might have had many a better fellow, he so greatly took her fancy that 'twas Jasper or nobody for her. He was a selfish customer, always thinking less of what he was going to do than of what he was going to gain by his doings. Jasper's eyes might have been fixed upon Netty, but his mind was upon her uncle's house; though he was fond of her in his way—I admit that.

"This house, built by her great-great-grandfather, with its garden and little field, was copyhold—granted upon lives in the old way, and had been so granted for generations. Her uncle's was the last life upon the property, so that at his death, if there was no admittance of new lives, it would all fall into the hands of the lord of the manor. But 'twas easy to admit—a slight 'fine,' as 'twas called, of a few pounds, was enough to entitle him to a new deed o' grant by the custom of the manor; and the lord could not hinder it.

"Now, there could be no better provision for his

niece and only relative than a sure house over her head, and Netty's uncle should have seen to the renewal in time, owing to the peculiar custom of forfeiture by the dropping of the last life before the new fine was paid; for the squire was very anxious to get hold of the house and land; and every Sunday when the old man came into the church and passed the squire's pew, the squire would say, 'A little weaker in his knees, a little crookeder in his back—and the readmittance not applied for, ha! ha! I shall be able to make a complete clearing of that corner of the manor some day!'

"'Twas extraordinary, now we look back upon it, that old Sargent should have been so dilatory; yet some people are like it, and he put off calling at the squire's agent's office with the fine week after week, saying to himself, 'I shall have more time next market-day than I have now.' One unfortunate hinderance was that he didn't very well like Jasper Cliff, and as Jasper kept urging Netty, and Netty on that account kept urging her uncle, the old man was inclined to postpone the reliveing as long as he could, to spite the selfish young lover. At last old Mr. Sargent fell ill, and then Jasper could bear it no longer: he produced the fine money himself, and handed it to Netty, and spoke to her plainly.

"'You and your uncle ought to know better. You should press him more. There's the money. If you let the house and ground slip between ye, I won't marry; hang me if I will! For folks won't deserve a husband that can do such things.'

"The worried girl took the money and went home, and told her uncle that it was no house no husband for her. Old Mr. Sargent pooh-poohed the money, for the amount was not worth consideration, but he did now bestir himself, for he saw she was bent upon marrying Jasper, and he did not wish to make her unhappy, since she was so determined. It was much to the squire's annoyance that he found Sargent had moved in the matter at last; but he could not gainsay it, and the documents were prepared (for on this manor the copyholders had writings with their holdings, though on some manors they had none). Old Sargent being now too feeble to go to the agent's house, the deed was to be brought to his house signed, and handed over as a receipt for the money; the counterpart to be signed by Sargent, and sent back to the squire.

"The agent had promised to call on old Sargent for this purpose at five o'clock, and Netty put the money into her desk to have it close at hand. While doing this she heard a slight cry from her uncle, and turning round, saw that he had fallen forward in his chair. She went and lifted him, but he was unconscious, and unconscious he remained. Neither medicine nor stimulants would bring him to himself. She had been told that he might possibly go off in that way, and it seemed as if the end had come. Before she had started for a doctor his face and extremities grew quite cold and white, and she saw that help would be useless. He was stone-dead.

"Netty's situation rose upon her distracted mind in all its seriousness. The house, garden, and field were lost—by a few hours—and with them a home for herself and her lover. She would not think so meanly of Jasper as to suppose that he would adhere to the resolution declared in a moment of impatience; but she trembled, nevertheless. Why could not her uncle have lived a couple of hours longer, since he had lived so long? It was now past three o'clock; at five the agent was to call, and, if all had gone well, by ten minutes past five the house and holding would have been securely hers for her own and Jasper's lives, these being two of the three proposed to be added by paying the fine. How that wretched old squire would rejoice at getting the little tenancy into his hands! He did not really require it, but constitutionally hated these tiny copyholds and leaseholds and freeholds, which made islands of independence in the fair, smooth ocean of his estates.

"Then an idea struck into the head of Netty how to accomplish her object in spite of her uncle's negligence. It was a dull December afternoon, and the first step in her scheme—so the story goes, and I see no reason to doubt it—"

"'Tis true as the light," affirmed Christopher Twink. "I was just passing by."

"The first step in her scheme was to fasten the outer door, to make sure of not being interrupted. Then she set to work by placing her uncle's small, heavy oak table before the fire; then she went to her uncle's corpse, sitting in the chair as he had died—a stuffed arm-chair, on castors, and rather high in the seat, so it was told me—and wheeled the chair, uncle and all, to the table, placing him with his back towards the window, in the attitude of bending over the said oak table, which I knew as a boy as well as I know any piece of furniture in my own house. On the table she laid the large family Bible open before him, and placed his forefinger on the page; and then she opened his eyelids a bit, and put on him his spectacles, so that from behind he appeared for all the world as if he were reading the Scriptures. Then she unfastened the door and sat down, and when it grew dark she lit a candle, and put it on the table beside her uncle's book.

"Folk may well guess how the time passed with her till the agent came, and how, when his knock sounded upon the door, she nearly started out of her skin—at least, that's as it was told me. Netty promptly went to the door.

"'I am sorry, sir,' she says, under her breath; 'my uncle is not so well to-night, and I'm afraid he can't see you.'

"'H'm!—that's a pretty tale,' says the steward. 'So I've come all this way about this trumpery little job for nothing!'

"'Oh no, sir—I hope not,' says Netty. 'I suppose the business of granting the new deed can be done just the same?'

"'Done? Certainly not. He must pay the renewal money, and sign the parchment in my presence.'

"She looked dubious. 'Uncle is so dreadful nervous about law business,' says she, 'that, as you know, he's put it off and put it off for years; and now to-day really I've feared it would verily drive him out of his mind. His poor three teeth quite chattered when I said to him that you would be here soon with the parchment writing. He always was afraid of agents, and folks that come for rent, and such like.'

"'Poor old fellow—I'm sorry for him. Well, the thing can't be done unless I see him and witness his signature.'

"'Suppose, sir, that you see him sign, and he don't see you looking at him? I'd soothe his nerves by saying you weren't strict about the form of witnessing, and didn't wish to come in. So that it was done in your bare presence it would be sufficient, would it not? As he's such an old, shrinking, shivering man, it would be a great considerateness on your part if that would do.'

"'In my bare presence would do, of course—that's all I come for. But how can I be a witness without his seeing me?'

"'Why, in this way, sir; if you'll oblige me by just

stepping here.' She conducted him a few yards to the left, till they were opposite the parlor window. The blind had been left up purposely, and the candle-light shone out upon the garden bushes. Within the agent could see, at the other end of the room, the back and side of the old man's head, and his shoulders and arm, sitting with the book and candle before him, and his spectacles on his nose, as she had placed him.

"'He's reading his Bible, as you see, sir,' she says, quite in her meekest way.

"'Yes. I thought he was a careless sort of man in matters of religion.'

"'He always was fond of his Bible,' Netty assured him. 'Though I think he's nodding over it just at this moment. However, that's natural in an old man, and unwell. Now you could stand here and see him sign, couldn't you, sir, as he's such an invalid?'

"'Very well,' said the agent, lighting a cigar. 'You have ready by you the merely nominal sum you'll have to pay for the admittance, of course?'

"'Yes,' said Netty. 'I'll bring it out.' She fetched the cash, wrapped in paper, and handed it to him, and when he had counted it the steward took from his breast-pocket the precious parchments and gave one to her to be signed.

"'Uncle's hand is a little paralyzed,' she said. 'And what with his being half asleep, too, really I don't know what sort of a signature he'll be able to make.'

"'Doesn't matter, so that he signs.'

"'Might I hold his hand?'

"'Aye, hold his hand, my young woman—that will be near enough.'

"Netty re-entered the house, and the agent continued smoking outside the window. Now came the ticklish part of Netty's performance. The steward saw her put the inkhorn—'horn,' says I, in my old-fashioned way—the inkstand, before her uncle, and touch his elbow as if to arouse him, and speak to him, and spread out the deed; when she had pointed to show him where to sign she dipped the pen and put it into his hand. To hold his hand she artfully stepped behind him, so that the agent could only see a little bit of his head and the hand she held; but he saw the old man's hand trace his name on the document. As soon as 'twas done she came out to the steward with the parchment in her hand, and the steward signed as witness by the light from the parlor window. Then he gave her the deed signed by the squire, and left; and next morning Netty told the neighbors that her uncle was dead in his bed."

"She must have undressed him and put him there."

"She must. Oh, that girl had a nerve, I can tell ye! Well, to cut a long story short, that's how she got back the house and field that were, strictly speaking, gone from her; and by getting them, got her a husband. When the old squire was dead, and his son came into the property, what Netty had done began to be whispered about, for she had told a friend or two. But Netty was a pretty young woman, and the squire's son was a pretty young man at that time, and wider-minded than his father, having no objection to little holdings; and he never took any proceedings against her."

There was now a lull in the discourse, and soon the van descended the hill leading into the long straggling village. When the houses were reached the passengers dropped off one by one, each at his or her own door. Arrived at the inn, the returned emigrant secured a bed, and, having eaten a light meal, sallied forth upon the scene he had known so well in his early days. Though flooded with the light of the rising moon, none of the objects wore the attractiveness in this their real presentation that had ever accompanied their images in the field of his imagination when he was more than two thousand miles removed from them. The peculiar charm attaching to an old village in an old country, as seen by the eyes of an absolute foreigner, was lowered in his case by magnified expectations from infantine memories. He walked on, looking at this chimney and that old wall, till he came to the church-yard, which he entered.

The headstones, whitened by the moon, were easily decipherable; and now for the first time Lackland began to feel himself amid the village community that he had left behind him five-and-thirty years before. Here, besides the Sallets, the Darths, the Pawles, the Privetts, the Sargents, and others of whom he had just heard, were names he remembered even better than those: the Jickses, and the Crosses, and the Knights, and the Olds. Doubtless representatives of these families, or some of them, were yet among the living; but to him they would all be as strangers. Far from finding his heart ready supplied with roots and tendrils here, he perceived that in returning to this spot it would be incumbent upon him to re-establish himself from the beginning, precisely as though he had never known the place nor it him. Time had not condescended to wait his pleasure, nor local life his greeting.

The figure of Mr. Lackland was seen at the inn, and in the village street, and in the fields and lanes about Upper Longpuddle for a few days after his arrival, and then, ghost-like, it silently disappeared. He had told some of the villagers that his immediate purpose in coming had been fulfilled by a sight of the place, and by conversation with its inhabitants; but that his ulterior purpose—of coming to spend his latter days among them—would probably never be carried out. It is now a dozen or fifteen years since his visit was paid, and his face has not again been seen.

March, 1891.

THE END